Chased by Grace
A Story of Victory

Kim Robinson

Kim Robinson

Chased by Grace – A Story of Victory

DEDICATION

To my daughter Laura and my son Walter, without whose support, encouragement and love Chased by Grace would never have been written. To my wonderful, beloved husband Paul I say thank you for your patience and love when this endeavor took so much of my time away from you. And I am forever grateful to my mother for raising me in a Christian home and in a sound, healthy church where I met Jesus.

ACKNOWLEDGMENTS

Special thanks to my earliest editors, Brenda S. and Jane M., for your direction, wise counsel, honest feedback and support. Thanks also to special prayer-buddy friends Audrey and Becky who listened and prayed during the long process that resulted in this book. These acknowledgments would not be complete without specific recognition of my dear AlAnon friends Barbara G. and Danni M. – your friendship and amazing strength in the face of unspeakable pain mean the world to me.

Prologue

Pamela's blood turned to ice as her eyes traveled across the words in the text message. The shock of what she read broke over her like a tsunami, wave after wave crushing the part of her brain trying to make sense of the message. Lily was in danger and she was powerless to protect her. What began as happily ever after had turned into a shocking nightmare...

Chapter 1

As Pamela walked ever so slowly out of the Gables Women's Medical Center the gray clouds overhead matched her mood. The "City Beautiful" usually had glorious weather but today it looked like rain. She felt anxious and unsettled. Spotting her car at a distance in the parking lot she navigated rows of ordinary-looking cars and made her way to her beloved candy apple red 1970 Mustang. It was her baby – pampered, loved and protected. Seeing it parked and ready for her to drive always made her feel happy.

Today was no different. Somehow it made her feel better to have it, just to know it was hers, something for which she was responsible to care for and maintain. Turning the key in the lock, she opened the driver's door, careful not to ding the paint. Pamela didn't like imperfection, not in her appearance, her home, her work or her car. Not in anything. She tossed her purse and the paperwork from the doctor into the passenger seat. The appointment for a routine well-check had not prepared her for the shocking news. The doctor's words seemed to hang in the air: *"This disease will make it very difficult for you to get pregnant. If you are able to conceive, then you have an 80% chance that the pregnancy will cure you. But your chances of pregnancy are low. I'm sorry."*

She sat there, letting the words sink in. Not able to have children? How could that be? No one else in her family had this type of problem. What she wanted more than anything was to have a family and be a mother. She had mothered her youngest siblings from the time they entered the family. She loved everything about children – their baby talk, laughter, smooth soft skin, big trusting eyes, the way they reached out to touch you or rested a head on your shoulder or simply patted your arm in the innocent loving way only a child can. Pamela had always planned to have children, and she did not like the saying "life is what happens while you are making plans." No, she was a planner and this was one plan she could not allow to be beyond her reach. She HAD to have children, it was her heart's desire. Tears welled up, threatening to spill over, only to be caught with the lace handkerchief she placed gently under her lashes. She needed to gather herself, not let her carefully applied makeup be ruined when she still had errands to run. Time enough to cry later, in the shower or at home alone. Besides, there was still a chance she would conceive and give birth. She needed to hold on to hope, stick to the plan.

She had been blessed with a family who loved her, a good husband, and a wonderful boss at her dream job. She knew how fortunate she was and did not take it for granted. But now it was time to start her own family.

She would give up her job in a heartbeat to be a stay-at-home mom. Pamela coveted the entire Motherhood Experience. Pregnancy with its morning sickness, the incredible miracle of a tiny life growing inside her, even the weight gain which showed the world she was to be a mother. The feel and smell of a newborn held close to her heart. Breastfeeding – how amazing that God's divine plan combined food and nourishment naturally with a special closeness that only mother and child could experience. Changing diapers, waking in the night, tiny hands to grasp her finger, innocent eyes to gaze up at her with complete trust and baby love – Pamela wanted it all. Her sister Riley had just given birth to her first child, a darling baby boy. Pamela longed to share motherhood experiences with her.

Pulling up to the exit gate she mechanically handed three one dollar bills and her ticket to the attendant. The wooden barrier lifted and she drove through, turning onto Hartford Ave. And what about Eduardo, she thought. He wanted children too. They had only been married for a few months, and while they had decided on a couple of years for "just the two of them" before they had children, they definitely planned on having a family. As the mustang steadily moved passed the stately oaks lining the lovely avenue she barely noticed the beauty around her. Usually she couldn't help but send up a prayer of thanks for the gorgeous Florida neighborhood where they were privileged to live. But now thoughts of Eduardo filled her mind. How would he take the news? He would be extremely disappointed of course. But would he be angry with her? That thought didn't even make sense, but he was a man used to getting what he wanted, and he wanted children. That's one thing they had agreed on early in their relationship.

Pamela recalled her and Eduardo's courtship. It had been filled with romance. He took her on creative dates and paid the kind of attention to her that most women only dreamed about. Like many men of Cuban descent he was very good about buying her expensive gifts. Eduardo liked to show that he was in charge; he was old school in terms of the man being the head of the household. He was also extremely charming. When he turned that smile and those eyes on her there was no resisting. He was serious about good food, both at home and when dining out, and they always dined at the nicest restaurants in town. His dreams were big and he fully intended to achieve them. Eduardo was passionate about his innovative work in the world of industrial technology. He was going to start his own company, build it from the ground up, have plenty of wealth and leave a business legacy for his sons when they came along. By anyone's standards, Eduardo successful and a good catch. He didn't settle and he always got what he wanted. Pamela was looking for a loving relationship with romance and security and a future. She found Eduardo attractive and exciting. He seemed so sure of himself and made her feel special. His authoritative presence impressed her and gave her a sense of safety.

They met at a Fleetwood Mac concert through mutual friends. He made his immediate interest in her quite clear, and she felt flattered. She had given him her number that first night and within a couple of days he had called to ask her out. He had taken her to his favorite coffee shop, Java and Juice; she sipped a non-fat latte while he preferred the strong coffee of the day. They had talked for hours. Pamela was mesmerized by his very presence. His wavy dark hair was combed straight back, no part, and the stubble beard only emphasized his handsome features. He was almost 6' tall but presented taller because of the way his presence filled a room. But it was his eyes – the color of bitter chocolate, so dark as to be mistaken for black, that really grabbed her. Set deep underneath significant black eyebrows, they bored through her with a piercing intensity that revealed nothing of himself but appraised everything about her. His dark good looks complimented her fair complexion and the combination of thick blonde hair with sky blue eyes. Unlike Eduardo, Pamela's eyes were an open window to her soul, quick to shine with happiness or fill with tears as they mirrored her heart. She had the looks of a model, with high cheekbones and perfect nose, and she knew it. She reveled in the way Eduardo looked at her. She was proud of her looks and worked out diligently to maintain her size 6 figure, not for the admiring glances of men but for her own self-satisfaction. Together they made a striking couple, and Pamela loved it.

Gradually he met her friends and she his business associates. Pamela was an avid reader, always had a book going and craved a significant amount of alone time. Eduardo was focused on his career and didn't have much free time. He enjoyed target practice at the shooting range, and occasionally worked in his shop designing beautiful custom metal art. Often he lost interest after he had solved a complicated design, not interested so much in the finished work as he was in the process and mastering the challenge of something never before constructed. Six months into their dating Eduardo told her he thought he was falling in love with her, and she was beginning to believe she was in love with him too.

Pamela's thoughts returned to the present, to the possibility she and her gorgeous husband would never have a child. It was unacceptable. As soon as she got home she would call her mother. She needed to hear her calm voice and ask for her wise counsel. During Pamela's teenage years her rebellious streak had caused significant strain with her mother, but after she moved away to college she began to realize how wise her mother was and how much she loved her. Roberta Rogers was down to earth with a great sense of humor, a deep faith in God and a strong sense of right and wrong. She was a homemaker and a loving mom to her four children of whom Pamela was the oldest. Adored by her husband Frank, Roberta raised her children to be honest, accountable, productive members of society, to love God and respect others, and to never take the love of family for granted. Pamela had come to appreciate how close her family was. What her Mom proclaimed often was right – most people didn't have what they had. They had formed a strong mother-daughter bond. Yes, she would call her mom as soon as she got home. Mom would know what to say.

Chapter 2

W. Eduardo Cohen, IV, looked down at his Rolex – 2:35 p.m. Would this meeting never end? They had gotten the business pleasantries out of the way over a two martini lunch at the Black Diamond, his favorite club. The representative from Fowler Construction had fawned over him throughout the meal. Now he was droning on about the reputation of their equipment, unique warranty provisions, and projected sales for the next fiscal year. Eduardo didn't need to hear it. He already knew he would get the deal on his terms – this guy wouldn't even know what hit him. He had other contracts to review and negotiate, a meeting with his install manager, and a conference call with his partner in Long Beach. Besides, he hoped to finish up early for the day and get out by four. He needed a massage to release the tension of his work day before he headed home to Pamela.

Pamela. His beautiful faithful wife. They were the perfect couple. She kept a neat house, was a decent cook, and never questioned his long hours at the office or his extended business trips. Her trust in him was one of the reasons he loved her. He had always believed that when he found "the one" he would know it, and he'd known it instantly when he met Pamela. She was interested in everything about him, appreciative of the gifts he gave her, and genuinely wanted to please. He wanted the right blend of submissiveness and intellect, and she answered that description. He hadn't wanted her to continue working after they were married; he could provide quite well for them and felt sure his income would explode in the next two years.

The importance of a quality education was ingrained in Eduardo from the time he was a young boy. His family was thoroughly credentialed. The right degrees and certifications made an important statement of who a person was, what he could accomplish. With them the sky was the limit; without them the financial ceiling was unacceptably low. Cindy Cohen had her B.A. in Art History and managed special artist exhibits at the Museum of Modern Art. Bill Cohen – W. Eduardo Cohen, III, to be exact – had earned his Bachelors at University of Miami and his MBA at Stanford. As an only child, Eduardo had benefitted from the full focus and attention of his parents and grandmother. He was used to being the center of their world and he loved it. Bill's success as an aerospace engineer enabled him to retire in his early fifties, with established wealth and time for the golf course. Eduardo had only a Bachelors in Finance but was already hailed as the expert in his specialty field of innovative technology management for large general contracting firms. Pamela had no degree, having only completed three years of college. Neither was it lost on Eduardo that her family was strictly blue collar. Her step-father was a fireman who never went to college; her mother attended college for only a few weeks and was just a homemaker. Pamela's marriage to him would set her up for a lifestyle she could not have otherwise.

Eduardo thought she should be focused on maintaining the perfect home. But she had surprised him with a stubborn streak when it came to her job. Pamela's job, her "dream job" wasn't high profile and didn't add much income. But it made her happy and she felt she made a difference at her company. She didn't want to quit until they started their family. Perhaps she needed that for now, until motherhood would become her life. Pamela would be a great mother, Eduardo was sure of that. They both wanted children. He hoped for a son that would carry on the family name, perhaps even share his love of business. Someone with whom he could one day share his expertise and watch a dynasty emerge. Pamela had the loving, nurturing qualities that he wanted for the mother of his children. Combined with her people skills and the way she presented to his important clients, he was on the fast track to the career he dreamed of. That was why he had courted her with such fervor, lavishing gifts and inordinate amounts of his time. He wanted her, and fortunately she had responded beautifully. He was passionate about her, telling her of his love even earlier than he had thought he would. The depth of devotion in her eyes had divulged to him even before her words that she loved him too.

Pamela was beautiful, smarter than other women he had dated, and had the charm and people skills to make up for what she lacked in formal education. To Pamela's credit, his mother adored her, and fortunately Pamela had instantly bonded with Cindy. They exchanged recipes, talked about their favorite music and authors, and shared what they called "God stories." Cindy and Pamela were both religious, something Eduardo saw as a weakness. He didn't need a crutch or an idea of a God. He was in control of his own life, thank you very much. Of course, while he and Pamela were dating he had emphasized his upbringing in the church, the fact that his grandfather had been a Baptist preacher and how his mother loved to go to church. He knew that was important to Pamela and he willingly let her assume he would get serious about going to church after they were married. Since their wedding, he had darkened the doors of her church just two times, and she had stopped asking him to go with her on Sundays. He didn't need to be preached at, and told what to do, or have someone try to convince him there was a God. He wasn't going and that was the end of it. He knew she was disappointed but she didn't push it any more. Getting up early on Sunday mornings, church meetings, helping in church business, feeding the homeless, Bible studies, standing around smiling and chatting about nothing important – that was for women.

Besides, he knew that once they learned of his position in the business world he would constantly be asked to give free advice, chair the finance committee, and, most ridiculous of all, give away his money.

Eduardo brought his mind back to the present. The Fowler rep was too slow to bring this thing to a close. Straightening his tie, he stood to his full height. This meeting was over.

Chapter 3

Roberta hung up the phone, distracted from the preparation of her latest op-ed piece for the local paper. Pamela had sounded so dejected, devastated at the possibility of not being able to have children. The odds were definitely stacked against her daughter. But Roberta had the wisdom accumulated from years of watching God work in her own life and the lives of her four children. What was that verse in the book of Luke – nothing was impossible with God.

When her first marriage failed leaving her with a young child, no money and no place to live except back home with her parents, Roberta had felt the situation was impossible. How would she support herself and her 5 year old daughter? But God. Despite her lack of training He had provided her with a receptionist job and loving parents who shared in her sorrow and willingly let her move back in while she got her life together. They were able to look after her little girl each day after school. And He brought her Frank.

God bless Frank Rogers! It was Frank who had shown her the difference between infatuation and real, lasting love. After two years of single parenting and an occasional date arranged by well-meaning friends, she met Frank on a blind date. Like her first husband, he was tall and handsome. Unlike Blake, he was a quiet man with a good reputation. Part of a large family, Frank was hard working and had two jobs. His position as a firefighter working shifts allowed for an additional part time job. He was frugal but fun-loving and his exceptional sense of humor made him the favorite in his group of friends. They hit it off immediately.

Frank was a quiet godly man, kind and gentle and with the driest sense of humor she'd ever known. His family was poor but their home was always filled with laughter and love. His mother had her hands full raising his twelve siblings so he had gone to work right out of high school to help support the family. After their first date they saw each other as often as work and family obligations permitted. His family enjoyed Roberta and had her and Pamela over often for dinner. Roberta felt not only loved but a sense of belonging, something she hadn't experienced with Blake's parents. Roberta's family was crazy about Frank. His sense of humor was an immediate hit with them, his quiet nature blending well with the loud family. Frank adored Pamela. He'd never married or had children but he was a natural father. Pamela was shy with him and he didn't push, just let the relationship unfold over time. A little over a year after the now famous blind date they were married and bought a small house. Roberta smiled as she thought of her husband. She'd never known marriage could be so joyful and fulfilling, that you could actually grow to love each other more instead of less as years passed. Frank had taught her that, and loved her more than she thought possible. He loved Pamela too, and treated her as if she were his own. And God didn't stop there. Over the next six years, God had blessed them with three more children – Riley, Luke and Tessa. By the time Pamela was in high school they had moved to a bigger house out in the country. Oh, she was a rich woman in all the ways that counted.

"Try not to fret, dear," she'd told Pamela after hearing the bad news. "There is a reason for everything and God has a plan. Pray, trust and let go of the fear or it will only make things worse." She knew that was sound advice, and she trusted God. But now that Pamela was happily married Roberta sure wouldn't mind another grandchild in addition to Riley's little boy. The family all liked Eduardo and was happy for Pamela. Frank was pleased that Pamela had married a good provider. Roberta loved seeing Pamela so happy. Riley and Tessa thought Eduardo was handsome and a good match for Pamela. Luke was glad to have another brother-in-law. He and Pamela were close and he knew how happy she was. He was also grateful she'd broken it off with the jerk she'd dated before Eduardo came into the picture. Eduardo could be a bit arrogant at times, but he was a nice guy and he was really good to Pamela.

Chapter 4

Mom is right, Pamela thought, as she began assembling ingredients on the kitchen counter to make the evening meal. She needed to let go of fear and turn it over to God in prayer. She was going to make that quiche with the cheese crust that Eduardo liked so well. Her cooking didn't measure up to his mother's, as he had commented. But she had her specialties and was learning to cook many of Cindy's dishes that were Eduardo's favorites. Cindy had even given her a new recipe box with many of her recipes all carefully written out. Cindy was the perfect mother-in-law. They both agreed it was a total "God-thing" they'd hit it off so well from their first meeting. Cindy told Pamela she was the daughter she had always wanted. Pamela learned different home-making skills from her that her own mother hadn't been able to teach her because they were always on such a tight budget. Roberta could stretch a dollar like no one else, and Pamela would always be grateful she knew how to live on less. Roberta's cooking repertoire had been limited because there was only so much you could do with ground beef, the occasional chicken and basic staples in the pantry. But Cindy was teaching her different sauces, how to select and incorporate freshly ground spices, and had introduced her to cookbooks she hadn't even known existed.

What Pamela really loved to do was bake, and in that area Cindy was practically peerless. Her secret recipe for homemade chocolate chunk cookies was the envy of everyone who knew her, her pie crust the flakiest, her cakes were always moist, and she could make any kind of cookie and make it flawlessly. Roberta was a good cook, but she wasn't as interested in baking except for birthday cakes for the children. Pamela could pour out her heart and soul to her mother and counted on her for wise advice, but with Cindy she could share her love of making cookies, trade novels from their latest favorite authors, and listen to classical piano music rather than country tunes. Both women were special to her in unique ways, and she couldn't believe her good fortune.

Pamela recalled the first time she stepped into the Cohen home. She couldn't believe her eyes. It looked like something out of a Better Homes & Gardens magazine, including the lovely garden out back. It was beautifully furnished with tasteful antiques resting on soft white plush carpet. But it was the built-in floor to ceiling shelves in the main living area that drew Pamela's attention immediately. So many books - the classics, reference, Christian reference, and children's story collections by famous authors. Nestled perfectly among the books were pictures of Eduardo as a child, ancestors long dead, and gorgeous pieces of exquisite china, Cohen family heirlooms accumulated over decades. She was captivated. Then Cindy had taken her into the library, and she feasted her eyes on the room filled with hundreds more books accented by decorative pieces. All the rooms were perfectly appointed, spacious, and comfortable. Classical music floated softly over them from hidden speakers. It was real but it felt like she had stepped into a fairy tale.

Eduardo's father, Bill, had emerged from the kitchen with a smile and offer of a drink. He was a man of few words but his gaze was so intense it almost reached out to touch Pamela. There was something momentarily unsettling about the way he looked at her. Probably just me being nervous, she thought. Then he disappeared back into the kitchen and she forgot her discomfort, lost again in the beauty and grandeur of this fabulous home.

The chime of the living room clock brought Pamela back to the present. She began using the pastry cutter to mix the flour, butter and grated cheese. Working the dough into a crust in the Williams Sonoma ceramic pie pan, she recalled that first visit. Pamela could not understand how as a part of this perfect family Eduardo had not yet found "Ms. Right" and married. She couldn't believe her good fortune. She wished he'd had siblings, they could have told her more about him in his growing up years. But she was gaining a wonderful friend and ally in Cindy, who looked to Pamela as her daughter.

Pamela folded three beaten eggs into the rest of the quiche filling mixture and poured it all into the cheesy crust pie shell. The oven was ready at 350° and while supper cooked she'd have plenty of time to straighten the house before Eduardo got home. He was rarely home before 7:30p.m. but Pamela wanted the table set and everything ready when he walked in. He was a busy man with a very successful business, and he often reminded her it took a lot more than working 8 to 5 to make the money he was making. Regardless of the lack of predictability in Eduardo's arrival, he liked to walk in the door and immediately sit down to a hot meal. Pamela prided herself on making that happen.

Chapter 5

Cindy closed the French patio door behind her, balancing a bunch of pink gladiolas from the garden in the crook of her elbow. These were as pretty as the ones she had cut for Pamela and Eduardo's wedding reception. It had been several months but she could still recall every detail of that beautiful wedding. She knew the full story of the courtship, engagement, the ring, the dress. Pamela had shared all of that with her.

She and Bill were thrilled with their new daughter-in-law. Pamela was a perfect fit, and already closer to Cindy than she had hoped for. Eduardo's attempts at other long term relationships had been below Cindy's expectation and at times she wondered if he would ever marry. More importantly, would she _ever_ have any grandchildren? But then Eduardo brought Pamela home to meet the Cohen family. Cindy began praying for them to marry that very day. The day Eduardo had called to announce he and Pamela were engaged was one of the happiest days of Cindy's life.

Pamela and Cindy visited often after the announcement. They eagerly discussed wedding plans. Pamela was close to her mother of course, and they were busy arranging for the minister, the location, invitations, the cakes, the attendants' dresses, and all the wedding details that a bride and her mother plan together. But the Rogers didn't have a lot of money, and Cindy knew Pamela wasn't sure what to do about The Dress. Cindy already had ideas about The Dress and about the ring too. Plus she'd get to plan the rehearsal dinner and a separate reception later in her home for their friends to meet the new couple. There was plenty to talk and dream about.

"I want an old fashioned wedding, complete with an antique-looking ring and an old fashioned gown!" Pamela had exclaimed one Sunday afternoon. As Cindy listened to her talk of white versus ivory fabrics, style and length, and the comfort factor she knew the moment had arrived. They were sitting in Cindy's formal living room where the two of them sometimes retreated, signaling to Eduardo and his father that wedding plans were being discussed and the ladies didn't want to be disturbed. Cindy had considered how best to tell Pamela about The Dress. It was perfect of course, there was no doubt about that. She felt confident it would fit with only minor alterations, and the history behind it was icing on the cake. She didn't want to push, but she would be deeply disappointed if Pamela didn't want to make it her own bridal gown. Last week she had taken the carefully wrapped dress out of its box and placed it on a silk hangar, strategically positioned in the front of the large closet in the rear guestroom.

Cindy stood up and reached for Pamela's hand. "Come with me," she said, "I want to show you something." As they walked from the living room down the long hallway to the rear of the house, Pamela said, "Tell me! What is it you want to show me?" Cindy entered the bedroom, smiling back at Pamela. "Over here, I'll show you." She opened the closet door and flipped on the light as they stepped in. There it was. The Dress.

Pamela stood there, speechless. Cindy watched her closely, delight dawning on her face as she realized Pamela was as taken with The Dress as she was. "I wondered if you might like to try it on," Cindy said. "It was worn by Eduardo's paternal grandmother on her wedding day. The Bartlett County Historical Society asked for it, but I wanted to keep it in the family."

Pamela caught her breath, putting her hand out to feel the soft, pale ivory fabric. She touched the lace high neck collar, ran her fingers lightly over the intricate lace bodice, full length puff sleeves to the cuff, and floor length slightly flared skirt. She turned it over to reveal dozens of tiny buttons and button loops down the back and reverently stroked the gauzy silk skirt-back.

"I've never seen anything like it - it's BEAUTIFUL!" she exclaimed. Pamela's questions came staccato as she turned to give Cindy a hug. "What is this fabric? It's soft like silk, sheer as gauze and light as cotton! Where did you find it? I can't believe it!! How did you know this was exactly what I wanted??"

"Here, let me help you with those buttons," Cindy said, ecstatic at her reaction. Pamela couldn't do those buttons without help, but she knew as soon as she slipped it on that this was The Dress. It was a perfect fit. She felt like she was dreaming. How could a dress made for someone else almost a century ago be such a perfect fit for her? Looping the last button at the neck, she observed carefully as she checked all the fitted areas. The collar was amazing, standing two inches tall but not stiff, gently hugging the air around her throat. The cuffs were about 6" in length, and they too encased her lower arms with a not-too-tight, not-too-loose feel and look, coming to an end exactly beneath her wrist bones, the lace barely touching the tops of her hands. The shoulder seams aligned as if they had been cut to her form, and the waist fit as if it had been custom tailored for her. Pamela turned slowly, catching sight of the sides and back in the three-way vanity mirror that sat atop the antique dresser. They studied the length critically. It would be too short if she wore much heel, but with the right pair of eggshell or bone colored sandals in a kitten heel it would be perfect.

Unbelievably perfect. Pamela looked in the antique vanity mirror. She felt as if she were starring in her own fairy tale.

"Oh Cindy, I simply must have it!" Pamela said. "It is so lovely – so 'me' – that I can hardly bear to take it off. Can you believe the fit??" Cindy laughed gently. "I thought it was your size, but I had no idea it would fit as if it were designed for you. I am pleased beyond words that you like it, I was so hoping you would." Together they said softly, "A meant to be." Pamela laughed. "Well, that's it then. I've found The Dress!" Cindy clicked off the closet light as Pamela gave The Dress one last caress. "I'll talk to the two cleaners I know that specialize in antique gowns and find the best way to have it cleaned. Will that be alright with you?" Cindy asked. "Of course," Pamela replied. "One less thing on my to do list." She ran down the hall to tell Eduardo about The Dress.

Cindy filled a large crystal vase with water and stirred in floral preservative, still thinking about that day. She recalled how pretty Pamela had looked in the antique dress, and how she'd decided to retrieve the antique family ring from the vault and give it to Eduardo. Later that evening Cindy had asked Eduardo if he would come sit with her for a while in the library. She told of the revealing of The Dress from her vantage point and told him how very happy she was it had worked out so well. He smiled, listening but occasionally checking his iPhone. "Have you purchased an engagement ring yet?" Cindy asked, motioning for him to put his smartphone away for the moment. Eduardo shook his head. "No, haven't had time."

"Let me show you what I retrieved from the safe deposit box yesterday." She went to the desk, opened the middle drawer and took out a small, square maroon box with a hinged lid and a tiny gold stud clasp. She opened it and showed Eduardo the diamond ring in the antique platinum filigree setting that had belonged to her mother. In the center was a round 2 carat diamond of the highest quality; another carat's worth of tiny diamonds shown below in the filigree, beautifully setting off the round like a supporting cast. "My father gave this to my mother when he proposed. He surprised her speechless with this gem. After his death it was stored in her safety deposit box for decades. Two years ago after her death I found this in the box with her important papers and valuable jewelry. I wasn't sure what to do with it so I just kept it locked up. Pamela says she wants platinum or white gold, so I thought this would be ideal" Cindy told him.

"It's quite unique, and the price is certainly right," Eduardo said with a smile. "I'll surprise her with it tonight. Thank you, Mother, it's perfect."

Eduardo walked into the guest room after dinner and found Pamela reading. "Now that you have the dress, I thought it would be nice for you to have the ring too," he said. Pamela looked up from her book. Eduardo sat down beside her on the couch. In his hand was the box, the lid open and resting on its hinge to reveal the ring. "This is for you, darling. A woman as beautiful as you deserves a ring that is worthy. I hope it's exactly what you wanted." He searched her face expectantly, watching her reaction. "Oh, Eduardo, it's lovely," she breathed softly. "Truly, it is more beautiful than I ever dreamed my engagement ring would be. How did you find such a stunning piece?"

Eduardo smiled down at her. "It was my grandmother's wedding ring – my mother's mother. I never knew my dad's parents so GiGi and I were very close. I lived with her during college and she told me often she wanted my bride to have it." Pamela slipped the ring on her finger. It was too big. How hard to have such an amazing engagement ring and not be able to wear it! Until now their engagement had been words she shared with family and friends. But once the ring was on her finger the whole world would know that she was engaged. Everyone who saw her, every cashier, waitress and retail attendant who waited on her, would know at a glance that she was taken. They would see proof that she was desired enough by a man to be promised for marriage. She felt so happy, so rich, so secure. The thrill of seeing the ring on her left hand was something she didn't think would ever get old.

"Eduardo, where should I take it to get it sized? I want to do it right away, tomorrow if possible."

"Why don't you ask my mother to recommend a place," he replied. "She'll know a reputable jeweler." Eduardo pulled her to him and held her close. She looked up at him, and he kissed her gently. "I'm glad you like it. GiGi would be so happy." Holding hands, they made their way slowly from the guest room through the rest of the house and into the kitchen where Cindy was waiting. Their happiness and hers filled the room.

Cindy brought her thoughts back to the present, to her own kitchen where she carried the vase of perfectly arranged flowers to the living room. She wished again that her mother had been alive to see Eduardo get married. How pleased she would have been to attend her grandson's wedding. Eduardo had always been her pride and joy, from letting him call her "Gigi" to giving him anything his heart desired from the time he was old enough to speak. Cindy smiled. She had been almost as bad, but Eduardo was hard not to spoil – he had been the sweetest little boy, a pleasure to be around. As an adolescent he had not been any trouble, the perfect son. And now he had the perfect wife.

Chapter 6

Pamela opened the oven door and inserted a knife into the center of the quiche. Perfect – another 10 minutes to set and it would be ready. Closing the door, she glanced up at the built-in shelves at the far end of the living room that joined her large, open kitchen. Her mother's face smiled back at her from a photo of Roberta and Frank on Pamela's wedding day. They had had such fun planning the logistics for the wedding. Roberta loved the fact that Pamela wanted a traditional wedding and had offered to help with finding the venue, florist and bakery. Roberta had discovered a beautiful historic home downtown, and after their site visit Pamela agreed it was the ideal setting for an old fashioned wedding. They had chosen local bakery Forever Sweet to prepare the wedding cake, and Pamela's cousin Heather would be their photographer. A friend of Roberta's owned a florist shop and agreed to provide flowers and the bridal bouquet. Pamela and Roberta were delighted to learn Pastor Kyle from their family church was available to perform the ceremony. Eduardo had suggested to Pamela that he focus on planning the honeymoon trip and she take care of the details for the ceremony. They could plan the reception together.

Choosing a date had not been difficult for Pamela. She had always loved springtime with its beautiful flowers and promise of new beginnings. She asked Eduardo about his travel schedule for the coming April and May; April was out but the first part of May was open. They chose the first Saturday in May and he blocked out the following week for their honeymoon. May 5th. Perfect. Hydrangeas, roses, gladiolas and gardenias would all be readily available, every bloom in peak fragrance. The flowers were one of the things Pamela enjoyed most about spring. Buds, blooms and the birds that were drawn to them all seemed to abound in hope. Brides too – and in the coming spring she would be one!

Pamela grabbed her favorite potholders and removed the quiche from the oven, pressing the red "Stop" button on the touch panel to turn the oven off. She set the dish carefully on the cooling rack. Using a clean table knife she gently eased it in between the ceramic edge and the perfectly browned crust, barely lifting each flaky fluted curve from the dish. A few delicate crumbs dropped onto the lip of the pie plate, lightly framing the 9" round. Just like the wispy tendrils of hair had framed her face on their wedding day, a few strands artfully allowed to escape the up-do that held the rest of her blonde hair atop her head surrounded by the flowered wreath with its slim satin ribbons freely flowing down her back. Her bridal portrait above the mantel showed the ultimate effect flawlessly, and she let her eyes travel across the room again to gaze at it. The quiche was left alone to fully set, letting her mind recall the full beauty of her wedding day.

Everything had been perfect. The gorgeous spring day allowed them to set up the reception out on the lawn and prepare for pictures in the garden gazebo. Her heart had filled to nearly bursting, pushing the remnants of old hurts out to make room for the hope of the new life that waited for her as soon as she said, "I Do." She had been ready to say it, ready to let God show her how to be a godly wife to her husband and encourage him on his own faith journey. Her father had guided her smoothly down the center aisle, her sister-attendants, his groomsmen and 200 relatives / close friends smiling as they witnessed her happiest of days. After the ceremony she and Eduardo drank champagne out of golden goblets that Bill and Cindy had used at their wedding. They fed each other cake bites piled with icing and gazed into each other's eyes. Tradition, sentiment, elegance and expectations permeated the entire day. It was the wedding she had always wanted, and the honeymoon cruise to the Mediterranean had been more wonderful than she had dared to imagine. Her dreams were coming true.

She was knocked off of Memory Lane by the sound of Eduardo's Tahoe pulling into the driveway. Pamela moved quickly to check on the quiche and take the salad out of the fridge. The tea was already brewed, ready for glasses of ice. As she heard the garage door close, the door opened and Eduardo's familiar "Dinner ready?" entered the room before him. Setting his briefcase down on the kitchen desk, Eduardo leaned over to smell the quiche. "Mmmm. Smells delicious. I'll go wash up for dinner, be right back."

Pamela had finished placing the food on the table and was pouring tea into crystal glasses when Eduardo walked into the dining room and sat down in his usual chair. Pamela sat to his right, close to the kitchen in case anything else was needed. She bowed her head in a silent meal blessing. She would have preferred him to join her in the prayer aloud but he wasn't comfortable with that. As she began filling their salad plates she asked about his day, and listened as he told of the Fowler rep and how the deal had closed exactly on Eduardo's terms. She smiled appreciatively. After a brief silence Eduardo asked, "How did your doctor appointment go today?" Pamela sipped her tea then cleared her throat, nervous about what she had to say. "It was my annual well-check appointment, but the doctor found something that caused the exam to take longer than I expected. And I'm afraid the news ... is not good."

Eduardo looked up, concern creasing his brow. "What do you mean?"

Pamela sighed. "I have endometriosis. It's a disease that causes abnormal growths on the uterine lining. They are rarely cancerous but they can grow, affecting the ovaries and other parts of the body. Sometimes they attach together forming cysts, and those can be very painful. The good news is that explains the abdominal pain I've been having. The bad news is it will make it very difficult for me to get pregnant."

The words hung in the air between them for a few seconds. Tears pooled at the corners of Pamela's eyes and she looked away, not wanting to see Eduardo's reaction. He asked quietly, "Is there any cure? Can they give you something for this disease?" The look on Pamela's face gave him his answer. She looked frightened, as if she might cry. Eduardo's face showed shock as he looked at her in disbelief. "So you're saying we might not be able to have any children?"

His immediate reaction of hope for treatment was replaced with the dawning realization that he might not get to be a father. His mind reeled with the unthinkable news, while at the same time mentally searching for a plan to reverse this impossible situation. Who would carry on the Cohen name? What about a son to carry on the business he was just starting to build? It had never occurred to Eduardo that Pamela might not be able to have children. Surely there was a way to fix this, they just needed to find the right doctor and the right procedure. No use getting upset at this point, he thought. They hadn't even explored all the medical options and Pamela had only seen her regular doctor, not a specialist.

He felt pity for her as she looked at him expectantly. She wanted so much to have children and he knew she didn't want to be a disappointment to him. He reached across the table and patted her hand. "Don't worry, this is all going to turn out fine. We need to find doctors with a specialty in this disease and learn what can be done. With the technology available today, I am sure there is a way to get this corrected and get you pregnant. My partner on the west coast has connections in the healthcare field. I'll have my assistant get to work on this first thing in the morning."

Pamela smiled weakly, relieved that he wasn't angry. She had been afraid he might see this as a personal defect, or view her as damaged or not good enough anymore. Now that the stress of waiting to tell him was gone, she let out a long breath, almost as if she had been holding it in for days. She was tired – the pain had taken its toll this past week – but happy that Eduardo was already looking at how to get past this obstacle instead of focusing on her imperfection, one that she couldn't help. "Thanks, I've been stressed about telling you," she admitted. Eduardo smiled and said, "You haven't even taken a bite of your salad. Why don't you let me take you to our favorite wine bar? We can sit out under the trees, have a nice glass of cabernet with your favorite shrimp appetizer and try to relax. This quiche looks good but let's refrigerate it for tomorrow night and get a change of scenery this evening."

Pamela felt the relief of sharing the news start to change her attitude. "That sounds great! Just let me put the food in the fridge and I'll be ready."

"That's my girl," Eduardo said, gathering her into his arms for a hug. "And when we come home, we can work on enlarging our family. No reason we can't continue trying while we wait to hear what the experts say," he smiled. Five minutes later they were in the car headed to Grape Escape, and Pamela was already smiling again.

Chapter 7

Riley put the ice mold in the glass punch bowl and stirred while Tessa arranged the sandwiches on the silver tray. Roberta finished setting out the mints, nuts and petit fours. Pamela loved petit fours and these were from her favorite bakery. The shower wasn't fancy since their budget was limited. But it was as elaborate as they could make it, with pink balloons tied to the mailbox out front, fruit punch in the punch bowl with its matching cups, delicate finger sandwiches of chicken salad and pimento cheese, lots of presents and everyone that Pamela wanted in attendance. Riley wanted this to be perfect.

Roberta still couldn't believe it – Pamela was going to have a baby! Pamela and Eduardo hadn't even needed their appointment with the second specialist in New York. Amazingly, five months after Pamela's devastating news, she was pregnant. She and Pamela both believed it was a miracle, an answer to prayer, which only added to her excitement. The moment the doctor called with the results from the lab she was on the phone to Eduardo. She got his voice mail at the office and excitedly left a message for him to call her right away. Then she called her mother. Roberta would always remember that call.

"Mom, you won't believe it, I'm pregnant!!" Pamela practically shouted into the phone.

"Oh, sweetheart, that's wonderful, I am so happy for you! Praise God! I had hoped He would bless you with children and the ability to experience the miracle of birthing a child. You are going to be such a good mother," Roberta said, her own excitement shining through her words. They talked for a few minutes about the tentative due date, how Pamela was feeling and how excited the rest of the family would be, especially Riley.

And now here they were, having a baby shower for her first granddaughter. Roberta knew God had answered their prayers. But God. Finally, her daughter was going to live her dream, becoming a mother. *Thank you, Lord, for this miracle and for how much you love us. We can't see the big picture; we only get to see the unfinished side of it all. But I know you are in charge and I praise you for this new life in our family. Amen.*

Pamela smiled at the balloons as she turned the Mustang into Riley's driveway. Riley ran out to greet her. The sisters had talked often since Dr. Sheldon had confirmed Pamela was indeed pregnant, against all odds. There was so much advice Riley wanted to share and Pamela had so many questions. Riley couldn't wait to rejoice in the birth of her niece.

Arm in arm they walked into the house, Pamela's baby belly bulging under her blouse.

Four hours later Pamela walked into her own home, immediately taking off her shoes and reclining on the couch. These days it was all about snacks and naps – and homemade chocolate cookies when she had the energy. She couldn't wait to show Eduardo all the gifts she had received at the baby shower given by her family. Now they had the stroller, pack-n-play, plenty of diapers and all the bathing accessories. Riley and her mom had outdone themselves, and of the aunts, family friends, cousins and work friends who had been invited almost everyone was able to make it. What fun painting onesies and guessing how big the baby would be. Pamela loved all of it. Her pregnancy had been a healthy one, no morning sickness or trouble sleeping, and Eduardo was treating her with special care. She smiled at the thought of his reaction when she had told him. Uncharacteristically he shouted "Yes!" and lifted his fist in the air. His excitement equaled her own and they had called every family member and friend they could think of with the fantastic news. Pamela had journaled her thanks and praise that morning at prayer time, using all the words of gratitude and worship that came to her for this gift, this miracle, this most precious of answered prayers. Yes, God was good. All the time.

She had known Cindy would be especially excited – unlike Roberta, this would be Cindy's first grandchild. For a woman who already had a full child's library and who had saved the quality wooden children's furniture from when her son was little, there was no more welcome news than "you are going to be a grandmother!" On their first visit to the Cohen's after the announcement Cindy showed Pamela the crib, dresser, table and chair, and child's rocking chair that had belonged to Eduardo. They had been preserved and were in mint condition. Cindy was delighted with Pamela's choice of a Jan Brett animals theme for the nursery, and began purchasing all of the matching books and toys she could find. But the most amazing thing was the poster-sized print of all the Jan Brett animal characters that Cindy found on one of her trips to New England. Together they unrolled it and marveled at its beauty and prime condition. "A meant to be," Pamela said. Cindy nodded and hugged her. "I'll take it to the gallery next week and see about getting it framed."

Just like her wedding, the preparation for her daughter was falling into place beautifully. They had chosen the name Lily, and Pamela couldn't wait to meet this little girl growing inside her. Pamela was still working for now, and those who had known her for so many years enjoyed hearing about the monthly doctor appointments and plans for the nursery. Eduardo's business had begun to really take off and he was spending more time at the office and traveling. Pamela was consumed with thoughts of the baby and how to prepare for labor and delivery and with her need for naps in the evening. She didn't like his late nights at the office or dinners out with clients, but she had her women's Bible study at church, Sunday School class and her family if she needed anyone. Eduardo's career was thriving, the way they both wanted it to. Pamela felt sure that once it was thoroughly established Eduardo would have more time at home. Time to spend with her and their children. Because now that she knew she could get pregnant, she wasn't going to stop at one. There would be more, hopefully at least 1 girl and 1 boy, until their family was complete. *Life is good*, Pamela thought, *life is good*.

Chapter 8

Eduardo had been relieved and elated when he got Pamela's voice mail, knowing instantly the pregnancy test was positive. He couldn't help but feel that his own virility had played a part in resolving the problem. He knew instinctively that he was more than capable of impregnating his wife, evidenced by the fact that he had done so despite the hindrance of a disease. At the time he had wondered if it would be a boy or girl, not really having a preference which came first. A girl first would probably make both Pamela and his mother happy. They would enjoy buying girl clothes and fussing with girly things. It was fine with him if the boy came next. Children were exactly what Pamela needed. This would motivate her to finally quit her job and devote herself fulltime to him, their home and their family. She wouldn't be able to spend the same amount of time volunteering at church or participating in Bible studies; she would need to be at home with the children.

The baby shower five months ago seemed a distant memory; now it was the Sunday after Pamela's due date. Roberta was staying with them for a few days and Eduardo had no problem with that. Having her there made Pamela happy and gave her an extra set of hands for housework now that she was in her last days of pregnancy – the "beached whale stage" Pamela called it. It also freed him to be at the office if he needed to or manage his email and pending projects from his office at home when he was there. With the baby coming any day he wasn't traveling but he needed to stay on top of things at work. There were two large pending projects, one on the west coast, that would be quite lucrative if his firm got the bid, and Eduardo was determined that it would.

Roberta finished unloading the dishwasher and began placing the few dirty dishes in the rack. Knowing that Pamela's due date had passed and Lily could arrive at any minute, Roberta told Frank the previous week she just had a feeling that she should be with Pamela. He understood his wife's longing to be with her oldest daughter at the Lily's birth. "Of course," he said, kissing her and giving his blessing for her to go. "Don't come back without a granddaughter!" he had joked as he waved her out of the driveway two days later. That was three days ago and she had called Frank every evening to check in. How blessed she was to have such a loving husband and be close with her daughter who wanted her there at this time.

Pamela lumbered into the kitchen and leaned against the island, looking bored. "What do you want to do for dinner, dear?" Roberta asked, walking over to gently rub her daughter's back.

"Oh, I don't know," she sighed. "I'm so tired of waiting. I'm ready to have this baby!"

Roberta laughed. "Believe me, I know how you feel," she said. "With Luke I gained way too much weight. He was past due also and by the middle of May it was already hot and very humid. The day before I went into labor I forced myself to move around a lot, even tried to clean out a closet. In the end, the baby always comes in God's timing. So often it feels to us as if He is moving too slowly but His timing and His ways are perfect."

Pamela smiled at her mom. "I know," she replied, "it's just that there's nothing to do at the moment. I've checked my packed hospital bag a bazillion times, read and re-read my notes and books about labor and what to expect, Lily's room is ready down to the stack of diapers at the changing table ready to be used. My due date was last week and I'm not having any contractions or sign of labor – not even Braxton Hicks!" She sat down on a leather padded barstool. "Are there any chocolate chip cookies left?"

Roberta's smile was filled with love and patience as she brought the cookie jar over and set it down in front of Pamela, who immediately reached in and grabbed two. Munching on the first one, Pamela looked up and said, "Maybe we could go out to dinner tonight? If I have to wait some more at least I could go to a nice restaurant and have some fish and grilled veggies, maybe even a margarita – I haven't had one of those in ages."

"That's a great idea," Roberta said, nodding as she thought about where to go. "The Wharf opened up a new place on the north side a couple of months ago and I hear the food is delicious."

"I'll ask Eduardo. Let's plan on that Mom, and the earlier the reservation the better. I can be ready in 15 minutes."

She found Eduardo in the office, poring over some spreadsheets displayed on the triple 24" monitors at his desk. "What are you working on?" she asked.

"That large bid due in a week for the west coast job. If I can land that job it would be a sweet deal for us." Eduardo forced his eyes away from the screens and looked at Pamela. "How are you feeling?"

"Fine. Still no contractions. I'd really like to go out to eat tonight and Mom suggested The Wharf. Is that okay with you?"

"Sure," he said. "Let me finish up this segment of the proposal and then we can leave when you are ready."

Thirty minutes later they were in the Tahoe headed north. At the restaurant Pamela relaxed a little, enjoying the beautiful view of the lake, the early evening lights twinkling across the water, and sipping a small, cool margarita on the rocks. She wasn't worried about a drink harming the baby's development at this stage and she needed something to take the edge off her nerves. Would this baby never come? After a fabulous meal of blackened red snapper, grilled squash and tomatoes with a spring mix garden salad on the side and a shared piece of chocolate meringue pie Pamela announced she was ready to go. Eduardo helped her out of her chair and they drove home in comfortable silence.

As they pulled into the garage Pamela asked Eduardo for the tenth time that weekend if the Tahoe's tank was full. He assured her it was and excused himself to his office. Pamela and Roberta headed back to the nursery to once again admire the room. The wooden crib was in the corner, outfitted with Jan Brett sheets, bumper pad and blanket. A stuffed bear that could produce sounds similar to inside the womb was in one corner. On one wall was a matching dresser, filled with baby clothes. Across the room were shelves, already filled with infant toys and books. The large Jan Brett print had been matted and framed and hung over the shelves. The closet had a pack and play, stroller, infant seat, boxes of diapers and the clothes hanging rod displayed a dozen smocked dresses. The changing table and diapers were ready and the shelves underneath held every accessory imaginable.

Pamela thought back to the Tea Cindy had given her, attended by Cindy's friends. Cindy hadn't wanted to do a traditional baby shower, but rather an afternoon tea where she could have her friends from church, the junior league and the museum over to meet Pamela. They had brought gifts of course, and it was at the tea that Pamela received the most elegant baby gifts. She had received Feldman smocked dresses with matching panties, lacy socks and several pairs of infant dress shoes for church, silver picture frames, autographed children's books by Caldecott medal-winning authors, a christening bonnet, and some savings bonds. The tea had been the perfect complement to Riley's shower – lovely, expensive gifts at one and practical, necessary gifts at the other. This pregnancy had been one big shower of God's blessings.

"What are you thinking?" Roberta's question brought her out of her thoughts to the present.

"Oh, just about the tea Cindy gave for me. We got some lovely things. Pretty things for the baby just delight my heart," Pamela replied happily.

"Yes, that was a wonderful idea Cindy had. You are so fortunate in your mother-in-law, my dear." Roberta gave Pamela a hug.

Pamela left the baby's room to go stretch out on her own bed, and Roberta told her she'd be in the guest room if Pamela needed her. Eduardo was still in the office. Pamela eased herself onto the king size tempur-pedic mattress, grateful for the bed's support. She loved their bedroom furniture with its mahogany sleigh-bed style frame and matching armoire, dresser with mirror, and night stands. She reached over to pick up her book. Flipping to the page with the bookmark, the contraction caught her by surprise. As it subsided she tried to read, watching the second hand on her watch to time the pains should another one come. And it did. For forty-five minutes she timed them, coming regularly now about 12 minutes apart. She knew that this type of early labor could last for hours, but when the next one lasted longer and was more intense she picked up the phone by her bed and pressed the intercom button. Eduardo picked up immediately in his office.

"Is it time?" he asked anxiously.

"Yes, I think so. I started having contractions an hour ago and they are getting longer and harder. Please call the doctor," Pamela answered.

Eduardo spoke with the doctor on call and was instructed to bring her to the hospital for admitting. Within minutes he and Pamela were on their way. Roberta would wait at the house until they knew for sure this was it, but they all felt sure it wouldn't be long now until they got to meet Lily face to face.

Chapter 9

Roberta couldn't get over it. Back in the day when Pamela was born the father wasn't even allowed in the labor and delivery rooms. But here she was in Pamela's birthing room holding her first granddaughter, a healthy 7 pound 9 ounce beautiful baby girl. Lily was swaddled in the striped hospital newborn blanket and cap and mewing softly to her grandmother. The lactation nurse was consulting with Pamela but Roberta could already tell the nursing was going to go fine. Lily had already latched on once, making the process look easily. *Thank you Father, please let the breast feeding be successful for Pamela and Lily. Pamela wants that so much.* She smiled down at Lily, amazed at the perfect tiny creature in her arms, and lightly kissed the cheek. A granddaughter!

Out in the hallway Eduardo was on the phone to Cindy and Bill. "She looks just like me!" he exclaimed. "Already I can tell she has my nose, mouth and chin. She's beautiful!"

"We can't wait to see her," Cindy said, excitement permeating her voice. "When can we come to stay with you for a few days?"

"The doctor won't release us until tomorrow, and Roberta will be with us for at least a couple of days after that," Eduardo said. "Why don't you plan on being here Friday? We'll see how Pamela is feeling and how things are going and then decide how long the visit should be."

"Friday it is," Cindy said, "we'll be there first thing Friday morning. Please give Pamela our love and tell her we are anxious to hold that darling girl!"

"I will, Mother. We'll talk before then." Eduardo pressed the End button on his phone. He was a father, and their daughter was healthy. Pamela had handled the labor and delivery like a trooper. Thankfully her labor had only lasted eleven hours, which he understood was not bad for a first pregnancy. Eduardo had carried Lily over to the bassinet for the nurse to clean and weigh her, get her feet prints and put the identification bracelet on. As if she needed that! She looked just like him, and he wouldn't let that baby out of his or Pamela's sight while they were there. He had simply stood there, gazing at this tiny person who was related to him, marveling at how he had helped produce another person. He felt fulfilled, satisfied. He had the perfect wife and now a beautiful daughter. His business had all the makings of an empire if he worked hard enough and life was good. Really good.

He had no sooner put the phone in his pocket when it rang. Not recognizing the number he silenced the call and glanced up at the directory in the waiting area looking for guidance to the cafeteria. He needed some coffee, it had been a long night.

That afternoon Luke, Riley and Tessa came for a visit. Pamela was happy to see her siblings and let them admire her gorgeous daughter. She was perfect – not just because she had ten fingers and toes, dimples, long lashes, hazel eyes and dark hair. She was perfect because she was a gift from God, and Pamela's very soul cried out to Him in gratitude and joy. She had not known she could love anyone as much as she already loved Lily. They had bonded during the 37 weeks she had lived in Pamela's womb, bonded at the heart level and to the depth of Pamela's soul. She loved this child with everything in her, this child God had blessed her with. She thought immediately of Psalm 139: "You created my inmost being; you knit me together in my mother's womb. I praise you because I am fearfully and wonderfully made." Despite disease and the odds against her being able to conceive, the God of the universe had blessed her with not just a pregnancy but a healthy one, filled with love and gifts and anticipation, ending with a mercifully brief labor and this beautiful, unbelievably amazing baby girl. Lily. What a lovely name. They had considered hundreds of names, and Eduardo was content to let her name the girl. He already knew what he would name a son. She wanted a name that was not just pretty but meaningful as well. The name Lily represented beauty, innocence and purity, a delicate flower. And little Lily was all of those things.

She looked over at Riley, holding Lily and cooing at her. Luke walked over to her bedside, smiling and bending down to hug his congratulations. He was the picture of Marlboro-man handsome. "How ya feeling, sis?" he asked. "Pretty cute little girl you have there."

"I'm sore and a little tired, but doing great! Can you believe it Luke? I have a baby, a beautiful baby girl," she said softly. God's grace was still amazing her on this day of her daughter's birth.

Luke patted her hand and stayed to visit a while, catching her up on life at the station and the latest pranks the firemen had pulled on each other. He had been a firefighter for only a few years, but his induction on the force had been a proud day for both him and Frank. They shared the same love of helping people, even at great risk to themselves.

Riley walked over, holding Lily carefully. "Oh Pamela, she's beautiful. Holding her makes me remember those precious newborn days with Brayden. There's nothing like those days." She turned to hand Lily to Tessa, who was eagerly awaiting her turn. A child in this family will never lack for love or support, thought Pamela. She looked at Riley. "I know.

It's only been a few hours and already I'm loving it. I want to savor every moment, every baby smell and every touch of her soft skin. My heart is singing!" she said.

The sisters chatted easily about nursing, changing diapers, how often to feed, and the importance of taking naps at every chance because you never knew when the baby would sleep. The nurse came in, asking visitors to step outside so she could take Pamela's vitals and do a post-delivery exam. The three said their goodbyes to Pamela and assured her they would see her soon. The nurse had just completed the exam when Eduardo walked in. He'd gone home to shower and change, and the nurse glanced up admiringly as he entered the room. Pamela smiled as she reached up to kiss him and feel his embrace.

Chapter 10

Was it time to feed Lily again? They had been home for less than 12 hours and already it seemed that all Pamela did was nurse, rock the baby to sleep and try to nap only to be awakened by Lily's cries. But that's why her mother was staying for a couple of days, to take care of meals, laundry and visitors while helping with Lily when she could. Pamela bent over the crib and picked up Lily, whose crying lessened a little. Roberta was quickly at her side. "Do you want me to change her while you get ready to feed her?" her mom asked.

"Thanks, Mom, yes please. I just have to go to the bathroom then I'll be ready for you to bring her to me," Pamela said, heading to her room.

After washing her hands and drying them thoroughly she settled into her favorite oversized rocking chair, both feet resting on the footstool. Roberta brought Lily to her, and they both smiled as the room grew quiet, the silence broken only by the sounds of the baby's sucking. As the milk flowed from mother to child Pamela felt the relief from the pressure of full breasts. She was thankful to have plenty of milk but had learned that she too could only go so long without nursing the baby.

"I'll bring you a glass of juice. Want anything to eat?" her mother asked.

"I'd love a grilled cheese sandwich if it's not too much trouble," Pamela replied.

"Not at all. I'll be back shortly."

Pamela gazed down at the infant attached to her, tiny hand resting against Pamela's skin. She would never get enough of this. Nursing and gazing and holding and cuddling with Lily. Sure, she had to contrast that with crying and lack of sleep and not knowing what to do when feeding or a dry diaper didn't still Lily's cries. But it was all worth it, oh so worth it. Her mom would only be here for the rest of the day, and Pamela wanted to enjoy every moment of her help, the easy way they had with each other, her mother knowing when to give Pamela some space. Pamela had always been one that needed her space, especially during times of stress, even good stress. She wasn't sure how she and Cindy would interact while the Cohens were staying with them. She had never had Eduardo's parents as house guests, and while she and Cindy got along great Cindy was very much a take charge person in her own home. How would she be in Pamela's home? Would she help with cleaning and laundry and meals as Roberta was doing, or would she only want to spend time with Lily? Pamela's instincts told her that Lily was a sensitive child, and watching her confirmed that. She startled easily, couldn't go to sleep unless the room was dark and very quiet, and if she heard a loud noise of any kind she jumped, even in her sleep. Cindy was so intense and this was her first grandchild. Would she know to be quite and gentle and go easy as she handled the infant? Or would she swoop down, overwhelming the child with the intensity of her feelings?

This is ridiculous, Pamela thought. I'm just tired, the lack of sleep is getting to me. It's going to be fine. Eduardo will help me. But then Eduardo hadn't been around all day today and Roberta had told her he planned to work extra hours to make up for the time out the past week. Yes, he'd been excited and taken video of them leaving the hospital and helped her get settled in at home. But the connection that had been so evident in their kiss at the hospital only hours after Lily's birth already seemed distant. She could tell he was chomping at the bit to get back to work full speed, make up for any lost ground. He had an extremely capable partner and excellent staff; his assistant managed his clients expertly when he was out. But he wanted to be there, to be in charge in person, and she understood. He was building something for them, wasn't he? She just wished he would be at home more during this first week, she wanted him near.

Goodness, the doctor was right about how emotional she was likely to be after the baby was born. Her emotions were all over the place. She eased Lily up onto her shoulder to burp her and glanced at her Bible on the side table. It was open to her life verse, Proverbs 3: 5-6. "Trust in the Lord with all your heart, lean not to your own understanding; in all your ways acknowledge Him and He will direct your paths," she quoted aloud without reading. *Yes, Father, I do trust you – with my life, my marriage, my child, my very soul. Protect my marriage, bless my husband's work and keep us close. Bring him closer to you in this new chapter in our lives that we may worship and praise you together. Amen.*

The smell of a perfectly cooked grilled cheese sandwich entered the room before Roberta. Pamela kissed the sleeping Lily and gratefully handed her over to Roberta to rock while she ate her snack. Mothering was hungry work, a grilled cheese never tasted so good. She smiled at her mom and leaned her head back against the pillow, falling asleep almost instantly. Roberta kept rocking Lily, gently patting her back and kissing her cheek. She was a grandma, and she couldn't wait for that word to come out of Lily's mouth.

The doorbell rang, waking Pamela. While Roberta finished changing Lily's diaper Pamela peeked out the dining room window and saw the Cohen's Lexus. This was it. Mom-time was over and mother-in-law time was about to begin. She couldn't shake the anxiety even though it didn't make sense. Taking a deep breath and squaring her shoulders she went to the front door and opened it.

"Hello!" Cindy exclaimed. "I hope we aren't too early, I just couldn't wait another minute to get my hands on that baby!" "No, it's fine," Pamela said. "Please, come in. Mom's in the nursery changing the baby." Cindy hugged Pamela as Bill followed them inside.

"Bill, you can take the bags into the guest room. It's down the hall, last room on the right," Pamela told him. Bill headed back to the car to gather the luggage while Cindy moved into the living room.

"I haven't seen the nursery since you hung the Jan Brett," Cindy said as she began walking toward Lily's room. Pamela told her she was going to love it and followed her down the hall.

Roberta had just settled Lily in her crib and turned to greet Cindy. The two women embraced. Cindy thanked Roberta for relinquishing the guest room and turned to the crib. She leaned down swiftly and gathered Lily into her arms. Lily immediately began to cry. There was no other word for it, Pamela thought, she swooped. Pamela noticed Lily's startle response as soon as Cindy picked her up from the crib.

"There, there, it's alright. Grandma CiCi is here now, shh, shh," she cooed, walking slowing around the room as the child quieted down.

"I'll just go help mom load the car," Pamela said to Cindy, who nodded at her approvingly and returned her attention to Lily. Pamela walked with her mother down the hallway.

"I'm sorry Eduardo's not here to put your bags in the car, mom," she said.

"Oh honey, that's not a problem, I only have one and it's small." Roberta turned to look at Pamela. "I know you are worried about how it will be while Cindy is here. Just relax and let things take their course. She's here to help, and she deserves her grandma time just as I did. It'll be fine."

Pamela attempted a brave smile. "I'm sure it will. I'm just going to miss you so much, Mom. It's been so great to have you here, you've been a huge help, and Eduardo is gone so much. It just feels like all of a sudden Cindy's become a mother-in-law, like it's awkward between us now that I have a baby. I'm not sure who should take charge. I didn't expect to feel so... territorial."

"Part of that is natural, dear, you're a new mother! Remember to rejoice in all things and pray without ceasing. Cindy loves you and she is obviously crazy about Lily, so don't fret. She can't feed the baby, only you can do that until you have a routine and are able use the breast pump. Let Cindy have her precious moments too," Roberta said, embracing her daughter as she prepared to leave. "Call me any time."

"I will. Thanks again, Mom and tell Frank thank you for letting us have you so long!" Pamela walked Roberta out to the car and watched as she pulled out of the driveway. Turning to walk back into the house she gathered herself and said a short prayer. This was to be a special time, not a time of anxiety. She smiled and opened the door.

Chapter 11

Eduardo walked into the house that evening to the delicious aroma of pork tenderloin, scalloped potatoes, and creamed spinach. As he entered the kitchen he saw Cindy pulling a thermometer out of the meat and check the ice in the champagne bucket. "Hello Mother, so glad you are here," he greeted her and gave her a bear hug. "Dinner smells delicious. Where's Dad?"

"He's just a few blocks away putting gas in the car. You know how he likes to keep it full, 'never drive with less than half a tank' as he likes to say." Cindy turned the oven off, leaving the potatoes inside. "How was your day?"

Eduardo smiled broadly. "Great. We got the west coast job and the client is really happy with our proposal. This one is going to propel us into the market as a major player, I just know it." He poured himself a glass of wine and one for Cindy. "Is Pamela sleeping? I'm so glad you are here, not just to help with Lily but I've missed your cooking," he said. "I assume you two are enjoying each other's company immensely as usual."

Cindy took a sip of wine and smiled. "Oh yes, things are fine. I can't get enough of holding Lily of course, but it's just that I'm so excited! She is such a darling little baby, perfect in every way. I think Pamela is a little uncertain about how it will be to have her mother-in-law here with a new baby, worried about whether I'll want to spend all my time with Lily and who will do the housework. But we are glad to have time together and already had a couple of nice chats today."

"Mom, that's ridiculous," Eduardo said. "Why should Pamela be worried about having you here? You two are peas from the same pod!"

"Exactly," Cindy replied. "Just a little normal territory issues, to be expected when Pamela's a brand new mother and it's my first grandchild. Not to worry, I've already taken steps to make sure things are smooth. Ellen, one of my friends from church, has a daughter who lives nearby and we've arranged for their maid to come for a couple of hours each day to do house cleaning, laundry, straighten the bedrooms and begin the meal prep for dinner. That way Pamela and I can focus on the baby. It's our gift to you both, a way of saying thank you for letting us come and stay."

Eduardo looked amused. "As if we could keep you away!" he said. "That's a wonderful idea. Pamela will be so pleased. You've been here less than a day and already you've reduced some of her stress. She couldn't have a better mother-in-law than you."

Cindy looked up at her handsome son, quite pleased with herself. She really did want to help Pamela, but she didn't want to waste time with cleaning and laundry when there was a baby to hold, rock, walk and read to. She knew Eduardo would love the idea, and if Pamela got upset over her mother-in-law hiring a maid for a few days Eduardo could take care of that.

"Why don't you go freshen up for dinner then check on Pamela," she suggested. "I'll just finish setting the table and set out the glasses. Dinner should be ready in 10 minutes."

Eduardo walked down the hall to his office and deposited his briefcase on the desk. It was so great to have his mom here to cook and help Pamela, and his dad could take care of any errands or small things that the ladies wanted done at the house. Women always wanted a piece of furniture moved or a picture relocated or a new plant purchased for the deck. Bill Cohen had always taken care of Cindy in that way and Eduardo knew his father would take care of those things for Pamela while he was here. That would keep him occupied and Eduardo could continue to work as usual and come home to his mother's delicious dinners.

He entered their bedroom and stepped over to the large closet, selecting a fresh shirt. He changed, checked his hair in the mirror and admired his figure. He was in excellent shape. In the business world the men either respected him for that or were jealous; the women loved his good looks and he could always count on getting just what he wanted whether it was a waitress at the club or a potential client. God, he loved his life. He turned off the light as he left the room and headed for the nursery in search of his wife.

Pamela heard his steps when he was just outside the door. "Shhh, Lily just fell asleep," she said quietly as she met him at the door. She stood up on her tiptoes to kiss him. "I've missed you. How was work today?"

"Excellent. Landed the job and we are preparing for the equipment order. Everyone is happy and it's going to really get me noticed in the industry. I'll have to be out in California a lot over the next few months. This job could be a turning point for us. Everything has to go perfectly, the client needs to be extremely satisfied. Which is what I do, of course," he grinned.

Pamela looked disappointed. She was tired and irritable and wanted to ask how he could possibly think of leaving her for several weeks at a time like this. But she didn't want to spoil his mood and she knew there was nothing to be done about it. "Eduardo I'm so happy for you. Congratulations," she said.

Eduardo took in Pamela's appearance, noting that her figure didn't look all that different from when she was in the middle of her pregnancy. He supposed it would take a while for her to shed the weight she had gained but he hoped it wouldn't be long. He needed her back in shape, gorgeous and at the top of her game for the corporate entertaining he had planned. She was probably just tired, and after all Lily was still just a few days old. Maybe it was time for them to have their own household help, give Pamela time for a personal trainer. He made a mental note to discuss that with his mother, she would know how to find the right people. "Thanks. Dinner will be ready shortly. Mom cooked one of my favorite meals and it smells delicious. See you in the dining room," he said.

They were all seated and sipping their wine when Pamela entered the dining room. She saw that Cindy was in her usual seat with Bill at her side, so she sat down on the other side of Eduardo, placing her napkin in her lap. Cindy smiled at her warmly. "How are you feeling dear?" she asked.

"Fine, thanks," Pamela said. "I didn't realize how tired I was until I put Lily down this last time. It's amazing what a difference a quick shower and change of clothes can make." She surveyed the table. "Cindy, this looks fabulous. Thank you so much for cooking," she said earnestly.

"Of course, dear. That's what I'm here for. You just relax, regain your strength and get plenty of rest. Hopefully you will be able to make use of the breast pump while I'm here and I can take some turns feeding the baby," Cindy replied smoothly.

"That idea sounds more appealing than it did last week, I'll admit," she said, and they all laughed. With that the tension in the house melted and they began to enjoy their meal.

When no one could hold another bite of tenderloin or potatoes, Cindy announced, "Bill and I are going to take care of the kitchen. You two just go on about your evening as usual. Pamela if you want to try to rest while Lily is still sleeping I will listen for her to wake up. Also, I hope you don't mind, but I took the liberty of hiring a maid for laundry and light housework while I'm here. I want to be totally available to you and Lily while I'm here. I'll continue to cook my son's favorite dishes, of course, but other than that I'm all yours." She and Bill cleared the first of the dishes from the table and took them to the kitchen. Pamela looked at Eduardo. "A maid? Is it anyone we know? Will she have access to the baby?"

Eduardo reached out his hand to pat her shoulder. "Relax, Mom has it under control. She's a referral from a reliable friend, and only you and Mom will be taking care of the baby." Pamela nodded. She didn't care who did the housework as long as she was taking care of her precious girl.

After dinner she went into the bedroom and took out the instructions for the Medela Breast Pump. Everyone had told her it was the best, and she had read plenty of opinions and advice on the internet about how to pump, when to pump, how to clean the pump. She hooked up the machine and turned the dial clockwise to start, adjusting the speed slightly. To her amazement in just over a minute she saw milk begin to pour into the bottle. She'd read that she would always have enough milk because her body was making it continuously while it was needed. That sounds just like a design God would think of, she thought. After fifteen minutes she turned off the machine, unhooked the apparatus and carefully zipped the bag closed. There, she had done it. One four ounce bag, ready to feed at a moment's notice. Until she saw the filled bag she hadn't realized how tied she was to Lily's need to eat. She wanted to be the one to feed her all the time, but that wasn't practical as Lily grew. After a few months she knew Eduardo would need her for occasional company functions where she couldn't take Lily. She would have to leave Lily for two or three hours at a time, and her mom or siblings would need to feed her. Now they would be able to. She felt proud of herself as she walked to the kitchen to put the milk in the freezer. She may be a new mother but she was figuring this out. Back in her room, head on the pillow, she drifted off to sleep. Thirty minutes later, Lily woke up.

Chapter 12

Lily giggled delightedly as the swing moved slightly up, then back down again. Her smile was infectious, the dimples showing off that cute face. Pamela looked down at her daughter and said, "Want to go up again? Just a little bit, not too high, you're only 6 months. Not a big girl yet. Don't get too big too fast, Lily. Mommy likes you just the way you are." Lily held on tight to the edge of the bucket swing and swung her legs, indicating to her mom to continue. Pamela gave the swing a slight push, holding on to the chain higher up. It was a cool, early spring afternoon and they were the only ones on the playground at Westlawn Park.

These days she and Lily had developed a routine that suited them both. In the mornings they had breakfast and spent time in Lily's room playing or reading books. Lily loved to read, and they never went anywhere without Lily's favorite board books tucked into Pamela's bag. A nap for Lily mid-morning while Pamela had prayer time and journaled. Usually she also had time to check Facebook and catch up on her email. For lunch Pamela liked to feed Lily out on the deck if the weather permitted. If not they would eat in the kitchen, Lily in her highchair and Pamela next to her seated on a barstool at the island. For after lunch play time Pamela liked to use learning toys, blocks or simple colored shapes. Then naptime, this time for both of them, and when they woke Lily was bundled into her stroller and they walked to the park four blocks away.

Pamela had given notice to her boss when Lily was six weeks old. He had thanked her for the years of service and assured her that while he would miss her she was doing the right thing. They both agreed motherhood was the highest calling and the value of a committed stay-home mom was without price.

She had quickly grown to love her life that did not involve working outside the home and felt blessed to have the option. She had endured two months of Lily's colic, and joked that during that time she basically strapped on a Snugli and wore her child all the time. It was the only thing that stopped Lily's crying. She learned she could do many things with a baby strapped to her body – fold laundry, prepare a meal, even put clothes into the washer and retrieve them from the dryer if she was careful. After that it was smooth sailing. Pamela adored this 6 month stage, where Lily was old enough to be not so fragile but not old enough to crawl away or say no. It was the perfect baby age and she loved every minute of it.

Although Brayden was already a toddler, Pamela and Riley scheduled regular play dates, more so the two of them could chat than for the children to play. Typically they met at a park or the children's museum, anywhere that had age appropriate areas for a toddler and an infant. She was so glad to have her siblings and parents in the same city. Roberta stopped by often for morning coffee and to play with Lily. Luke came by sometimes on his off days and Lily was quite charmed by her dashing uncle. Tessa loved to come play with Lily during the hour of dinner preparation, and she and Lily would sit on the kitchen floor playing with plastic dishes while Pamela prepared supper for them.

It was especially helpful to have her family around with Eduardo gone so much. After his parents had left, Eduardo was at home in the evenings for one week before his regular traveling to California began. Pamela loved those evenings when he was home, willing to take a break from work to play with Lily or read her a story or take an evening stroll. That's the way she wanted all of their evenings to be, and one night in the middle of that week after Lily was asleep she told Eduardo so.

"Honey, you know I have to travel for this job. It's the biggest thing that's ever happened to my company, and if it goes well the opportunities for future growth are practically limitless," he had told her.

"But you are going to miss so much! Lily is growing so fast, changing or learning a new skill almost every day. Don't you want to be here for that?" Pamela asked, her eyes searching his.

"Of course I do. But my presence on this project is integral to the progress of the job, crucial to our success and the client's happiness. Without that I may as well not have taken the venture. Pamela, I love what I do and this is an incredible opportunity. Besides, you have the weekly maid now, your family is here in town and you have lots of help if you need it. I need this project to go well; I want it to be a major success. I'll be the talk of the industry if I can pull it off and I know I can. I've got the staff, the critical path management plan and the right equipment. All I've needed is the chance to show the international big boys what I can do and now I have it. I'm not going to let this chance slip through my fingers. Besides, don't I provide well for you? You don't have to work, you have a maid and as much money as you need for the household, nice clothes, expensive hair and nail color and now plenty of money to take care of Lily. Try to be a little more appreciative of all I am doing for you. And please, don't bring up this subject any more. I'll be home as often as I can."

He had turned his attention to his laptop after that, and she had let the subject drop. It wasn't what she wanted, and she was concerned that this was only the beginning of "big opportunities" that would keep Eduardo away from her and Lily, away from the life she wanted to have with her husband, not just her daughter. He had been quite firm that there was to be no more discussion on the matter, and she knew even if she tried it wouldn't make any difference. She decided to make his remaining three evenings at home as pleasurable as possible, hoping to entice him to cut down on his travel. She was fitting into her pre-pregnancy clothes once more and she made sure to be dressed in her most flattering outfits by the time he was home each evening. She was extra careful to keep Lily on schedule and put her to bed on time now that she slept through the night. She prepared his favorite meals and served his preferred beverages, which now included expensive wines and cognac for after dinner. She made sure the living areas were cleared of Lily's toys and everything was in its place. On two of those nights she enticed him away from his computer and into their bedroom. As with any couple their passion had waned since the early months of marriage, but Pamela sensed something else, the beginning of a disconnect. She couldn't put her finger on it but it bothered her, and long after Eduardo was on his side lightly snoring she lay awake, wondering.

Chapter 13

Applying the finishing touches to her makeup, Pamela stood up from the dressing table. She eyed herself critically in the mirror. The cap-sleeve, above-the-knee length fitted dress in a shade of blue to match her eyes was perfect for an evening out to celebrate their anniversary. She accented it with the antique pearl ring that had been GiGi's, pearl stud earrings and the string of vintage Marvella pearls Cindy had given her. Pamela felt elegant, and ready for a night out with her husband. He had been traveling a great deal since his first trip months ago out to the west coast. She was happy he was home this week and eager for some time alone with him. He had promised to be home early to pick her up, and assured her his cell phone would be turned off. She had engaged Tessa, already busy in the kitchen, for the night to take care of Lily and she smiled as she heard Lily bang her tray while Tessa heated the child's favorite meal of mac-n-cheese and green peas. The spike heels of Pamela's silver sandals clicked as she made her way down the hall and into the kitchen.

"Are you having fun with Aunt Tess?" Pamela asked Lily, stroking her hair.

"Cheese," said Lily firmly, and both sisters laughed.

"The list of emergency numbers is on the kitchen desk, and of course you can always call Mom or Riley if you need. This night is for me and Eduardo, and I'm determined to make it totally about the two of us," Pamela said smiling, checking the list one last time.

Tessa nodded. "I'm all over it. I'm looking forward to having Lily to myself – at our family gatherings I don't get much one on one time with her. You two have a great evening and don't worry about a thing. I mean it."

"Thanks. It seems like it's been forever since we've had a date night. I really appreciate your coming and spending the night. That takes all the stress out of it," Pamela said.

The sound of the garage door opening caught their attention. Seconds later the door opened as Eduardo walked in, talking on his cell phone. "Yes, Randy, that will be fine. Just send me all three reports first thing in the morning. I'll call you after I meet with the install team." Eduardo clicked off his phone and slipped it into his pocket. "How are my girls?" he asked, tousling Lily's hair and kissing Pamela on the cheek. He gave Pamela an appraising look. "Wow, you look great." He turned to Tessa. "Hi, thanks for coming."

"Lily and I are set for the evening," Tessa told him. "After dinner we've got bath time, play time, then stories and prayers until lights out."

Eduardo turned to Pamela. "You ready? Let's go celebrate!" he said, taking her arm. "Don't wait up, Tess, we are off the clock tonight. No calls unless it's a real emergency." Pamela gave Tessa a hug, Lily one last kiss and left the kitchen without another look.

As they entered the garage Pamela looked from the car to Eduardo. "Where's your car?" she asked, confused.

"Right here," he said, waving to the brand new Cadillac Escalade SUV parked in his spot. "It was time for something new." Pamela took in the sparkling vehicle – cream colored paint with platinum interior, all the bells and whistles. She knew he liked to have capacity for both clients and the occasional cargo, but this was more extravagant than anything he had purchased before. "Isn't it a bit much?" she asked, tentatively.

Eduardo grinned. "It's amazing what a dealer will do for you when you show up with cash. This baby's got it all. My newest clients expect first class. Besides, it won't be long before Lily's brother comes along and we'll want the extra room. Your Mustang is not exactly a family vehicle. Come on, let's see how she drives."

They climbed in and Pamela settled into the luxurious leather seats. As she adjusted her seatback and fiddled with the passenger A/C panel, Eduardo commented on the amenities. "Everything is fully adjustable; separate climate controls, Bluetooth, Onstar, Wifi and two TV-DVD players in back with streaming." Pamela had to laugh. "We'll have to be careful that our children don't grow up spoiled," she said. Then she sank back into the plush seat and let herself relax, gazing out at the city lights as they made their way to Nappaliano's. It was fun to feel like more than a mommy, as wonderful as that was. Tonight she was an attractive, desirable young woman, and she would let herself be treated as such.

Eduardo guided the Cadillac smoothly into the restaurant's parking lot, pulling up to the entrance. The valet was at his door in an instant and Eduardo handed him the keys, pocketing the ticket. Their hostess greeted them warmly, found Eduardo's name on the reservation list and gave Eduardo a flirtatious smile. "This way, please," she said, "your table is ready." She led them to a secluded but spacious table near the back and motioned for them to be seated. Rather than handing them menus she turned to Eduardo and said, "Tony will be with you momentarily." She retreated and was replaced by a young man bearing a tray with water, a steaming basket of fresh sourdough bread and dishes of butter.

Pamela looked puzzled. "Where are the menus?" she asked Eduardo. Before he could answer, a tall dark haired man appeared at the edge of their table and announced, "I am Tony, I will be taking care of you this evening. Mr. Cohen, per your instructions we are ready with wine whenever you say. There will be four courses from our private menu, served at your leisure, followed by after dinner drinks if you wish." Smiling, he waited at Eduardo's right side.

"We'll have the wine now, please, followed by the appetizers. I'll motion when we are ready for our salads and the entrée. Thank you Tony." Eduardo's demeanor made it clear he was accustomed to being in command of the situation.

"Very good sir," Tony replied as he exited quietly.

"Oh Eduardo, how fancy!" Pamela exclaimed. " I feel like royalty. What are we having?"

" Knowing how you love seafood I ordered the lobster bisque, and the main course will include both lobster and gulf shrimp so I don't think you'll be disappointed," Eduardo answered, pleased with himself.

"Perfect!" Pamela moved her arm as the waiter appeared with their wine. She waited for Eduardo to taste it and nod his approval, watching as the server poured their glasses. Eduardo lifted his glass and his eyes to her. "Happy anniversary, sweetheart," he said.

"Happy anniversary, dear," she agreed, happiness settling in the deepest layers of her heart. Oh she was blessed!

Relaxed and happy, Pamela began to bring Eduardo up to date on Lily, her Bible study and friends from church, and her latest ideas about landscaping for the back yard. She told him about Lily's newest developed skills, how she was cruising all around the house and would be walking any day now. "She's so smart. She works with her manipulatives as well as Brayden, and her matching and sorting skills are really advanced. Lily loves the music toys of course, and I love the way she is focused when she makes her selection. You should see her at the park, the swings are her favorite!" As Pamela talked, Eduardo listened attentively, nodding occasionally or saying "Oh?" to encourage her. But mentally the wheels of his business brain were churning relentlessly. He couldn't stop thinking about the call he'd had that morning from the potential client in Minnesota. After hearing of the success of his project out in California, the Project Development Director for Primus, Ltd. was interested in meeting about fleshing out a new concept their development team was working on. Eduardo knew he didn't have an equal in his market niche and as he'd known the opportunities were opening up everywhere. He would have to open and staff a central office; where was he going to find the right Operations Manager, someone who could be trusted and also knew the technical side of the firm? He considered how he would return the call tomorrow. His approach needed to convey enough interest to gain traction but not so much that he lost his bargaining edge. He had been looking in Pamela's direction while she was talking but not seeing or hearing her. Now he saw her lips moving and began to register sound coming out of her mouth. Something about Daniel and revelation. She was talking about church now, he recognized, and said, "Tell me about that."

"Well, the study involved both books, focusing on the book of Daniel and tying in Revelation to give us a better understanding of prophecy, end times, and the very real nature of judgment and hell. It's fascinating. Our pastor is incredible with his fresh insight. I love the way he makes me think in new ways about familiar scripture. It would be so nice if you'd attend with me one Sunday, you might really find it interesting," Pamela said, trying to sound anything but wheedling or pestering in that last sentence.

"Pamela, you know church is not my thing. We've talked about it before. Let's not ruin a great evening with that discussion." Eduardo's tone said he was finished with the subject.

"Alright," she said softly, her disappointment evident. She decided not to let it envelope her and asked, "Tell me what's going on with California. It's taking you way from home much more than I thought it would but I can tell you are pleased with how everything is coming together." Pamela smiled engagingly at him, wishing him to share not just the details of the project but his hopes and dreams and goals as they moved forward. "What's the latest?"

Eduardo refilled their glasses and took a sip of the expensive sauvignon blanc. He gave her the layman's version of the project and talked about how his presence in California lent not only expertise and motivation to meet the deadline but assured his brand new client of his total commitment to satisfaction. Eduardo prided himself on delivering what the client wanted and showing off his creative technology interface skills in the process. He could come up with a solution when everyone else was at a loss. He told her of the facility, talked about traffic and the weather, and mentioned the challenges with local tradesmen who were used to a different set of expectations. He neglected to mention the night life that he and his new client regularly enjoyed together at the expense of their companies. Just part of the cost of doing business.

Pamela put her fork down and nudged her plate away. "Absolutely superb," she cooed. "Honey, this was a really special treat. Thank you."

At her left a tray appeared. Delicately seated atop the small round dish was a generous serving of Tiramisu, the drizzled caramel dripping down onto the chocolate designs criss crossing the plate. "Oh, I couldn't!" Pamela exclaimed, her eyes almost as big around as the saucer. "There simply isn't room!"

Eduardo motioned for him to leave the dessert and lifted his fork. "Well, I certainly can. This place is famous for its desserts." Pamela excused herself to the powder room while Eduardo settled the check. He had been quite pleased with the quality and the service, as his gratuity showed. Waiting for Pamela in the lobby he gave the valet his ticket. When she emerged from the ladies room their car was waiting for them at the curb. She melted into the seat and leaned back for the ride home.

As the garage door slowly closed behind them they entered the house quietly, listening for sounds of a baby crying. There were none. Only the welcome sound of silence. "Score one for Tessa," Eduardo whispered. They stepped softly through the house making their way to the master bedroom, passing the closed doors of Lily's nursery and the guest room where Tessa was sleeping for the night. Once inside, Eduardo closed the door. He loosened his tie, watching Pamela as she moved toward the bathroom. "I'll only be a few minutes," she tossed back over her shoulder as she shut the door.

Shedding his shoes, jacket and shirt, Eduardo leaned against the leather head board of their massive bed and clicked the remote. The TV screen displayed picture but no sound.

Pamela had changed into a new nightgown. It was soft and filmy, feminine and alluring but not provocative. She desired her husband's genuine love and his respect, not just a physical connection that was satisfying in the moment. Glancing in the mirror one last time, she opened the door and switched off the light. Stepping into the room her eyes caught a glimpse of the television screen before Eduardo flicked off the TV. She felt her mood evaporating at the disturbing image that had flashed across the screen.

He walked across the room, holding out his arms, noting the anxiety on her face. "Sorry, darling, I was channel flipping and that last one was a surprise. They'll put anything on cable these days." Pamela grimaced. "That garbage shouldn't be on any channel," she sighed. He took her hand and looked at her approvingly. "Let me look at you. Wow, this evening just keeps getting better," he smiled as he reached behind her to turn off the light.

Chapter 14

Sunlight streaming through the top row of windows coaxed Pamela's eyelids open around 7:30 the next morning. She let herself awake gradually, stretching and rolling her head over onto the cool part of the pillow. What a luxury to sleep in, knowing that Tessa was there to take care of Lily who was an early riser. Pamela hadn't slept this late since Lily was born. It felt strange, but in a good way. She remembered the night before, and a prayer rose from her heart to thank God for a good husband, a wonderful anniversary night and the means to have it, and the promise of her future.

Eduardo's side of the bed was empty. She listened for the sound of water running in the shower but heard nothing. He must already be in the kitchen for coffee. He didn't have to leave town until the next day and she wanted to have breakfast at home as a family. Pamela slipped out of bed and removed her favorite pink robe off its hook. She slid her feet into a pair of slippers and padded down the hallway.

The smell of freshly brewed coffee greeted her in the doorway, but Eduardo was nowhere to be seen. There were no breakfast remains, no sign of any activity except the warm coffee maker. She poured herself a cup and stirred in some Splenda. Pamela let the taste and warmth of her first cup work its way into a smile on her face as she leaned against the counter.

"Mama!" came Lily's excited cry as Tessa carried her into the kitchen. Pamela set down her mug and reached for her daughter, covering her face in kisses. "I missed you! Were you a good girl for Aunt Tessa?"

Tessa poured herself a cup of coffee and sat down at the island. "We had a great night. She loved her bath, of course, and I got to read my favorite story books while I put her to sleep. Lily went right to sleep and so did I. I forgot how much energy it takes to play with a little one!" she admitted. "Lily has been awake for about an hour. I fed her cereal without waiting for you because she was hungry. Oh, and Eduardo was on his way out when we came in for breakfast. How was your anniversary date?"

Pamela stared at Tessa. "Eduardo has already left town? He wasn't supposed to leave until tomorrow. I had plans for us this morning," she said, the corners of her mouth drooping. She placed Lily on the play mat with some toys. "Did he leave a message?"

Tessa slid two English muffins into the toaster and pressed the lever down. "He said he had to leave a day early, something about another new client and a short window. I'm sorry, Pamela, Lily was hungry and I didn't try to get any more information than he offered."

"That's okay, not your fault, I'm just disappointed. We had such a great night out that I hate for it to end so abruptly. Thank you a million times for keeping Lily. The food was fabulous, I got to have Eduardo's undivided attention and it felt like we were back to our old selves, before his work got so busy and his time at home so scarce. I hate the distance that his schedule creates. Besides, I didn't sign on to be a single mother!" she joked.

Tessa walked over and gave her a hug. "It'll be fine. He's a good provider and he works hard. Give him a few years and you'll probably have him at home so much you'll want him back at the office." Pamela squeezed Tessa's hand. "Thanks, Sis, you always know how to bring perspective to the moment. Can you stay for a while?"

"No, I've got to get to class. But call any time, I enjoyed it and always love a chance to keep the Lil'ster." Tessa grabbed her overnight bag from the entry way and called out, "See you soon. Call me this weekend."

Lily played quietly with her play dishes while Pamela spooned some flax seed into her morning yogurt. With Tessa gone the house seemed suddenly emptier than it should be. What an emotional roller coaster. One minute she was sharing an intimate evening with her husband, the next she was left with the briefest of chats and a hug goodbye from her sister. And now it was just her and Lily again. She knew she shouldn't complain, her life overflowed with blessings. But she wanted more than the occasional anniversary date or infrequent Sunday afternoon in the park with Eduardo. She wanted to share life daily - enjoying each other's company, working out disagreements as they arose. She hoped to get to know him better, learn what was behind his reluctance to attend church or talk with her about God. She wanted abundant life. Together.

Lily's hand on her leg made her look down. The toy teapot was hooked over her left big toe and she held tightly to a plastic fork and knife in her right hand. "Swing?" Lily said.

Pamela bent down to scoop up her little girl. "Yes, sweetheart, we will go swing," she said, holding Lily close. Thank God she had Lily. Her shining star, she thought to herself. My precious girl. Together they walked to the closet to get the stroller.

Chapter 15

A postcard view of the Pacific Ocean stretched out as far as Eduardo could see from the balcony of his Long Beach condo. He had been lucky to snag one of the few ocean fronts available. His first trip out to California quickly convinced him that the monthly rent was a much better deal than weeks of hotel expense. Besides, he was going to be out here enough that he wanted a place convenient to his west coast office at a few hours' notice. Here he could take an early morning swim in the ocean if he chose or have his morning coffee on the beach, without interruption of hotel staff and with unlimited privacy. He shared housekeeping service with one of the other business tenants. The kitchen and bar were constantly stocked, and laundry and dry cleaning were done while he was at the office so that his apartment was always ready.

He walked over to the desk, selected a report and sat down in the executive chair to read. Eduardo had an efficient but complete office area along one side of the spacious living room. Here he could access his state of the art computer, three large monitors and high speed printer. There was an office for him at their local branch of course, but he preferred it here. He maintained close contact with his assistant, Barb, back in the home office. Only she and his partner here in Long Beach had his private work cell number; everyone else, including Pamela, could reach him on his main cell.

Eduardo placed the report back on the desk sat back, deep in thought. Cohen Technologies had established itself as a player in the main market, and he wanted to make the most of this window. He needed to secure the clients he coveted the most and become thoroughly entrenched before the next newcomer on the scene. Fowler, High Branch and a few lesser but solid clients were his, and Primus was nibbling at his lure; who next? He sent a quick text to Barb asking her to email him the latest updates to his ongoing prospect and companies of interest list. Eduardo knew that he would be key in gaining the interest and trust of the CEO's and key personnel for each firm. He also knew he was the perfect man to close the deals. He had the expertise, the charm, the right team assembled, and now he had the stature in strategically targeted market sectors. All he needed to do was execute his plan.

The problem was going to be Pamela. She wanted him home more. Home, with its routine dinner conversations and mundane expectations of playing with Lily, evening strolls in the neighborhood and constant hints of her desire for him to join her at church. Eduardo was pleased with his personal life. He had a beautiful, status-appropriate home and car, a pretty wife who was the perfect corporate companion, and a daughter, with plans for more children. But those things were the basics, base line for what he wanted to accomplish in life. The right home, wife and children were expected; that part was already done. It was time to pursue more important interests, the things that excited and drove him. And that meant travel, more than he had been doing recently and much more than Pamela would be content with.

It was time for her to be pregnant again, he decided. Lily was almost a year old and Pamela was happy, handling motherhood beautifully as he had known she would. She had her church activities and her family close by. But he knew she would be very upset when she found out his planned itinerary for the remainder of the year. She was gaining confidence as a wife and mother, and she wouldn't hesitate to make her feelings known expectantly when it came to family. She wanted him to spend time with her, time with Lily, and time with both of them. He would put his foot down, of course, and remind her that he had to capitalize on this time in his career. He would assure her he was working hard for the family, and increase her household account to allow for some more discretionary funds. He could afford it, and it would be money well spent to avoid an argument or, god forbid, Pamela turning into a nag. He had neither the time nor the inclination for that. Yes, it was time for another baby. Eduardo had clients to conquer and entertain. Clients who favored the same type of upscale establishments he did with excellent food, gorgeous women and tables in secluded corners.

He picked up the phone and punched in a number. "Victor, it's Eduardo Cohen. Yes, I'm back in town for a while. Can you reserve table 5 for me this evening, say 8 o'clock? Great. I'll be entertaining clients; leave room for additional guests should they be so inclined." Clicking the phone off he stood and stretched, admiring himself in the wall mirror. He was on the top of his game in every way; he wouldn't have traded places with anyone. It was going to be a good day, and an even better evening.

Chapter 16

Her Bible Study group was having brunch after the morning session. Lily was with the other children in child care at the church. Pamela enjoyed the lively discussion of the material they had covered that morning. God's Word was so alive, so relevant and rich with promises. She listened as Beth and Katelyn speculated about details of the end times, the rapture and when would Jesus return. She felt so blessed to have friendships with godly women who shared her interests. It was good to be reminded there were other women who felt the study of God's Word was important enough to set aside time each week from their family and household duties to read, study, share and pray. The group had challenged each other to begin a daily prayer time and record their praises and prayers. Pamela found it hard to discipline herself each morning at first, but lately she had started to look forward to her alone time with the Lord. She was learning to listen for the different ways God spoke to her: through scripture verses that sometimes leapt off the page, through devotionals and prayers written by others, and occasionally in that silent sensing in her spirit which Pamela called the God-nudge. It was a time of spiritual growth and she loved it. She only wished she could share it with Eduardo. But he was not interested.

The waitress came with their check and they began dividing the check among them, adding tip together at the end. They said a short parting prayer for the coming week, hugged each other and left to gather their children.

When Lily saw Pamela's face in the doorway she toddled over and put her arms up. Pamela entered the safety gate and swept Lily up into her arms. "Did you have fun?" she asked. Lily pointed to some of the toys on the floor, saying something that was meaningful only to her. "Don't you wish you could understand what they are saying at this age?" the caregiver asked. "You can see their minds working but they speak a different language."

Pamela laughed. "Yes, I do. Thanks for taking care of the children, Lily really enjoys her time here." She shouldered the diaper bag and waved goodbye to the remaining children. In the parking lot she buckled Lily into her safety seat in the back. Hard to believe her mother and that generation had simply placed their children loosely in the car, relying on their free arm to keep a child from injury if they had to brake suddenly. She was glad she lived in an age of technology.

Technology. As in Cohen Technologies. Pamela felt the seeds of resentment beginning to germinate in her heart at the demands the company placed on Eduardo's time. As she drove through the neighborhood streets between her church and her home, she couldn't help but be discouraged about the immediate future. She knew she should just count her blessings and be grateful for the wonderful life Eduardo provided. But she had never envisioned that life would involve so little of him in her daily life. He had been in Long Beach for over a month now since leaving so abruptly the morning after their perfect anniversary date, and he'd told her this morning he wasn't sure when he'd be home.

How was she supposed to react? Her fairytale marriage was becoming a long distance relationship, with more 'ship' than 'relation.' Her friends thought she was living her dream, and she was – except for the fact that the perfect husband was slipping out of the picture. Didn't he miss her? Miss taking her and Lily to the playground or swimming with them in the pool? When Eduardo was home he seemed to still desire her, but the nagging feeling that something was coming between them wouldn't go away. There it was again, that feeling of a disconnect. She didn't have a clue why or what it could be, they were so blessed. But Eduardo's time away from home was truly beginning to bother her, and when he was home his attention was usually diverted by his laptop, cell phone or the news on Wall Street. Conference calls with either coast made his hours in bed erratic. She was beginning to feel alone in her own marriage.

Pamela's friends and family, especially her mother, knew how disappointed she was at the way things were. She suspected Roberta was more than little concerned at Eduardo's distance not only from her but from anything God-related. But her mother simply continued to pray with her, encourage her and advise her to be the best wife she could be and let God work out the details. "He who began a good work in you…" she would say, and Pamela knew it was true. They were each works in progress; God wasn't finished with any of them yet. She would simply have to be patient.

The next morning Pamela woke to a wave of nausea. She could think of no reason why she should be feeling sick. As she made her way into the bathroom she hoped she wasn't coming down with something. Riley was bringing Brayden over later for a play date to plan Lily's first birthday party. She didn't want to have to cancel. When she was finished being sick she rinsed her mouth and sat weakly on the chair at her dressing table. She didn't have a fever, no additional symptoms other than feeling tired after a full night's sleep. What was wrong with her?

Then it hit her. She was almost two weeks late. She hadn't thought much of it until that moment. She had been irregular all her life and the endometriosis made it even worse. A smile began working its way across her heart up to her lips. Could it be? Was she pregnant? *Oh Father, please let that be it! It was supposed to be hard for me to conceive, but with You all things are possible.*

Pamela pulled on her robe and padded back to bed, thinking about their anniversary night. That had to be it. Eduardo hadn't been home since then and the timing was right. She couldn't wait to find out for sure so she could call Eduardo. Surely he would want to rush home and celebrate. He loved it when she was expecting. She would call Riley and ask her to pick up a pregnancy test from Walgreens on her way over. She could count on Riley to keep it secret from the family for now, and she wanted someone to share the good news with. Pamela turned on her side and sighed happily, drifting back to sleep.

Chapter 17

Two weeks later the lab confirmed what the over-the-counter test had shown. Pamela was pregnant! Her due date was February 14th – Valentine's Day. She practically danced out of the doctor's office and walked on air to her car. Less than two years ago she had walked out of the same doctor's office across the same parking lot to the same beloved car. But this time she walked out as a mother of a precious little girl expecting her second child. *Oh God, my heart is so full. Thank you, thank you, thank you.*

She drove the short distance to Riley's house to pick up Lily and share her fabulous news. Riley was ecstatic. "Mike and I have been trying again – maybe we'll get to be pregnant at the same time!" she said excitedly. "When are you going to tell Eduardo?"

Pamela hesitated. "Part of me wants to get on the phone right now, tell him the wonderful news and hear him say he'll be on the next flight home. Another part of me wants to wait until he returns and surprise him in person. But I don't think I can wait, I'll call him tonight after Lily is in bed. On Riley, another baby!! I wasn't sure I'd ever have any children, and now God is raining down His blessings upon me." Suddenly famished, she headed toward the kitchen. "Do you have any more of those brownies left? I'd love one with a big bowl of vanilla ice cream."

Riley chuckled. "Oh, that's a great breakfast for a pregnant woman," she said sarcastically. "Yes, I have several, and you deserve as many as you want. So, with all Eduardo's travels I didn't know if you two would ever have time to get together. When do you think it happened?" she asked.

"It had to be on our anniversary night," Pamela answered, spooning ice cream into a bowl on top of a very thick brownie. "That was such a magical night. We weren't trying to have another child, I wasn't even thinking about. I was so relaxed, feeling pampered and happy to have my husband home AND spending time alone with me." She paused, then continued. "Riley, please pray for me. Eduardo's time away and having sole parenting duty is really getting to me. I find myself resenting his work, even resenting him. He is always so excited to leave, so focused on 'client acquisition and retention' as he calls it. It's like he achieved his happy little wife and home and now life is all about work." She looked up. "That sounds awful, doesn't it. When I say it out loud it makes me sound like a selfish, ungrateful spoiled brat. I don't mean to be, but I thought being married would mean having a husband at home. Not just someone to sleep with, but someone to laugh with, dream with and share our heart's desires.

Now I wonder if I'll ever have that. I'm in a long distance relationship with my own husband and he seems perfectly fine with it."

Riley went to her sister and placed her one hand on each shoulder. "Now look at me. Eduardo loves you. Look at all the effort he made to get you, to bring you in as a part of his family. I know it must be hard but it's just where you are right now. It won't always be like this. At some point he'll have his clients and the business right where he wants it, and you'll be there ready to enjoy that husband at home. Tell you what, let's pray about that right now." The sisters bowed their heads and prayed.

That night after Lily was tucked in bed Pamela fixed a mug of her favorite Lemon Lift hot tea. She had a jillion things going on in her head and needed to sort them out before she called Eduardo. She and Riley had planned most of the party for Lily's first birthday, and she wanted to make sure Eduardo would be home for it. She hoped he would schedule his trips around the party, but she was not going to take "No" for an answer. Should she talk to him about coming home for the party first, or spring the news that she was pregnant? She decided on the latter. That should put him in such a good mood that committing to be home for Lily's birthday would not be a problem. As she picked up the phone and punched the number, Pamela couldn't escape the feeling that her marriage was beginning a new chapter.

Three thousand miles away Eduardo couldn't hear his cell phone ringing. He and Chad Brunson were having cocktails in the bar, in no hurry for dinner. The meetings had gone well today, very well, and Eduardo was in the mood to celebrate. Victor had saved this particular round booth for him. He knew it was Eduardo's favorite. Service in the club was faultless no matter where he sat, but this booth had the most privacy and the best view of the dancers. Chad had eagerly accepted the invitation to this exclusive club and Eduardo would see to it that he had the full experience, leaving the man wanting more. The way it always left Eduardo.

Their waitress had just left with the order for their second round of drinks when he saw the girls. Brandy, the tall brunette was leading the way with blonde Alisha close on her heels. Brandy came and stood at Eduardo's side of the table. He smiled up at her.

"What's this?" Chad asked, eyes wide with surprise.

"Your first table dance," Eduardo replied. "Just relax and enjoy yourself. It's on me."

Chad shifted uncomfortably in his seat as Alisha slid in beside him. Eduardo laughed. "She just wants to get know you a bit before performing for you. Nothing to worry about, and you aren't doing anything wrong.

This is business." He turned his attention to the tall brunette as she stepped up onto the table directly in front of him.

Chapter 18

Pamela's head rolled off the couch cushion, waking her with a start. The face of her watch displayed 12:30 a.m. Blinking her eyes a couple of times she realized she had fallen asleep on the couch. She grabbed her cell phone, wondering why Eduardo's call hadn't woken her up. She checked the missed call log – nothing. She had waited all night to give him the news but never got the chance. This was ridiculous, couldn't he take a break from work to return a call to his wife? She sighed, shaking off her irritation and walking toward the bedroom. She had to remember that pregnancy hormones made her extra-moody. Eduardo would call tomorrow and she could tell him then.

The phone rang at 7:30 the next morning. Pamela picked it up on the first ring. "Did I wake you?" Eduardo asked pleasantly.

"No, I just finished the breakfast dishes. I'm in the den with Lily who is playing with her blocks." Pamela took a deep breath. "I tried to call you last night but got your voice mail," she said lightly.

"Sorry, I couldn't pick up when you called. The meeting ran very late and I didn't get a chance to call back until it was too late," he said smoothly. "The meetings went great, by the way, another satisfied client in the bag."

"That's great," Pamela said, trying to sound enthusiastic. "Congratulations. I have some news to congratulate you on as well. You're going to be a father again," she smiled into the phone.

"Honey, that's wonderful news!!" Eduardo was genuinely excited. "Wow, looks like that problem you had has been corrected." Eduardo preened in the mirror, holding his phone with one hand and smoothing his hair with the other. God, he was a stud.

"Yes, apparently I don't have trouble getting pregnant anymore," she agreed. "Eduardo, I'm so ready for you to come home and spend some time here! We've got Lily's first birthday coming up and now with another baby on the way, well I just want you at home. When are coming back?" she asked anxiously.

"I'll be home in 10 days," he said firmly. "That'll give me time to wrap up Phase 2 and then I can return to the home office and spend some time in town. In the meantime, take care of yourself and remember you're eating for two now."

They talked briefly for a few more minutes then said their goodbyes. Eduardo put the phone down, almost unable to believe his good fortune. Was he becoming that powerful, that he could make a decision and practically think the thing into existence? No sooner had he decided it was time for Pamela to get pregnant again than she calls with the news that she is. He knew of course that it had to be from their anniversary night, but even that confirmed his prowess. He'd only been with his wife a few times during recent months but that was all it took.

Eduardo knew that Pamela would give the credit to "God". She would talk about how they were blessed and should be grateful to someone, something she couldn't even see or prove existed. He despised the concept. He was in command of his life, he made his own destiny and he alone was the reason for his successes. The notion of a god was a crutch for weaklings, the stuff of fools.

He picked up his briefcase and headed out the door to his rented convertible. Only a few more nights and he would have to say goodbye to his west coast girls. But there would be other cities, and other girls. He worked hard and he deserved to treat himself to the perks so many other businessmen had. His thoughts stopped short of admitting that what began as a perk was now a need. A serious need.

Chapter 19

Pamela was tired. It seemed she was always tired these days. She'd forgotten the need for naps during the first trimester, and this time around she could only nap if Lily did. Thankfully Lily still took a short morning nap and a long one in the afternoon. Eduardo would be home this evening and she could hardly wait. She wanted to see the excitement in his eyes about his second child, see his love for her and Lily.

They were in the nursery when Pamela heard the door open. Picking up Lily she walked down the hallway to greet Eduardo. He met her halfway and gave them a hug. "Welcome home, dear," Pamela said. "Look Lily, Daddy's home." Eduardo kissed both their cheeks. He looked tired – no, he didn't look tired, his eyes looked tired. Pamela stroked his back. "Why don't you just relax and take your time freshening up. You must be exhausted. I'll go see about dinner."

"Yes, I will admit to being a bit tired. The trip was exhilarating but I could use a short nap before we eat," he said.

"That's fine, dinner can hold. We'll check on you in a bit," Pamela said easily. She was just glad to have him home.

After dinner they played on the floor with Lily until it was time for bed. Pamela filled him in on all the details for the party, which would be the following Saturday at their house. She was going all out with decorations. Her mom and sisters would be over early to blow up balloons, help ice the cake, arrange the candles, and make sure everything was ready for Luke to cook hotdogs and hamburgers. It was going to be a good old fashioned back yard birthday. He smiled at her excitement and was reminded how little it took to please her.

"Is there anything you want me to do?" he asked.

"Yes, I'll need you to pick up the helium balloons and set out the toddler riding toys on the back deck. But I'll tell you when it's time," she said. Then she put away Lily's toys and picked her up to change her. "I'll put her to bed now. It's so good to have you home for playtime. Lily reached out to touch Eduardo's face, as if to emphasize her mother's statement.

"Good to be home," he said. "I'll be in the office if you need me."

The party was set for 11:00 a.m. Saturday. By 10:00 everything was done and Eduardo had returned with the balloons. "Why so many?" he had asked her. "Because it's her *first*, of course" Pamela had answered laughing. Laughter was everywhere in her voice these days, her heart was happy again. Cindy and Bill had driven in the night before. Everyone in Lily's family would be there to celebrate her turning 1 year old.

Luke started cooking the dog and burgers at 11:30. "The kids are already hungry," he told Pamela. "Let's get them fed and then the adults can wait a bit if they want. I'll keep the food warm."

"That'll work," she said, turning to go back into the house. I'll just get the salad and fruit. Riley and Tessa are bringing out the water and tea." Pamela took the empty meat tray back into the kitchen as her sisters were coming out. Inside, Roberta and Cindy were chatting. She smiled at them as she passed. Her house was full of family and those who loved her. Her daughter was a full one year old. And she was carrying their second child. Her mom had been right, she had to pray, trust and wait on God. Things would unfold in His time and His way, and His timing was always perfect.

It sure seemed that way now. She wondered if she would have a son. She rather hoped so, yet she really wanted Lily to have a sister who would be her best friend. *Your will in this, Father. Just please give us another healthy child. And thank you for the gift of children.*

That night as she put Lily to bed she hugged her close. Lily had been the star of the party, of course, paying the usual attention to some of the toys but showing more interest in the boxes and packaging. Everyone knew the first birthday was for the adults. The day had been exactly what Pamela wanted. Lily had looked darling in her smocked dress, covered with an apron when she was eating the smoosh cake. Eduardo had taken some video with their new camera, and Frank and Bill had taken turns vying for grandfather of the day. Pamela had enjoyed baking and decorating with her mom and Cindy. They hadn't told anyone yet about the pregnancy. This was Lily's day and Pamela didn't want any attention taken from her daughter. True to her word Riley had told no one. They would wait a while, let her recuperate from Lily's party and get further into the first trimester, then tell everyone the happy news.

The next morning she and Lily went to church, where the teacher in Lily's class had special snacks to celebrate her birthday. Pamela went to the early service and was there in time to visit with other parents whose young children were up early. They were used to her attending without Eduardo and had stopped asking about him, not wanting to embarrass her. She told them about the party and settled in to a chair. The praise band started with "How Great is Our God", and Pamela felt the worship rise within her. Here she could lay her resentment and jealousy at the foot of the cross and focus on the greatness of her God.

Chapter 20

Pamela was in labor, and the baby was coming much faster than her first time. She had asked for an epidural but was told it was too late, it would be time to push soon. Eduardo was standing behind her, holding her hands and letting her pull on them as the contractions came. Pamela tried to focus on her breathing, resting before the next one hit. She could do this. She had done it once before and she could do it again – this time for her son.

They had known it would be a boy since her 20th week. Eduardo was enormously pleased, eager for a son to carry on the family name. He had surprised Pamela by adding the name Maxwell as one of the middle names. "We'll name him W. Eduardo Maxwell Cohen," he had said. "I'm W. Eduardo Cohen the fourth. We've already had William, Bill, Will and Eduardo in the family. My son will carry on the family name but with his own unique addition. I will call him Maxwell, after my great uncle." In her heart, Pamela added, "And I will call him Max."

Her pregnancy with Max had surprised her too. Unlike with Lily, she had terrible morning sickness and weight loss in the first four months. She had heard that each pregnancy was different and found it to be true. She supposed each labor and delivery would be different too.

Their parents were in the Labor and Delivery waiting room. Bill read the paper while Cindy and Roberta chatted. Frank was on shift that day and Lily was with Riley. Suddenly Eduardo burst through the doors. "He's here!" he said proudly. "Maxwell is here, safe and sound at 9 lbs 8 oz. Mother and son are doing fine." He shook hands with his dad and let Cindy envelope him in a huge hug. "I'm so happy for you, son," Cindy said with tears in her eyes. "What a happy day."

Pamela leaned back against the bed and let out a sigh. The nurse was preparing Max and had just announced his weight. No wonder she'd had such a hard time – 9 ½ pounds! She'd needed stitches but she'd done it, had her boy naturally. She was ready to hold him, put him to her breast and let her love for him envelope them both. As Max was handed to her she gazed in awe. Such beautiful blue eyes, already. Not much hair but the most beautiful features. She had worried that she couldn't love another child as much as she loved Lily, her shining star. But now she understood. With each child her capacity to love had increased. She loved Max with a limitless love, as much love as she had for Lily but a different love because they were different individuals. Just as God the Father loved each of His creations with boundless love that embraced their uniqueness. She guided

Max's mouth and smiled happily as he greedily began to suck. *Thank you God for another healthy child.*

Two days later they were home. Eduardo was scheduled to leave on a trip out of the country for four weeks, and Pamela had criticized him for going. "Couldn't you postpone your travel for once?" Pamela had asked, unable to keep the annoyance out of her voice. "I'm tired, I need help with the children, and I need you."

Eduardo had answered calmly. "Pamela, this trip was scheduled by the engineering firm that makes the primary component for our equipment. All my competitors will be there. It's not one I can skip." His tone had been patient but firm. "Besides, your mother will be staying with you for the first two weeks then my mother said she could say for two. I'll be home by then."

Knowing once again that she wouldn't win this fight, she shoved her resentment down into a drawer at the bottom of her heart. She needed to focus on the baby. It would be wonderful to have her mother there, and Cindy had asked to keep Lily for a few days. Pamela gave her consent and Cindy was in grandmother heaven. She watched as Eduardo packed his bags, wishing things would be different.

Pamela's emotions swirled around inside her, bumping into each other, sending her feelings in all directions. She knew it would be a good thing for Lily to stay with the Cohens for a few days, and she was looking forward to her mother's stay, helping her with Max and bringing her perspective on this life adjustment of child number two. But she already missed Lily, and Eduardo was leaving, and things just didn't seem right. She had said some things to him she shouldn't have, and she didn't want to part on unhappy terms.

"Eduardo, I'm sorry I've been so cross. You know how I hate it when you leave, and so soon after I've had the baby … well, it just feels so unfair. I get upset and can't control my tongue." Pamela crossed the room as he zipped up the last bag. He turned to face her. "And I'm sorry I can't stay. If it were any other trip I wouldn't go. Take care of Maxwell and the days will fly past before you know it." She walked him to the door and kissed him goodbye, then listened to the garage door open. And close.

Chapter 21

Three Years Later

Had it really been three years since Max was born? The days had flown into weeks and months. Max was a happy boy from the moment he arrived, always wearing a smile and bringing laughter and joy with his presence. Lily was her shining star, and Max was the laughter in her soul. Her mother-days were full now, rich in all the things that mattered like sticky kisses from her active three year old son and special drawings from her five year old, very creative daughter. Walks to the park, afternoons on the playground, splashing in puddles after a brief rain, play dates with cousins. The three of them never missed any of her family gatherings, going without Eduardo most of the time because of his schedule. Breakfast outside on the kids' picnic table eating waffles with banana faces and hair, visits to the Children's Museum, sandwiches of bread cut into cookie-cutter shapes, arts and crafts, and lots of homemade cookies. Sunday School, Vacation Bible School, Children's Choir. Pamela loved it all. She didn't want this phase of being a mother to end, but Lily was already in kindergarten. First grade next year would change everything. For now, she relished the time she had alone with Max while Lily was in school, and the time she had with them both in the mornings, afternoons and evenings.

She had thrown herself into all of it, busy with children and church while Eduardo traveled and grew his business. He had apartments in several cities now for his long term stays, and she never knew how long he would be home when he did make an appearance. To be fair, there were pockets of time he would spend with them on the weekends. He occasionally took the children to the neighborhood park, and had even helped build the playscape at the elementary school, much to Lily's delight. The year before he built a small float for Lily and Max to ride in the HOA July 4th parade and they won first prize. Those times made Pamela very happy. Lily and Max loved doing things with their dad, and she hated to see them so sad each time he left. But over time she grew to be angry. He was able to do all those wonderful things, yet he chose to withhold them, doling them out sparingly like crumbs to his family while spending most of his time with clients. There would be music performances, science fairs, school plays and homework projects; she wanted her children to have an involved father. Eduardo's children needed more of his time, and so did she.

Pamela knew that holding on to her anger and resentment was not healthy, but then neither was her marriage at this point. She was starving for real connection with her husband. She tried everything she could think of to get his attention, to get him to communicate with her about her feelings and how concerned she was about their relationship - voice mails, hand written notes, recorded messages that he could listen to when he got home long after she had already gone to bed. When she did get him to talk about it, he assured her that he was working hard for their future, that he had to be gone. He told her she should be happy that she was so well taken care of and had a husband who was faithful. She didn't have it in her to be confrontational; she wanted to keep the peace.

Worst of all, she had resigned herself to the fact that he did not even believe in God, had no interest in her faith. How could she have been so blind? Scripture was clear about being unevenly yoked, and yet she had walked willingly into marriage with an unbeliever. She had wanted love and security and financial freedom so badly that she deliberately put blinders on when it came to Eduardo. Eduardo hadn't wanted to discuss his faith. She should have known then to put a halt to everything until she was confident their union would be founded on Christ. But Pamela had told herself that of course he was a Christian – his mother had such a strong faith, he had been raised in the church, his grandfather was a Baptist minister for goodness sake. His faith was just private to him. Now she felt foolish, helpless, and stuck.

She also felt guilty. Because of the discord between them, her desire for physical intimacy had diminished to almost nothing. For Pamela the connection came in moments of sharing and focused time on each other. For Eduardo the connection was in the sex; he no longer expressed interest in her thoughts or hopes, only in her body. The intimacy she had felt briefly during the first year of marriage was gone, replaced by a sense of obligation mixed with futility. Part of her was relieved when he left on one of his trips; there would be no uncomfortable demands in the bedroom while he was gone.

She could not bring herself to share any of this with her prayer partners or even her family. She felt like such a failure. On the surface her life was better than that of anyone in her circle, and for the most part they thought she was happy. How could she disappoint them with the truth? It would only upset them, cause them concern for her over a situation they could do nothing about. She had made her bed, and she would lie in it. She knew it could be so much worse. She had her precious children, the love of her family, and she did not have to worry about money. And there was always prayer – for her husband to find faith, for her to feel desire again, for the miracle of renewed intimacy and restored connection. With God it was possible.

The morning had begun with a light drizzle which turned into a steady rain. Good thing Max was at Riley's with those two boys, she thought. She was behind on the laundry, and Eduardo was supposed to be home tomorrow. Pouring a capful of detergent into the washer she tossed in the kids' clothes, then reached for the laundry hamper from their closet. She pulled out a pair of Eduardo's khaki casual slacks. Checking the pockets, she noticed a stain near the bottom of the zipper. Taking a closer look, she saw another smear a bit higher up. Slowly she sank to the tile floor as the sight registered in her brain. The pink stain on the crotch of her husband's pants was lipstick. Lots of it.

Chapter 22

Pamela closed the door behind Riley as she followed the boys inside. "Thanks for bringing Max home," she said.

"Of course, no problem," Riley smiled. "They had a great time and with any luck will be tired enough for naps this afternoon." She looked closely at Pamela. "What's wrong? You look as if you've seen a ghost."

Pamela glanced into the living room where Brayden was picking out a DVD. "Ok if the kids watch a short movie? I need to talk to you," she said quietly. Riley answered quickly. "Sure. I don't have to leave for another half hour."

They settled the boys on the floor then Pamela led Riley into the kitchen. She pulled a pair of khaki paints out of a plastic bag. "I found this in the laundry today." Riley stared at the lipstick stains, stunned. Pamela continued. "I'm going to have to talk to Eduardo but I'm scared. I don't know how he'll take it."

"Oh, Pamela, I'm so sorry," said Riley, tears forming in her eyes. "How awful. Has there been anything like this before?"

Pamela sighed. "No, nothing. I feel like I've been kicked in the stomach. There's just no acceptable explanation for this…" She hung her head.

Riley moved closer. "Look, you have to confront him about this. This is a problem, and it won't go away by ignoring it."

Pamela looked up. "Once, a few months ago when he was working in town, I went by his office to surprise him. Leaving their offices was a very attractive woman wearing too much makeup and too short a skirt. I didn't think anything of it at the time, but now I wonder… do you think he's having an affair?"

Riley was quiet for a moment. "I don't know. You don't think he's going to one of those 'gentlemen's clubs', do you? Whether it's an affair or not this is a problem. I know you don't like confrontation, Pamela, but you can't let this slide. When is Eduardo due home?"

"Tomorrow," Pamela said. Riley stood and said firmly, " I'll keep Max with me tomorrow and pick up Lily from school. The children don't need to be around when you do this. You need to get to the bottom of this." Riley gave Pamela a long hug.

"Thanks, I needed that. You're right, I can't ignore this, and I can't confront Eduardo with the children here. I appreciate your help more than I can say," Pamela said tearfully.

"I'll be praying for you. God will make a way," Riley said, then left the room to gather her boys.

The next morning Pamela dropped Max off at Aunt Riley's. He was quite happy to have two days in row with his cousins. Pamela was nervous as she drove back to the house. Exactly how was she going to broach this subject, and regardless of what Eduardo would say how should she react? *God help me,* she prayed, *I feel scared and I don't know what to do. I know you value marriage, You love both of us. Help me be brave, guide me in what I should say.*

I will be with you, my child. She heard the reply in her spirit and relaxed a bit. Yes, God would be with her every step of the way.

Chapter 23

Pamela was in Max's room putting away his clothes when she heard Eduardo come into the house. She closed the last drawer and walked through the house. She found him in the living room, seated in his leather recliner watching the news. She asked him how his trip was, he said fine. The usual. Eduardo flipped a couple of channels and she left to get the plastic bag. It was time.

"We need to talk," Pamela said re-entering the living room. He looked up, surprised. "Right now? I just got home. Can it wait? And where are the kids?"

"No, it can't. This is serious. Lily and Max are with Riley." Pamela sat across the room on the ottoman clutching the plastic bag. "Please turn off the TV."

Eduardo clicked off the screen and turned slightly in his chair to look at her. "What's wrong?"

"This is what's wrong," she said, fear and anger rising in her throat at the same time. She pulled the pants out of the bag and held them up, the pink smears on full display.

Eduardo blinked. "Where did you find those?" he asked, buying some time, not able to believe he'd made such a mistake.

"I found them when I was doing laundry yesterday. You can imagine my shock. I suppose this explains all those late night meetings," Pamela said, hating the sarcasm in her voice.

Eduardo's voice was matter-of-fact. "As you know, part of my work involves entertaining clients. I take them to places where the service and food are excellent, and where they can get a private table dance if they want. It's very common in the business world, Pamela, there's nothing wrong with it."

"Nothing wrong with it? Nothing wrong with discovering lipstick covering the crotch of my husband's pants? Eduardo, this is not a tiny spot on your shirt collar. This is disgusting!" Pamela said, unwanted tears collecting behind her eyes. "How do you think this makes me feel? This is not right, surely you don't expect me to be okay with this ... sordid lifestyle. And I can't believe that all of your clients want this sort of thing."

"No, I'm sure you can't, but it's true. I'll bet even some of your church-going buddies are occasional patrons. Look, Pamela, it's no big deal, just some talented dancers giving special attention to some tired businessmen for a few extra bucks. I can't tell you how many deals I've closed after those evenings," Eduardo said calmly.

Pamela looked him full in the eye. "Do you enjoy it?" she asked.

"Hell yes, I enjoy it. What guy wouldn't? But honey, it's just scenery. There is no affection, no making out, no sex. These are working girls, and their job is to provide enjoyment for men. It's not like I'm having an affair. I told you, I'm not unfaithful to you. You need to be appreciative of that too, because the opportunities are out there. You shouldn't let this upset you so much. Like I said, it's no big deal. It's no reflection on you; you're my wife and I love you. You are the one I provide for, those girls just get a few minutes of my attention when I'm not at home with you." Eduardo reached for the remote control, satisfied that he had handled the situation well.

"So you're saying you're going to keep on going to these places, even though it hurts me? I feel cheap, degraded and disgusted by all of this," Pamela said, a tear sliding down her cheek.

Eduardo's voice was slightly louder now. "No, I'm saying that it doesn't hurt you and you shouldn't feel cheap – especially the way I take care of you. This is something I have to do for work, so yes I'm going to continue doing what it takes to grow the business." He locked eyes with her for a few seconds, saying nothing. Then he turned on the television and settled back in his chair.

Pamela sat in stunned silence for a few minutes, unable to think or speak. Then she got up from the couch, slowly as if she were an old woman, shoved the pants back into the bag and walked to the laundry room. Mechanically she applied stain removers and started the washer. Then she broke down and cried, the sound of her sobbing drowned out by the water pouring over the dirty, dark part of her life. The stain might be lifted but the scar on her soul would never go away.

They ate lunch in silence, Eduardo reading a magazine while Pamela picked at her food. She couldn't stand the sight of him, couldn't get the image of that lipstick out of her head. She had no appetite but didn't know what else to do. There was no more fight left in her, and she needed every minute before she had to pick up Lily and Max to compose herself. She didn't even want to talk to Riley about it but Riley would certainly ask. She was trying to decide what to say to her sister when she heard Eduardo's chair legs scoot back on the floor. Dropping his napkin on the table he looked up at her and said "I'm going out. Don't wait up." Eduardo picked up his keys and left the house without another word.

She sat there for the next few minutes letting the silence envelope her. Pamela hated arguing. She was old enough when her parents divorced to remember how awful it made her feel inside, how small she felt when they fought. One look and a few harsh words from Eduardo could bring back her insecurity, her desire to do whatever it took to keep the peace.

How had they gotten to this point in their marriage in such a short time, she asked herself again. And again she knew the answer, or at least part of it, and she felt sick to her stomach. She wondered if he was going to the office, or to one of those places. Pamela forced herself to stop going down that road in her thoughts, it would only make her crazy. She needed to get back into mommy-mode and do it quickly. Her children were waiting.

Chapter 24

Christmas was one of Pamela's favorite seasons. She shared Cindy's passion for decorating, baking, special church services and a special time of preparing her heart for receiving anew the Christ child. It was still early in December but each week there was a party, a lunch at Lily's school, or a children's event at church. Tonight the children's choir would be performing at church. Pamela couldn't wait to see Lily in her golden tinsel star costume singing with the others about the baby Jesus.

She called out to Lily and Max, "time to get dressed for church." "We're playing, mommy," Max said. "Five more minutes?" Pamela relented. "Five more minutes, then I'll come in and change your clothes." "Ok," Max said happily.

She hoped Eduardo would be on time. He had promised to attend and video the choir. Pamela and her family would get to the church early and save him a place. She thought about how their relationship had changed since the lipstick incident. Wrapping a piece of cling wrap over her tray of cookies for the bake sale, she stifled the thoughts that came to mind. They were like roommates now, though on the surface nothing looked any different. He had his work, she had her children and church. They had dinner as a family when he was home, and he would oblige her with his attendance at children's functions like tonight. They even continued to share a bed. But she was usually fast asleep by the time he crawled into it, and he was either gone by the time she woke or sleeping late. She knew better than to try to wake him. The few times he chose to sleep in she had learned to leave him alone until he emerged from their room, ready for work.

So far she was managing it. She had decided to be grateful for all the wonderful parts of her life and accept her marriage the way it was. That was much easier said than done, of course. At her prayer bench her heart cried out for resolution, for courage, for Eduardo to change, for her to be a confident wife stating reasonable expectations instead of a people-pleasing doormat. But things continued as they were. On the bright side the children were happy, doing well, and so much fun. They brightened her days like nothing else could. Pamela couldn't imagine life without them. She had more blessings than she deserved, and she was grateful.

Walking into Max's room she smiled at the city of Lincoln logs the two had built. It covered the floor in Max's room. Lily was putting the last piece of fence up on the corral. "Time to get your robe and costume on, honey," Pamela said. Lily looked up. "Tonight's the night I get to be a star!" "You're my shining star every day, sweet pea," Pamela told her, hugging her close. Then she turned her attention to Max, who was eyeing the jacket and tie. In this area she could assert herself. "Come here young man, let's get you into these handsome clothes."

Half an hour later they walked into the narthex of St. Luke's to be greeted by Frank, Roberta and the rest of Pamela's family. Riley's oldest boy was in the choir too, looking shy in his shepherd costume. They assembled all the children next to the Chrismon tree for the annual picture. Max was hamming for the camera but Luke managed to get a good picture of the cousins. Pamela took Lily and Brayden to the choir room while the rest found seats in the sanctuary. Pamela returned, asking Luke, "Is Eduardo here yet?"

Luke shook his head. "Haven't seen him."

Tessa said, "I'm on the end of our row so I can save him a place. I'm sure he'll be here."

"Thanks," Pamela said, "I hope so. He's supposed to take the video. I told him 6:30 sharp."

The music started and the narrator stepped to the pulpit. The room was beautiful with its inset, stained glass windows, their shelves lined with greenery and candles. She took it all in as she listened to the words pastor Kyle read from Isaiah: "For to us a child is born, a son is given, and the government will be on his shoulders. And he will be called Wonderful, Counselor, Mighty God, Everlasting Father, Prince of Peace." Oh how she wanted the peace of this moment to stay in her heart.

The children's choir filed out and took their places on the steps. Luke was on the end of the back row, Lily towards the center on row two. Pamela readied her camera, turning around again to look for Eduardo. Where was he? They were starting and he wasn't here.

She turned around and Roberta patted her knee. "Look at Lily, isn't she precious in that star? Her voice is very good for a 6 year old," she smiled. Just then Luke, sitting on the other side of Pamela, said, "Move down, Eduardo is here and we need a little more room." Pamela looked down the end of the row and saw Eduardo, messing with the video camera. He didn't look her way. The children were on their second song and she hoped he would at least get part of that. They would end the program with Silent Night.

The last refrain of "sleep in heavenly peace" still hung in the air as the parents and grandparents in the audience burst into applause. On Christmas Eve they would leave the church in silence, but this night was for the children. Pamela was so proud. Lily had remembered all the words and hand gestures and sang well. Her little star. Max clapped loudly, pointing to his sister. Then he saw Eduardo. "Daddy, make room for me, I want to sit by you!" he said, getting off his seat and moving to the end of the row.

Eduardo patted his head. "Sure, want to look at the video camera?" Max nodded as Eduardo showed him the image in the screen. Pamela was greeting those around her, inching her way to the end of the row. When she reached Eduardo she said tersely, "Glad you made it. Did you get the video?"

"I got most of it. The battery died before the end, didn't have time to make sure I had a fresh one before I left the office," he replied. He picked up Max. "Let's go, buddy, you can ride home in daddy's car and we'll beat the girls." "Yeah!" Max said, waving his mom goodbye.

Pamela was left fuming in the aisle. Beth from her Bible study came over. "Wasn't that darling?" she asked. "Oh, and I'm pleased to see that Eduardo came. Has he left already?"

"Yes, he was able to make part of the performance. He left to take Max home, I have to wait for Lily to get out of her costume," Pamela said, turning to leave. She didn't feel like talking.

At home she got the children ready for bed and asked Eduardo to come in and hear Lily read some of her book. The child was a phenomenal reader for her age. Eduardo came in and sat down on the edge of the bed, listening as she worked her way through a couple of short pages. "Wow, that's great Lily. You're a smart girl," he said. "Give daddy a goodnight kiss." She complied, adding a hug around his neck.

"Goodnight, daddy. Sleep tight and remember the angels are watching over you," Lily said.

Pamela followed Eduardo out of the room and into their living room where a basketball game played on the television. She asked Eduardo, "Can we see the video on the big screen?"

"Sure," he said, and switched the input. There on the screen was the choir, looking adorable. Lily was perfect. They watched as the choir sang half their second song and began the last one. The picture stopped midway during the last song.

"What happened?" Pamela asked. "Where's the rest of it?"

"I told you, I didn't get it all because the battery died. We saw it in person, and you have enough here to show that Lily did a good job," Eduardo stated flatly.

Something snapped in her head. Eduardo may be fine with showing up for half of their child's special night and be satisfied with a partial video of the performance, but she wasn't. She went off on him, her voice soft enough to keep from waking the children but ugly in its tone. She told him what she thought of his arrogance, his selfishness, his thoughtlessness. She chided him for not putting his family first, for always having excuses but rarely showing up. She told him how miserable she was, how she felt lonely in her own marriage.

Eduardo looked at her coldly, contemptuously. "Why don't you take a lover?" he asked. "It wouldn't bother me, especially if it will keep you off my back."

"Eduardo, you can't be serious! We need help to get things back on track. Would you at least consider getting some counseling with me?" Pamela pleaded, horrified at her outburst but feeling the freedom of honesty.

"I don't need counseling," he replied, condescension dripping from his voice. "This is getting ridiculous. You're ungrateful, you're turning into a nag, and there's nothing for me in the bedroom any more. I don't have to stay here and put up with this."

"No, you don't," Pamela said, she sound of her own words shocking to her ears. "Maybe we should separate, maybe some time apart would be good for us, give us a chance to sort things out and remember what brought us together in the first place."

Eduardo snorted. "You'd better be careful what you ask for. You wouldn't last without me. You need me."

Pamela stayed silent, not sure where the conversation was going and not trusting herself to saying anything more.

"Fine," he said. "I can be out of here in no time. I'm leaving for Long Beach day after tomorrow anyway, I'll just get a hotel until then." He stood up. "I'll be in the bedroom packing if you need me. And trust me, Pamela, you will need me."

Chapter 25

The shock of what had happened didn't fully sink in for Pamela for a while. Eduardo had left, bags packed, shortly after their argument. Pamela had gone to bed as soon as she heard his car back out, her tears a mixture of exhaustion, relief and grief. The children didn't question her the next morning when she told them Daddy was on another trip, they were used to that. Nothing felt any different. Their argument was almost like a bad dream.

But it wasn't a dream. Days passed without a call from Eduardo. She didn't try to reach him either. There wasn't anything to say. Her mind raced with possibilities, none of them feasible. She couldn't see herself staying in a marriage of convenience the rest of her life. Yet divorce was unthinkable. She didn't want to be a working single mother with the children in child care. And what would she do? She hadn't worked in years, had no idea what that world was like now. Pamela wasn't naïve enough to think that Eduardo would simply divorce her with a settlement enough to keep her and the children in their lifestyle. She didn't even know how much money that would take, or whether they had that much. Eduardo was right in one sense; she did need his financial support. Oh, this was a mess. *God help me, what have we done?*

Three weeks later the call came. Pamela looked at the Caller ID and her heart skipped a beat. It was Eduardo. She pressed the talk button and said, "Hello?"

"Hi Pamela. I've been expecting you to call," Eduardo said smoothly into the phone.

"Hello Eduardo. I was hoping you would call, and now you have," she said lamely. "How are you?"

"I'm great. Are the children well?" he asked.

"Yes, they're fine. Lily still loves her teacher and Max is as adorable as ever," she replied.

"Good. Listen, I've been talking with my attorney, and I think you and I should meet. These loose ends aren't going to work forever for either of us. We need to decide how we are going to handle things going forward," Eduardo said.

"Handle things? What do you mean?" Pamela asked, not sure of anything anymore.

Eduardo's voice was calm. "Let's have lunch tomorrow and I'll explain. Meet me at Sinclair's Grill at noon?" he asked.

"I'll see if Riley can keep Max, but yes that should work," Pamela answered hesitantly.

"Perfect. See you tomorrow." The phone clicked off before she could say anything.

Pamela wasn't sure where this was headed. He sounded very business-like, talked of attorneys and 'handling things' but it was their family he would be dealing with. Did he want to reconcile? Divorce? Something else? She was weary of thinking about all of this without any answers. She knew that the God of Bible hates divorce, and until recently she'd never considered it as an option in her life. What if Eduardo didn't give her a choice? He controlled the money, and if he didn't want to be with her he could easily make it happen. She called Riley. "Hey, can you keep Max tomorrow during the lunch hour? Eduardo's in town and he wants to have lunch."

"Of course!" Riley said cheerfully. "That's wonderful, you two haven't gone out for lunch in a long time."

"Thanks a million, I'll have him there by 11:45," Pamela said.

Sensing something else, Riley changed direction. "Is everything alright between you? I mean, you haven't talked about it in a while but I know there have been issues. And lately you don't talk about Eduardo at all. What gives? There's something else, isn't there?" she pressed.

Pamela hesitated. If she could confide in anyone it would be Riley. Perhaps it was time to begin letting her family know the truth. If Eduardo didn't come back they'd know soon enough anyway. "Yes, things are not good. Actually, we've been separated since the night of the children's Christmas program at church."

"What?? Why didn't you tell me? Oh, Pamela, I'm so sorry," Riley exclaimed, concern obvious in her tone.

"I didn't want to worry everyone, and frankly I just haven't been up to talking about it. We had a big fight, I told him what I thought and how miserable I've been and he left. He's gone so much on business I figured no one would be the wiser, and I didn't know how temporary it would be. We didn't speak for almost a month, then today he called and wants to meet. Said he's talked to his attorneys and thinks we should 'decide how to handle things.'" Pamela hated hearing her own words. How could this be happening to her?

Riley was silent for a moment. "Pamela, if he's talked to his attorneys it doesn't sound like he has reconciliation in mind. Do you have an attorney?" she asked.

"Are you kidding?" Pamela shot back. I've started saving some of my discretionary money but no, I don't have an attorney. Didn't think I'd ever need one!"

"Never mind," Riley said quietly. "Just go to lunch and find out what he wants. You've got my number if you need me."

"Ok, thanks. And please don't tell mom. I'll tell her myself when I have a better idea what is going on," Pamela requested.

For lunch at Sinclair's she chose gray slacks and a short-sleeve black cashmere top. She wanted to look her best. Mascara was applied sparingly, however; she wasn't sure if tears would be involved in this lunch and she didn't want to end up looking like a Halloween costume. Dropping Max off at Riley's, she arrived at Sinclair's a few minutes early. No sign of Eduardo's car yet. She walked in and waited in the hostess area.

At 12:10 p.m. Eduardo walked into the restaurant. He took her arm and let her to a table, where they ordered salads and water. He got right to the point. "I actually considered going to counseling with you," Eduardo began. "Some people say it's helpful. But I'm not willing to invest my valuable time, not to mention money, in a process where the outcome I want is not guaranteed. I'm not going to change and I don't expect you are either."

"I'd say we've both changed, in a way," Pamela ventured softly. "You're not the same man who courted me and pulled out all the stops when it came to romance. And I've grown in my faith, learned more about the steps I should have taken before getting married. But I'm willing to go to counseling and see if we can work things out. I don't want to put the children through a divorce, or be a divorce statistic myself."

"The kids will be fine," Eduardo said confidently. "Children are resilient. As they get older I'll be able to be more a part of their life, especially Max. I've got big plans for him."

"Eduardo, you have to build relationship starting when they are young. I'm already having some discipline issues with Max because he knows I'm not the stern one. Children need a father in the home," she said earnestly.

"Look, I don't want to argue. I never thought I'd contemplate divorce either. But it's not uncommon anymore; in the business world being divorced is quite acceptable, much more so than being single. This isn't working. It was great when we got married but you've become a nagging, ungrateful housewife, and now that I've had a taste of freedom outside your expectations I want more of it. I don't want anything to do with your god, but I will have influence in the lives of my children. I thought we could settle things up front. No need for a nasty, expensive battle."

Pamela watched, speechless as he drew out a document from his briefcase. "My attorney helped me draft this. I think it's fair, and I've allotted enough funds for you to take care of things until you can get a job," he said, handing her a copy. "Inheritance for the children will be put in a trust, of course."

She stared at him, then began reading the paper in front of her. Their salads were delivered, and she pushed hers aside. Eduardo picked up his fork and started eating.

"Eduardo, what is this? This says that we'll divide everything evenly except for the business. Are you seriously suggesting that we sell the house, divide the proceeds, you give me some money from your business while holding a chunk of it in trust for the kids, and we divide the children too?" Pamela was incredulous.

"Yes," he said, "that's exactly what I'm suggesting. "You said yourself you needed a hand with Max. I can afford the right supervision and boarding schools for him until he's old enough to start in the business. You can keep Lily, and your share of the proceeds from the house should enable you to get a small place comfortable enough for the two of you. As for Cohen Technologies, there is debt associated with it like any business, of course. We've assessed the net value, separated out what I want the children to have as inheritance, and that leaves you with a nice sum for the near term. I don't think I could be fairer than that."

Pamela couldn't believe what she was hearing. Had he gone mad? Split Lily and Max, like they were two assets on his corporate balance sheet? It was impossible for her to agree to that. He was never around to care for either child, and she wasn't going to let her baby be raised by a nanny or boarding school. She didn't care about the business, but the amount of money he was allotting for her didn't seem like enough to buy even a small house in their school district. She looked up at him in disbelief.

"I can't agree to splitting up the children. And I need to get up to speed about the housing market before I can think about the rest of it. I guess I'm naïve, but I didn't realize until this lunch that divorce is where we are. I don't know anything for certain, but I know this. I'm not going to let you split up those children. They need to be with me and you can have generous visitation whenever you see fit to come to town." Pamela was indignant.

"I'm afraid I have to insist on joint custody. Divorce is one thing, but it would look very bad if I agreed to give up custody of my children. Pamela, you really need to take this deal. You don't have the money for an attorney or the stomach for a fight," Eduardo said, looking as if the conversation were over.

"What about your parents?" Pamela asked. "Have you talked about this with your mother? She's going to be heart broken."

"Yes, she probably will, at least for a time. But you aren't going to keep her grandchildren from her and neither am I. She'll get over it in time. This can't be about my parents. It's about us. There just isn't any 'us' left," Eduardo said gravely.

Stifling the panic spreading through her body, Pamela unhooked her purse from the back of the chair. "I think I need to get some legal advice," she said in flat voice, standing to leave.

"My attorney has drawn up an excellent arrangement. He's the best in local family law. You're making a mistake if you try to fight this." Eduardo took a sip of water. "For now I'll continue to pay the bills and your allowance," he said. "But at some point that will stop. Go ahead, find a lawyer and then call me back when you decide to accept my plan."

"I'll contact you when I have thought this through and have done my homework," Pamela replied. "You are welcome to visit the children, take them to the park or dinner any time, you know. They miss you." She waited hopefully for his response, and when there was none turned and walked out of the restaurant.

Outside the entrance she just stood there, unmoving, car key dangling from her right hand. The sun gave off its beautiful bright light, shining glorious against the blue cloudless sky. How could the sun be shining and the day be beautiful when her marriage had just ended? She didn't want to be another divorce statistic. Why would God allow this to happen to her? She had been faithful, prayed and tried everything to keep her marriage together. It wasn't fair. What was the point of living to please God if He was going to let her life go to hell in a hand basket?

As the situation began to sink in anger began to warm her insides, starting in her gut and moving through her veins as if flowing from an IV. Pamela had never been so mad, never felt such righteous indignation. Her anger flared, rising to greet all of the justifiable resentment she had stuffed until that moment. *Thanks a lot God. If this is what Your help feels like, I don't need it.*

Stepping off the curb she quickly took the few steps to her Mustang. She flung open the driver's door and threw her purse into the passenger seat, not caring that her cosmetic bag flew out into the floorboard. Grabbing her cell phone, she typed out a brief text to Riley: "Just left lunch, need some time to think, will call when I'm on the way to pick up the kids." Then she started the car, slammed the gearshift into reverse and stepped on the gas. Only the furious honk of the driver she almost hit prevented a collision. Ignoring the angry one finger salute, Pamela waited until it was clear then exited the parking lot. She needed some open road, some highway speed to keep pace with her racing thoughts. She headed north on S. Dixie Highway, driving as fast as traffic would allow. She drove for several miles, passing cars that were observing the speed limit and out pacing the ones that weren't. But the speed couldn't get past her emotions, and after a few minutes her anger dissolved into the beginnings of a good pity party. She took the next exit, looking for a restroom. At the edge of the frontage road an orange neon sign boasted the words "Cryin Shame". Perfect, Pamela thought. That's exactly what this is, a crying shame.

Pulling into the half-full parking lot she left the Mustang at the far end. Entering the building she immediately pulled off her sunshades, letting her eyes adjust to the dark interior. The bartender looked her up and down, giving her a wink and a smile. "What can I get for you?" he asked. "Where is your ladies room?" Pamela responded. "At the end of the counter take a right, the door's on your left," he said.

She washed her hands and waved one in front of the motion sensor on the paper towel dispenser. A long piece of brown paper towel ejected and she tore it off, drying her hands thoroughly. Pamela looked in the mirror, reaching into her purse for her cosmetic bag. She realized it was still in the floorboard of the car. It didn't matter anyway at this point, she thought, no need to freshen my makeup before going to get the kids.

Country music played through the speakers as she walked back into the bar. The patrons were mainly old men, interested only in their beer and whiskey and not letting their glasses get empty. Suddenly Pamela wanted a drink too, something strong that would numb her brain from all the thinking, something that would overpower her own cocktail of emotions. She sat down on a barstool, resting her purse on the counter. "I'll have a Jack Daniels on the rocks, please," she said to the bartender. He wasted no time in pouring a generous glass and placed it directly in front of her. "You running a tab?" he inquired. She pulled out a twenty and laid it beside the glass. "No thanks," she said. He picked up the bill and Pamela picked up her glass. She took a long sip, surprised that the strong drink actually tasted good. Almost instantly she felt the effect of the liquor and followed it with another sip. Her shoulders relaxed as she focused on the feeling, gladly letting her thoughts slip away. She deserved this, to be 'off' for a while, not responsible for anything and not worried about anyone or the future. Shock and anger, worry and sorrow gave way to warmth and a pleasant light-headed numbness. I could get used to this, she thought, it feels great not to feel anything, not be accountable to anyone.

The ice cubes clinked against the bottom of the glass, and before she could signal the bartender he brought her another. How nice to be served, no questions asked, anything available at the flash of cash. She put the glass to her lips, closing her eyes. Eduardo may leave me, God has obviously left me, but I've got my family and my children. And this comfort in a glass. Comfort. From the edges of her brain came a verse: "Yea though I walk through the valley of the shadow of death I will fear no evil, for Thy rod and Thy staff comfort me." Pamela's eyes opened abruptly. *Where is your comfort, God? I feel like You have left me. My life is a mess, I don't know what will happen to me or the children or my home. Where is the comfort in all of this?* Pamela was startled by her own prayer. Yet now she didn't feel so mad at God, only alone and low on hope. *I will never leave you or forsake you, my child. Trust me. Wait. I will be with you and I will show you the way.*

All of a sudden she no longer felt deliciously warm and numb. She felt weak and ashamed. She set the glass down, pushing it away from her. What was she thinking? What was she doing in this bar off the beaten path drinking straight bourbon in the middle of the afternoon? Her life verse immediately flooded her mind, "Trust in the Lord with all your heart, don't lean on your own understanding… and He will direct your path." Of course. Trust and wait, that was the answer. She certainly wasn't going to make things better sitting around getting sloshed.

Pamela stood up, holding on to the back of the chair as a wave of dizziness came and went. She asked for a glass of water, emptying it completely in just a few seconds. *Thank you, Father. Thank you for saving me from myself. This isn't me, running from You and trying to drown my sorrows. I am so sorry, please forgive me. And please get me safely home, with my children. And with You.*

She slipped her purse off her shoulder and walked to the exit. She didn't even hear the bartender's friendly, "Come again!" as the door closed behind her.

Chapter 26

Pamela pored over the legal documents spread out on her bed. Lily and Max were asleep but it would be a while before she could sleep. It was summer. Lily had just completed first grade and Max would be in kindergarten in the fall. And her legal battle with Eduardo had been going on forever, it seemed, but in reality it had only been nine months.

She had broken the news to her family, had endured that painful process. They were concerned but supportive, and everyone was praying for the miracle of reconciliation or at least an agreement that would prevent a nasty public divorce. Her Bible Study group had listened caringly, offering prayers and help with the children. As frightened as she'd been to share her 'dirty laundry' with the group, it had brought them closer. She learned that two others in the group were on their second marriage, and was reminded that they served a God of infinite second chances. She had called her old boss, explained the situation and asked him to consider her for any positions that might be available. He assured her he would make a place for her but was sorry for the reason. She had made it through a talk with Pastor Kyle and his wife, who prayed with her and counseled her to do everything in her power to restore the marriage. She had even survived the difficult conversation with Cindy, who had called to say how upset she was. Cindy had asked if there was anything that could keep the marriage together, and Pamela advised her to talk to Eduardo about that. She didn't go into detail or explain that she wasn't about to give up her faith or go through life waiting for the chance to get lipstick stains off her husband's pants. That would have been tacky; she loved Cindy too much to tell her the whole truth. She was Eduardo's mother, he could tell her if he chose.

She had accepted the fact that they were getting a divorce. They had met one last time at the house to tell the children – she insisted he do that with her – and the kids had acted unaffected by it. But Pamela knew that divorce is always, *always* hard on children, no matter the circumstances. Eduardo had been gone long enough that they had noticed the difference. Lily was coping by withdrawing, spending lots of time reading and drawing. Max handled it by acting out, and now at the age of 5 he was becoming a handful. Still a charming and happy little boy, but when he chose to disobey she was having a hard time administering discipline. She had an appointment with a children's counselor, a woman referred to her by a friend at church, in a couple of weeks and hoped that would help.

What she could not figure out was how to come to agreement with Eduardo on their divorce terms. She had found an attorney who agreed to help her for a reasonable fee. Pamela had chosen him after consulting with

Don Philip, head of a law firm she had worked for part-time in the years before she met Eduardo. Don had given her three names. She called all three, then met with the third one, Jeff Baxter, after conducting phone interviews. She liked Jeff immediately, warming to his friendly, easy manner as he told her about his law practice and what she could expect in a contested divorce. Pamela could pay his initial fee from her savings if they could work things out. But if an agreement could not be arrived at and they went to trial, she told him she didn't know how she could pay. They discussed various scenarios, and when he discovered she had legal secretary experience he smiled. "Tell you what," he said. "If it goes to trial I'll let you work off some of the fees by preparing my trial documents and doing some of the word processing. Deal?"

"Deal!" she said, feeling like she had an advocate.

In the course of their meeting she had learned that Jeff was also a Christian. She told him she was praying for guidance in this situation. He nodded. "Always remember that God hates divorce, but he doesn't hate divorced people."

Now here she was at the decision point. Godly people were praying for her, she had prayed for wisdom, and the most recent counter settlement offer from Eduardo's attorney was spread out before her. Jeff had given her some sound advice about how to approach receiving her share of Eduardo's business assets, recognizing immediately the disadvantaged position Eduardo's initial offer had placed her in. She kept telling Jeff she didn't want Eduardo's money; she wanted the house, paid for, and primary custody of the children. Jeff showed her how to use Eduardo's assets as bargaining chips in their negotiations but left the back and forth to her and Eduardo. Eduardo was still intent on splitting up the children, one for each of them. Pamela had never heard a more ridiculous idea. She knew he didn't really want the day to day responsibility of a child, he would just end up paying someone for full time care. She suspected it was more a way of getting to her, knowing that she would give up everything to have her children. And she would, but they needed a place to live that she could afford. Didn't her years as corporate wife, homemaker and the 'care and feeding' of her husband count for anything? He wouldn't have heirs if it weren't for her. She'd offered every compromise she could think of. Jeff was adamant that she not give up her claim to part of his business, telling her she needed those assets to start building for retirement and to help with unexpected expenses that came with children and owning a home.

Pamela slid off the bed and knelt beside it, grabbing her Bible. "Trust in the Lord with all your heart," she read, feeling their ring of truth begin to ease her angst. "Lean not on your own understanding, but in all your ways acknowledge Him and He will direct your path." She bowed her head and began to pray.

Father, the last thing I ever wanted to talk to you about was divorce terms. I am ashamed of my failed marriage, and I ask your forgiveness for my part in not working this out. It's always a two-way street. You see the paperwork spread before me, you know how much I love my children and desire to care for them. I'm scared, God, really scared. How are they going to be scarred by this divorce? Will their father be in their lives, and if so will he be a good influence? He doesn't know you and doesn't want to. Please show him you are real, open his heart to you for his children's sake. I don't know what to do. What do you want me to do? How can we shift this thing off dead center? Please guide me, guide Jeff, and let this be over with soon. The kids start school in a few weeks and I'll have to go back to work. I need to know where I stand financially. In Jesus' name, Amen.

She didn't know how long she'd been kneeling there when she heard it. "*Give him the business,*" the voice said. Pamela looked up. There was no one there but the voice had been so obvious she almost expected to see someone. It wasn't an audible voice, but a strong powerful voice that she clearly heard nonetheless.

"God, is that you?" Pamela asked in a whisper. "I'm listening, please tell me what to do."

A few seconds passed, then she heard it again, as clearly as the first time but with an additional message. "*Give him the business. In exchange, I want you to ask for the children and your home, but nothing else — not any part of the business. And when you ask you must tell him the reason you are doing it.*"

Pamela sat up straight, completely alert. Was this Almighty God, telling her the divorce terms she should offer? Why would He do that, she thought, He hates divorce. On the other hand, she reasoned, why wouldn't He? She knew God answered the prayers of His people. He knew she didn't want any of Eduardo's business, only a place to raise her children. She felt a peace wash over her, along with a glimmer of hope. Would Eduardo do that? Would he let her have the house and primary custody of the kids if she would give up her right to any of his business?

Then a doubt entered her mind. Could God really want her to give that up? That asset was supposed to put her kids through college and be her future. And as for telling Eduardo why she was doing it, the only thing she could dread more that getting divorced would be to talk to her husband about God. She could not imagine proposing divorce terms to Eduardo saying: "God told me to tell you….."

Jeff had said she would need those assets. But God said to trust in Him and not lean on the understanding of man. Pamela knew she had to look at things through the eyes of faith. As a believer she was to walk by faith, not by sight, in obedience to God each and every day, even if it meant giving up something she wanted or thought she would need. She decided to do what God had told her and let the dollars fall where they may. She would work hard to earn all she could but trust her financial future to God. She would obey what she was now certain was the voice of God.

Pamela stood, moved the papers to the side, and got under the covers. She fell asleep as soon as her head hit the pillow.

Chapter 27

Pamela called Jeff first thing next morning. "Can you see me today?" she asked. "I think I have the settlement terms worked out."

"I have a 30 minute window if you can be here at 10:30," Jeff answered.

"I'll be there," Pamela said, hope surging through her.

Pamela arrived promptly and was shown in to his office by Jeff's legal assistant.

"What's on your mind?" Jeff asked. Pamela told him what happened the night before and of God's terms she wanted to offer. Jeff looked her for a long minute, then spoke.

"As your attorney it is my job to advise you in what I think is your best interest, and I must advise against this. As your friend, I don't want to see you lose all this. But as a Christian, I have to counsel you that if God has said this to you, who are we to disobey God?"

Pamela jumped up, clasping Jeff's hands. "Thank you, I know this is the right thing to do. I've been asking God for guidance, and He showed up in the most unexpected way. Do you think Eduardo will agree?" she asked, suddenly nervous.

Jeff laughed. "He's crazy if he doesn't. I'll draw up the settlement agreement and send it to his attorney this afternoon. If you hear from Eduardo, let me know."

Pamela left the attorney's office with a wide smile on her face. She did some grocery shopping, stopped by the post office and picked up the dry cleaning. By the time she got home it was almost 1:00 p.m. She unloaded the groceries and had just hung the dry cleaning in her closet when her phone range. It was Eduardo.

"Pamela, my attorney just emailed me your proposed settlement agreement. Is it true you've decided against asking for any of Cohen Technologies?" he asked breathlessly.

"Yes, Eduardo, it's true," she said calmly. "There is only one catch. I request that you meet with me in person so I can explain my reasons."

"Sure," Eduardo said. "How soon can you meet?"

"I'll be at your office tomorrow morning."

"I'll be here," Eduardo said, trying to hold off the excitement in his voice. He could not believe this turn of events. If he pulled this off, he was THE man.

Pamela was nervous about the meeting, but she was on God's territory now. She felt a strange calm descend as she pulled the Mustang into the parking lot of Cohen Technologies the next morning. Eduardo's assistant ushered her into the modern office, seating her at the small conference table.

"Thanks for meeting with me," Pamela said when Eduardo walked in. She declined the assistant's offer of coffee.

"Of course. When I saw the terms Mr. Baxter sent over I couldn't believe it. It'll take a few weeks to get the house deeded over to you, and I want my CPA to go over tax implications for this year with me. I'm good with the amount of child support but I'll want to use the term joint custody for my visitation. Other than that the terms will read exactly as you have set forth," Eduardo stated. "Why are you doing this?" he asked.

Pamela took a deep breath. "Because I've prayed about it and I believe this is what God wants me to do. And, He wants you to know it was His idea."

She could tell by the look on his face that Eduardo completely discounted the "God" explanation. He didn't say anything, just shook his head in disbelief. He was anxious to get the deal in writing before she came to her senses, so he handed her two cleanly printed copies and a pen. Pamela signed her name and passed the agreements across the table. Eduardo drank in her signatures then added his own. Then he picked up the phone and pressed the intercom button. "Melissa, can you come in and bring your notary stamp please?"

"That's it, then," he said. "I'll have Gary prepare the divorce decree. Once the house is cleared we'll file it at the courthouse and let your attorney know.

Pamela stood up and offered her hand. "Goodbye Eduardo, we'll talk when the visitation schedule is finalized."

He shook her hand and said goodbye.

Two months later the divorce was final.

Chapter 28

At least she had a reserved parking space. Going back to work was hard enough without scavenging for a place to park her Mustang every day. Pamela's space was on the end of a row, and she parked as far as possible away from the car next to her. She locked the car and took the stairs. She was in her fourth week of the new job. Things were going well; she'd forgotten how well she and Scott worked together, how appreciative he was of her administrative skills. He had been right, she was well suited to the position.

God had blessed her mightily in the past few months. Her old boss, Scott Woodster, had called her the day after she signed the settlement agreement. His office manager had retired and he was looking for a replacement. Thank God she had called to give him the heads up she might need a job or he would never have thought to call her. The position didn't start until September 15th, another blessing. Lily and Max had started school on the 3rd so she had had time to get her affairs in order and put the pencil to her budget.

It would be tight to save for property taxes and insurance, and she could forget about shopping, hair color or getting her nails done for a while. But she calculated that she could handle utilities, groceries, routine car maintenance and nominal gift giving with her salary. Working would also provide her health insurance. The children would remain covered under Eduardo's policy, and child support would cover after school care, incidentals for school, and any out of pocket copays or medicines for them. If she was careful, she would be fine. She now had an asset of her own, their home. She was concerned about how she would pay for its upkeep over time and the fact she had no emergency savings, but for now God had taken care of her beautifully and she would continue to trust in the Lord, leaning not on her own understanding.

The children's counselor had assured her that while the kids were dealing with grief and loss over their father's leaving they would be fine in time. She told Pamela the fact they were open in sharing about it was a good sign. Lily talked about it more than Max. Max talked about almost everything else, but in a few more sessions they would be released. Pamela still struggled with guilt over the children having to go through the ripping apart that divorce is. What little time they'd had with their dad had dwindled, and they missed him. They would soon begin some weekend visitation and she hoped that would go well for all of them.

The custody arrangements were basic, with rotating holidays and the children scheduled to have every other weekend with Eduardo. Because of his travel Pamela knew she would have the children the majority of weekends, and that is exactly how the arrangement functioned in reality. She and Eduardo kept things civil when the kids were around. She knew that he would take the children to visit Cindy and Bill often, and that pleased her. Pamela missed her mother-in-law greatly, but at least Lily and Max didn't have to.

She did her best to provide her children with a happy, healthy home, and relied on her extended family and church family for help. That part had been harder than she thought, asking for help. But she knew how much she enjoyed helping others so she swallowed her pride. She shared in the car pool, took turns keeping the cousins so that she and Riley each had a little down time. Her mother had taken to dropping by on the weekends for a while to play with the children. That gave Pamela a chance to cook ahead and prepare a couple of casseroles for the coming week.

She had found that the time right after they got home was the most challenging. She missed the immediate sharing that came with picking her children up from school. By the time she retrieved them from aftercare the memories of the day's events weren't as fresh or they were no longer interested in talking much about them. Fortunately her job didn't involve overtime – she couldn't afford the extra dollar per minute fee if she was late to pick them up. She was determined that they would always have dinner at the table, even if it was sandwiches. Dinner time was family time. She didn't need the studies to tell her how important it was for the development of her children to have a shared meal at table with family. Even if that family no longer included their father.

The children had a chore chart, taking turns setting and clearing the table. Then homework if they had any, a little play time, baths and then to bed with time built in to read. Pamela was a firm believer in no TV for children on school nights while they were this young. One night a week she had family game night, where they played Sorry, cards or Monopoly. One week the Monopoly game lasted three days; they all wanted to play to the bitter end so she left it set up until the game was won by a very happy Max.

Life developed a new routine, one that kept her too busy to think much about Eduardo. The months after the divorce was final folded into years, almost without her noticing. She drew strength from her faith and from frequent family gatherings. They got together as much for the adults as for the children. Pamela, Riley and Luke loved the fact that their children adored each other. Luke's two girls, Riley's two boys, and Pamela's "one of each" were all close in age. The siblings marveled at how much the cousins loved to play together. They knew that kind of camaraderie couldn't be forced.

The first holidays she had to spend without her children were hard. She spent them with her family, but it was hard to see the other children playing without Lily and Max. Her only consolation was that Cindy was getting time with them; that was a win-win. Cindy was good about sending little notes detailing the things they did while they were with her, cute things they'd said, and always how much she loved having them. How grateful Pamela was for her children's grandparents.

Her life wasn't perfect but it was real, filled with the love of God and a great support system. Pamela often commented that single-parenting was everything it was cracked up to be - she wouldn't wish it on her worst enemy. But God. He had provided her with a home, her children, and a good job with a Christian boss. She and her children were in a good healthy church, surrounded by godly people who loved on them weekly. They weren't perfect, they simply shared being a forgiven people who knew Love and wanted others to know it too. By God's grace she was making it. Lily and Max's elementary school years yielded many sweet memories and special moments during the ordinary times. Pamela wouldn't have traded those times or their closeness for anything.

She prayed daily for her children to grow their child-faith into true saving faith, and for Eduardo's heart to be touched by God. She couldn't undo the mistakes of her past but she could trust her future to the One with whom all things were possible.

It seemed impossible that one day she found herself on the front porch, snapping first day of school pictures of Lily, now in eighth grade, and Max, starting his first day of sixth grade. How could they both be in junior high school? Not until years later would she remember that that was the day she first noticed the crack across the ceiling of the living room. She couldn't know it at the time, but both the foundation of her home and the new life she had so carefully constructed were starting to crumble.

Chapter 29

Eduardo was restless. He didn't know why, he should be feeling on top of the world. He was now the sole owner of Cohen Technologies. Never again would he worry about losing part of it to a spouse - if he ever married again the pre-nup would tie things up so tight there would be no question. He had developed most of his potential clients and all of them were extremely pleased. Business was doing very, very well. The trust for his children had been established, his estate planning complete.

His new condo on the southwest side was luxurious, tailored specifically to his taste with two small bedrooms for Lily and Max. He didn't have them very often, but when he did typically they would watch movies and play the latest in video games. Occasionally he would take them out to eat but usually he preferred to order in. Every now and then Lily would talk him into making homemade hamburgers, the kids seemed to love those. They vegged out while he kept up with work emails, slept in on Saturdays, then by Sunday mornings he was ready for them to be picked up at 9 a.m. so Pamela could take them to church with her. Max had begun to resist getting up early on Sundays, and sometimes Eduardo let him sleep. But not often.

He continued entertaining his clients at his favorite clubs. New clients were usually up for the experience, but many of his existing ones had stopped joining him once the work relationship was solidified. Lately he had taken to going alone. The table dances were getting old. They didn't satisfy the way they had in the beginning. Eduardo had laughed about that to one of his newer clients, who suggested that what he needed was a massage. He explained that he wasn't talking about massage therapy, but a true, personalized massage. Eduardo had taken the card the man handed him and placed it in his wallet.

In the six weeks since receiving the card, Eduardo had purchased four massage sessions. He now understood what the man meant. The skilled hands of his masseuse helped him release the tension of his work day. She had quickly learned his preferences, selecting a variety of massage oils that made his skin tingle from the sensation. It dawned on Eduardo that the restlessness he now felt was a sign that it was time for another session. He picked up the phone and made the appointment.

He pulled his car into the parking garage and stepped out, taking the stairs two at a time. Once inside, Eduardo sat down, noting with satisfaction that his favorite massage oils had been replenished and waited on the side table. An assortment of DVDs lined the shelf underneath the player. He might try one of those during his session tonight to enhance the experience.

Tawny appeared in the doorway, wearing her signature smile. The feeling of power and control began to ripple through him. He closed his eyes. In this place he was in total command and full control. He smiled as he anticipated the rush of feeling and the delicious sense that here it was all about him.

Chapter 30

The crumbling started mid-way through Lily's eighth grade fall semester. She tried out for the JV football team and made it. It was so out of character for Pamela's shy, feminine daughter. Lily excelled academically and was doing well socially but had never been interested in sports. In addition, she began having extreme stomach aches, often on alternate Fridays, and sometimes after the kids had been with their dad she would have outbursts that seemed extreme. She seemed the happiest at home with Pamela or when involved in church youth group activities, a group in which she was very active. It was so hard to know what behavior was 'normal' for an adolescent girl, when to be truly concerned and what to do if there was reason for concern. Pamela began to be extremely concerned about her daughter.

By the spring of Lily's eighth grade year Pamela knew something was wrong. She racked her brain considering how to address it. She had asked Eduardo's opinion and he had said Lily was just a teenaged girl. When the school counselor called Pamela at the end of a work day in late February about a suicide note that Lily had passed to a friend, Pamela became truly alarmed. She called Eduardo to inform him and ask his advice. He insisted it was "just hormones", that Lily didn't need any 'help', that it was embarrassing enough to have received the call about the note. Pamela told him she was very worried and, knowing his opinion of counselors, stated bluntly that she was going to seek counseling for Lily. He repeated that it wasn't necessary. She couldn't understand why he wasn't worried. Surely he loved their daughter; she could not think of any reason he wouldn't want to consider professional help if Lily needed it. That night at home when Pamela asked Lily about the note she apologized, called it 'dark teenage humor' and said that it was a joke. Lily assured her mom there was no reason to be concerned, but Pamela was not convinced. The "mother-gut" is strong, and not easily dismissed.

It had become Pamela's habit to start each day at her prayer bench, the wise Word of God at her fingertips and a list of joys and concerns before her. This concern was by far the most major she had ever dealt with, and she was reeling in shock at the thought that Lily – her beautiful smart accomplished beloved daughter – would contemplate suicide. She called her mother, still and always the best source of advice, and after discussing the matter they agreed – it was time to call a counselor and get to the bottom of this.

Pamela made a "well-check" counseling appointment for Lily, who to her surprise did not object at all. There was a waiting list and they couldn't get in for a month, but she felt better having acted on the school counselor's call. The next few weeks passed fairly smoothly. The every other Friday stomach aches continued though, and the worst one happened the day before Lily was to leave with her dad and Max on a week-long cruise. Grandma CiCi would join them at one of the ports of call.

"Joining my grandchildren on a cruise has been a dream of mine, "Cindy had told Pamela over the phone when discussing the travel arrangements. "I can't believe Eduardo is making my dream come true," she had gushed. Pamela knew the children would love it, knew also she would never be able to afford it so she had given her blessing for them to go

Just days before departure Lily began making comments about not wanting to go on the cruise. She even asked Pamela if she had to go on the trip. Pamela was stunned; how could she not want to go on this trip of a lifetime? She asked Lily why she didn't want to go. The answer was vague: something about wanting to stay home for spring break and hang out with friends, but that didn't make sense to Pamela. Besides, the tickets and other arrangements had been made long in advance, and if she was going to call Eduardo to say Lily wasn't going she would need a *really* good reason. Even if there were a reason Pamela knew he wouldn't accept it; he would only think she was trying to keep Lily from him during his allotted time. Sighing, she reminded Lily that this trip had been her grandmother's dream for years and that her father had already paid for everything in advance. Lily said yes, she knew, and she would go on the trip.

Oh how she would wish she had kept her daughter home.

Truth is always strong, no matter how weak it looks;

and falsehood is always weak, no matter how strong it looks.

Phillips Brooks

Chapter 31

Wednesday morning following the children's return from their trip Pamela sat at the breakfast table, picking up her cell phone to check email. She pressed a button and the screen came to life. Pamela's blood turned to ice as her eyes traveled across the words displayed in the text message. The shock of what she read broke over her like a tsunami, wave after wave crushing the part of her brain trying to make sense of the message. It took several minutes to realize she had accidentally picked up Lily's phone thinking it was hers. She couldn't breathe, couldn't think, couldn't get the weight off her chest.

The text was from a good friend of Lily's, responding to Lily's message about what had happened to her on the cruise. On the last night Eduardo brought Lily to his cabin and raped her; then he threatened to kill her and other family members if she told anyone. Lily's text said she couldn't bear the pain of what her father had done or the fear that he would kill her to keep her quiet.

Pamela was horribly shocked; her mind didn't know how to process the information. Surely not, this couldn't be. It was a nightmare. Not her *father!* She couldn't believe Eduardo would do such a thing, but also couldn't escape the raw emotion in the note combined with Lily's recent behaviors that suddenly started to make sense if this were true. From the moment she stepped out of Eduardo's car and walked up to the porch Pamela had known something was different. There had been a look in Lily's eyes, a deadness that was disturbing. At the time Max had been dying to tell her all about their adventures and Lily said she was tired, but the look never went away and for five days now Pamela had been puzzled and concerned.

Pamela called in sick to work. It wasn't a lie, she felt physically ill. Then she called her mom and told her what she had found.

"Honey, you get that child in to see a counselor TODAY," Roberta told her. "We don't know for sure what has happened, but something is terribly wrong and you mustn't delay in getting her help". Pamela knew it was the right thing to do – the next right thing. She pressed the counselor's office number into the phone. When the receptionist answered, Pamela said, "My daughter needs to see a counselor today, please. We have an appointment scheduled for later in the month but this is an emergency." She explained the situation, still not believing the words that came out of her mouth. She was placed on hold briefly, then told to be at the office at 11:00 a.m. that morning.

Pamela felt a hint of relief. At least she'd done something. She called the school and arranged to pick up Lily at 10:30, asking them to send her teacher a note. It was all she could do to calm herself enough to take a shower and get ready. She prayed the entire time, not knowing what to believe but knowing they needed help desperately. At 10:30 she pulled up to the front of the school and parked. Lily was waiting out front for her, and as she got into the car she looked at her mom with concern. "Mom, what's wrong?" she asked, her hazel eyes wide with fear. "The school counselor told me I had to leave early today, that you'd pick me up."

Pamela breathed out slowly. "I'll explain on the way. Glad you got the message," Pamela said, with more assurance than she felt. Lily buckled up and Pamela pulled out of the driveway. She told Lily that she had discovered the text that morning, and how she came upon it by accident. Lily said nothing but was listening. Pamela explained that after the recent "joke" suicide note, finding the text this morning had prompted her to make the call to get the counseling appointment bumped up to today. She hesitated, then added, "Lily, I want you to know that I will do everything I can to help you, to keep you safe. The place we are going to this morning is a safe place, the counseling office has Pastor Kyle's recommendation and I trust him. Do you trust me?" She looked at Lily, who nodded, still saying nothing. "Ok, thank you darling. When we get there I'll be with you. I'm going to get help for you from someone who knows what they are doing. You know that I support you 100% and am praying for you always." They drove the rest of the way in silence, but somehow it wasn't as tense as before. There was a hint of anticipation too, and it gave Pamela the confidence she needed to forge ahead. This was her precious daughter. Whatever was wrong, they'd get to the bottom of it together. If Lily had been harmed, Pamela would protect her and never let it happen again. Never.

Inside the counselor's quiet, calming office they sat down, Lily on one end of the couch and Pamela on the other. The counselor was compassionate and kind, with a calm manner that made Lily feel at ease after the first ten minutes. She explained the process, reiterated why Pamela had made the appointment and showed her a copy of the text message Pamela had brought with them. She asked Lily to tell her about some of the stresses in her life. Lily talked of being shy, of feeling the need to excel with her grades, the pressure to fit in. After a while, the counselor said gently, "Lily, if the text is true, please tell me so I can help you. If you are in danger we can help, your mother and I. There are others to help you also, but we have to know if it's true." A few seconds passed, until Lily gathered the courage to say, "Yes, it's true. I'm not supposed to tell anyone, he threatened to kill me, and my mom and my brother!" she said with great agitation. "Dad wasn't bluffing. I didn't mean for mom to find out."

The woman gave Lily a few moments, then said, "Well, I'm glad she did. When someone, especially someone you love, hurts you like this the others who love you need to know. Your mom wants to keep you safe, and that is our first priority." Pamela moved over to put her arm around Lily, and Lily didn't resist. The counselor told Lily she was very brave, and that over time she would be just fine because she was willing to be honest and get help. They were told that when a child made an "outcry" to a counselor she was bound by law to report the incident to Child Protective Services and explained that someone would be contacting them. Lily asked if she would have to talk to that person about what had happened, and was told yes but that the lady who would call from CPS was specifically trained to help teenage girls.

"Do you have any other questions?" the counselor asked.

"Do I still have to go to my dad's for visitation? I don't want to be around him, don't want to be alone with him," Lily said, quietly.

Pamela quickly answered. "Honey, you don't have to go any more. I'll deal with your dad, you just focus on healing and getting help to deal with this. You've been hurt a great deal, and you won't be put in harm's way ever again if I can help it."

They discussed the need for further counseling targeted to Lily's needs and made an appointment for later in the week.

On the drive home, Pamela was torn between the shock of what she had learned and the need to nurture and comfort Lily. She suggested that they go home, and Lily looked relieved. "All I want to do is watch one of our favorite movies and snuggle on the couch with you, Mom. Can we do that?" Lily asked.

"You bet we can, darling. I'm here for you," Pamela said, fighting back the tears. She was, and she would be. Forever.

And so it began. Eduardo was questioned by Child Protective Services and denied everything. There were no witnesses, not unusual with the crime of incest. The incident had happened out of their home state, and it was Lily's word against her father's. He insisted she was lying. Although Lily did not want to see him, he was insistent on trying to see her. The pressure on Pamela to accept Eduardo's word as truth and to believe that Lily was "just emotional due to hormones" was enormous. That simply did not make sense with an accusation of this magnitude. Why would Lily lie when she had so much to lose by telling the truth: relationship with her father; relationship with her grandmother; financial support – inheritance, college tuition, car, insurance, gifts; privacy – she would be interviewed by counselors, police, social workers, court-ordered psychologists, attorneys; legal hassle – she, her brother and friends would be subpoenaed for depositions and possibly have to testify in a criminal trial. Pamela considered what she knew. In her heart she knew Lily was being honest, even though it killed her to think that her own ex-husband had done this to their daughter. Lily's eyes had been filled with sadness from the moment she returned home from the "dream" vacation. Lily's fears had escalated constantly. Over the weeks she had asked Pamela to check locks on doors and windows. Lily had started to have problems sleeping. She had nothing to gain by a false accusation.

Pamela had a decision to make. Believe Lily, accept the unthinkable, and get help for her daughter as best she could. That would mean dealing with Eduardo, facing expensive legal battles in court over her father's access to her, possible criminal charges that would be brought against him, and interviews by the police. It meant that Lily would have to endure questioning from CPS, attorneys and others, have a complete medical and psychological exam, and who knew how it would all end. Max would have to be questioned also since he had been on the trip. Or, Pamela could believe Eduardo, accept the equally unthinkable idea that Lily was lying, get her into counseling to figure out what was going on, and support visitation with her father. The only thing she knew for certain was that God would give them the strength to face whatever happened, and that if she stood on the truth and trusted God they would be fine. He would get them through whatever was to come.

Logic and human pressure told her to believe Eduardo. But instinct and a strong mother-gut told her to believe Lily. After all, the pain Pamela saw in her daughter's eyes could not be denied. Her behavior had changed too drastically, she was too frightened and despairing to be making this up. Pamela had a decision to make. She chose to believe her daughter.

It was that belief, and Lily knowing how grieved Pamela would be if she succeeded in killing herself, that ultimately helped keep Lily alive. That and the grace of God.

Lily's Story
Part One

Chapter 32

What happened to Lily went far beyond the immediate pain and horror of her father's crime. Her soul was damaged. The sense of loss was tremendous. She lost so much; the loss of ability to trust those whom she'd believed to be trustworthy was crushing. A question formed in Lily's mind: if her father had betrayed her, could she still trust that others she had always believed could be trusted utterly and completely? Then there was the weight of the false sense of guilt and shame that is common to victims of incest: the heavy sense of no self-worth; the false perception that if her father loved her only for her body then that was the only thing any man could love her for. She felt great, unfathomable sorrow; and the desire to end the pain by death became harder to fight. Pamela learned that the medical diagnosis for her condition was Post Traumatic Stress Disorder, but as they lived out the results the term "disorder" seemed vastly insufficient. Pamela worried whether counseling would be enough to heal her daughter.

Max was greatly affected as well. Pamela had been encouraged by CPS to get him a counselor. Through a referral from an associate of Jeff's she found Miguel – a godsend delivered straight from the angels in heaven. Miguel was working diligently with Max. At the age of eleven, the effects of the trauma slammed Max and collided with the adolescent hormones just beginning to bubble up. On the surface he seemed to be only slightly bothered by how his life was turned upside down. He didn't talk about what happened, or his feelings, or much of anything. He was still very social and always more interested in friends, video games, paintball or his bike and ramps than in school. But Miguel in his wisdom spotted the signs of a major storm brewing and was very concerned. Max was caught in the middle between his sister and his father, a Max sandwich created by Eduardo. Miguel told Pamela that only time and the truth was holding back the storm of conflict Max was yet to face. He, like his sister had been deeply hurt. He had been ripped and torn by trying to discern truth from two people he loved. Eduardo continued to see Max and had told him repeatedly that Lily was disturbed. Max's father owed his son the truth, but until that was forthcoming he was a disaster waiting to happen. It would be only a few months later when the storm broke and Pamela would become a believer in Miguel's prediction.

Max began to have problems going to sleep. He simply could not get to sleep unless his mother was with him. Pamela spent most nights on a cot in his room, but sometimes she wanted to be in her bed so badly that she laid a pallet on the floor of her room and Max would sleep there.

Before sleep would come they would talk, or he would try to use the relaxation tapes Miguel had made for him, or she would read to him. She kept her well-worn red leather Bible at her bedside. At the beginning of those awful years reading scripture was the thing that most often brought Max a measure of peace, and slumber.

The nightmare progressed. CPS came to their home and interviewed each of them. Pamela began to glimpse the legal ramifications of Lily's admitting the truth about what her father had done to her. She would have to help her children balance their emotions, their need for help and healing through counseling, their daily lives, the pressures from Eduardo to see them. She had no idea how she would handle it all, and she had no time to think of her own needs. Her children were in crises. CPS gave her information about County Victim's Services. Pamela read everything and learned much about what Lily was going through and the emotional danger she was in. It scared her to death.

In the meantime, Eduardo seemed to be living in a world of his own. He and Pamela were still communicating but only by email and only when necessary, usually about court-ordered items. Because he had threatened Pamela with legal action if she didn't let him have Lily for visitation, she had gone to Jeff who promptly filed a Protective Order citing a "clear and present danger of family violence." The tension between Pamela and Eduardo had exploded. Eduardo was furious, shocked that Pamela had taken such action. He was not allowed to have the children, go near their home or her place of employment, go near the children's school, or communicate with them in any threatening way. His emails to Pamela were about the children's grades, or requesting documentation for medical expenses he was supposed to reimburse under the divorce decree, anything to keep in contact. After years of non-communication, now it was all he wanted to do. His tone was unpredictable – at times it would be conciliatory and friendly, then it would switch to accusatory and intimidating. He was angry and seemed unable to believe that Pamela would not believe whatever he said. He seemed at a loss as to how to communicate with her if he could no longer direct her actions.

Pamela began to feel very uncomfortable with their correspondence. She didn't want to anger him by not responding, and was concerned that she should come across neutral, not antagonistic. She started to feel as if she were being watched. She told herself that was ridiculous, that Eduardo wouldn't do that, that she was just exhausted from the fight and not thinking clearly. She certainly didn't need any more drama, even in her imagination.

It had been almost a month since the discovery of Lily's note. Pamela was still reeling from the events, trying to find her way in this "new normal." One thing that really helped was talking to Riley. Riley was supportive, knew how to keep a confidence, and she knew how to listen. Three days after the CPS interviews she called Pamela and said she was coming to take her to lunch.

Riley arrived at Pamela's office around 11:45, took a brief tour of their new space, and they decided on their favorite Mexican food place for lunch. Two cheese enchiladas and an hour later Pamela was feeling much better. They walked up the steps to the building, laughing over the latest escapades of Brayden and his brother. The lobby was empty when they walked in, the receptionist still at lunch. As they entered Pamela's office, Riley walked over to the window while Pamela turned toward her desk. She stopped, staring at a small brown paper grocery bag sitting in the middle of her desk. What in the world....? She set her purse down and walked around to the other side, joined by an equally curious Riley. Inside the bag was a pair of horse blinders, and they saw a folded white paper taped to the side. Pamela's name was on the outside of the note.

When her eyes dropped down to the edge of the desk, she sat down slowly, trembling. Next to the bag was a pile of horse manure. Little pebbles of manure were dripping over the edge of the desk and onto the floor, forming a small pile. This was creepy. Pamela began to tremble. "Riley, I can't read the note, will you open it?" she asked. Riley pulled the note free from the bag, unfolded the page and began to read.

"People who wear blinders create messes."

Pamela was silent. Questions bombarded her brain. Who would do this? What could they possibly be thinking? Was it Eduardo? It wasn't his handwriting on the note. What about the Protective Order? Her co-workers must have seen him come in. How embarrassing. This was crazy. Tears began to trickle down her cheeks – this was turning into a serious nightmare. Eduardo had to be connected in some way. What kind of man was he? Was she safe? Were any of them? Riley stayed for a while to calm her then left to return to work. All afternoon Pamela pondered the manure, the bag, the note, and the stranger who'd written it, wondering what if anything she could do about it. She was dealing with psychotic behavior for which she had no frame of reference. If Eduardo was involved what had happened to turn him into a monster?

Two weeks later she found evidence that someone had been in her house. Inside. They entered a locked house without a key and rearranged several things. Nothing was missing or broken, but the placement of her keepsakes and decorations was so unusual she knew she wasn't imagining it and it was too weird to be the work of pranksters. Now Pamela was beyond creeped out, she was scared. She called Luke to come change out the locks at her house.

Jeff scheduled a hearing on the Protective Order, bringing the note and affidavits from each of Pamela's co-workers who had witnessed a man enter the office with the bag and leave without it. During the legal proceedings the court appointed a Guardian Ad Litem for the children and mandated that Max would be allowed to visit his father. The Guardian Ad Litem immediately stated his concern that Max was not safe alone with his father. He explained how visitation could work if they used an agency called Kid Swap. When a visit was scheduled Pamela would take Max, drop him off, and leave, arriving at an exact time so that she would be gone when Eduardo arrived to pick him up. The time of the visit varied, but the rule was that a Kid Swap staff person had to be with Max and his father at all times during their visit. When the allotted time was up, Pamela would arrive to retrieve her son. He too had endured interviews by Child Protective Services and was subjected to a process to which no child should ever be exposed – certainly not an eleven year old boy being pressed hard by his father to believe a lie.

Lily had an excellent individual counselor and was also in group therapy with a psychiatrist on a regular basis. Julia, her counselor, was a godsend. She guided Lily up the challenging path to healing. God only knew where they would be were it not for Julia. The irony was that Julia had been a court ordered therapist assigned to evaluate Lily after the initial outcry. The request for an assessment of Lily's emotional stability towards supporting or discrediting her outcry of sexual abuse had come from Eduardo's attorney Gary Flint, the most expensive criminal defense lawyer in the state. Eduardo was fighting in court every step of the way. His attorney loved filing motions with short deadlines for any reason or no reason, driving Jeff Baxter crazy with the demand for responses. Jeff had been charged with finding a therapist within the few remaining days prior to the next hearing that had the required credentials and upon whom both sides could agree. At the end of the business day before the hearing, Jeff finally got the approval of the other side to secure Julia Foster's services. All he had to do was contact her and get her to agree by 11:00 a.m. the next morning. He left a voice mail and asked for a call back night or day. At 10:50 a.m. the next morning when Pamela checked in with Jeff there was still no word from Julia. As Pamela replaced the cordless phone in its cradle she sent up another "arrow prayer" – *God, please let Julia agree to do the assessment, and within the next 10 minutes. Jeff says she's reputable and good.* At 11:00 Pamela's phone rang. It was Jeff: "Pamela, you won't believe this but I just got a call from Julia. She said yes."

Julia and Lily bonded almost instantly.

Chapter 33

Julia's Report of Psychological Evaluation was thorough. She stated the allegations and noted that her evaluation was court ordered to assist in the decision making process regarding continuance of the protective order. She used five different tests during the evaluation. The results were clear. The report stated that none of the test results suggested Lily had any significant emotional disturbance, personality dysfunction or reality distortions. There were no indicators of psychopathology which might prompt a false outcry of sexual abuse. As difficult as the evaluation may have been on Lily, Pamela felt affirmed and strengthened in her position. She had done what she felt necessary to protect her daughter, and her instinct had proved to be right. Now it was time to face Eduardo in the courtroom and find justice.

The courtroom in the county courthouse reminded Pamela of the ones she had seen in old Perry Mason re-runs. It was fairly small with only a few windows, and the wood paneling on the lower half of the walls looked as aged and weary as she felt. The jury box was to the left of the Judge, whose massive bench was in the center of the main wall. Seated in front and to the right of the bench was the court reporter, a young serious-looking woman with a mane of red hair. She busied herself with setting up her machine, adjusting the positions of her chair and equipment. Pamela looked over at Jeff, who was just unloading the last box from the dolly he had used to cart in the four boxes of legal documents pertaining to the Protective Order and her current motion for full custody of the children.

Jeff sat down beside her at their table facing the judge's bench. He emptied his briefcase and placed a clean unused yellow legal pad in front of him. He turned to face Pamela, patting her shoulder reassuringly. Her face tried unsuccessfully not to show the fear she felt. She had not seen Eduardo in person for over a year and with all that had happened since then she had no idea what to expect. Based on the ugly emails she had received from him and the barrage of distasteful discovery documents with which his attorney had harassed hers she was dreading being in the same room with him, even with Jeff at her side and in an public place where she knew she was safe. This was about as far from happily ever after as she could get.

"I don't expect Eduardo and Mr. Flint much before 9:00 so let's go over why we are here today and what you can expect. First off I can assure there will be no more postponements of this custody hearing. Judge Mitchell made that very clear the last time Mr. Flint filed a motion to continue; I think he is as annoyed by Flint's shenanigans as we are. Our motion requests that you be granted full custody of Maxwell and Lily, that the terms of the Protective Order regarding Eduardo's contact with the children be made a permanent part of the custody arrangement, and that Eduardo be ordered to pay all your legal fees, all counseling fees – past, present and future – for the children. We still don't have the results from the court-ordered sexual offender risk assessment of Eduardo using the Colorado Sex Offender Risk Scale, or SORS for short, conducted by the renowned Dr. Keimig at the University of South Florida. If it comes back that Eduardo is high on the risk scale, Flint will of course vehemently maintain that the assessment doesn't mean anything, that his client is a fine upstanding member of the community, etcetera. But I am more than confident based on all the evidence gathered – Lily's and Max's statements to the police, CPS, the guardian ad litem, their counselors, your own testimony, plus Julia's professional evaluation of Lily and the information obtained in all the depositions that were done – that we will win today. Eduardo's own interview with the court-appointed psychologist uncovered his sexual addictions, denial of reality in other areas, and some serious pathological tendencies. The irony is that all of this information was initiated by Eduardo's attorney to try and support his denial of the rape charges. I strongly suspect his actions are about to come back and bite him full force, and I for one can't wait to see that.

"Pamela, I don't know what happened to him that made him the way he is now, but the Judge is just as familiar with The National Criminal Justice Reference Service Report as I am, which yielded the statistic that 75 percent of victims are first time victims where the accused has no reported history of molestation or abuse. And we all know the statistic that in about 90 percent of sexual abuse cases involving children, the perpetrator is someone the child knows and trusts. The myth that sexual abuse is performed primarily by strangers was debunked years ago. There are multiple studies where research has proven the routine presence of denial on the part of the offender in cases like this. I realize this proceeding is going to be uncomfortable for you, but let God's strength sustain you and don't be afraid. You have the confidence that can only come from standing on the truth.

"If our motion is granted this will be the end of it. No more hearings, no more counseling notes subpoenaed, and no more chance that Eduardo can gain access to Lily ever again. I supposed there is one blessing to come out of all the months of motions, court hearings and discovery – Judge is not going to let this thing drag on any further, one way or the other it is going to be settled today. I included the request that Eduardo be registered as sex offender. That is likely not going to happen today but it will give Flint something to motion against and the Judge a bone to throw

Flint's way. Don't worry, just pray and trust while this thing goes down." Jeff picked up his court-stamped copy of their Motion for Full Custody and began jotting notes on his pad.

Pamela swallowed. Could it really be over today? Was it possible that she and the children could begin to live their lives on a more normal basis, free from fear and subpoena notices? Knowing Eduardo she couldn't believe he would lose without more fighting. But she reminded herself of Luke 1:37 – "for nothing is impossible with God." She silently said a prayer then focused on regulating her breathing. She wanted to appear as calm and confident as Jeff told her she should feel, trusting that her God was in charge. She glanced back at the spectator's box and was surprised to see Max's counselor Miguel seated in the back row. Pamela felt better just at the sight of him.

The door to the courtroom opened and Gary Flint strode in, followed closely by Eduardo and two runners bringing boxes of legal documents. It was 8:59 a.m. Flint knew better than to risk angering the Judge by arriving late but he was determined to make a show of his entrance. Pamela watched as the group made their way to their own table, not 10 feet away from where she was sitting. Eduardo looked fabulous in his dark grey pinstriped suit and starched white shirt, a pale pink handkerchief peeking out of his suit coat pocket. He ran his hand over his perfectly arranged hair, then turned to his right to look at her. She managed to hold her eyes to his, trying not to be dismayed at the smug coldness she saw there. No nod, no smile, just a cold hard stare. Pamela looked at the court reporter, not able to look at him any longer. The room suddenly seemed chilled, and all fell silent as the bailiff rose and said in a loud voice, "All Rise! Judge J. J. Mitchell presiding."

Everyone stood and watched as the judge entered the courtroom from a door behind the bench. His black robe was pressed and surrounded his slight frame with dignity and authority. He was seated in the big leather chair and took the folder of documents that was handed to him by the bailiff. "Be seated," he said in a deep voice that needed no microphone. They sat. The silence in the room was deafening as he leafed through the papers then looked down at the court reporter to ask if she was ready. She nodded. Judge Mitchell wrapped the gavel on the matching wooden block. "Cause No. 735289, Cohen v. Cohen. Counselors, are you ready?"

Jeff pushed his chair back and stood. "Yes, Your Honor, we announce ready for trial."

Gary Flint also rose. "Your Honor, at this time we announce ready for settlement."

Judge Mitchell raised an eyebrow skeptically. "Mr. Flint, I've already made it abundantly clear that no further delays of this hearing on your part will be tolerated. None. Unless you are ready to sign off on the motion by Mr. Baxter as filed and currently pending before this court, we are proceeding with this trial."

Flint looked earnestly at the Judge. "Judge, other than vigorously opposing the motion that my client be registered as sex offender, which we will not agree to, we wish only a few moments to confer with opposing counsel regarding clarification of the amount of attorney's fees in question and some very minor wording in the section of the motion that pertains to Mr. Cohen's visitation with his son."

"I'm warning you, Mr. Flint, if I release you two groups to a conference room and the results are anything less than satisfying to the Defendant I will grant this motion with prejudice. Do you understand?" The Judge looked unwaveringly stern.

"I do, Your Honor. Thank you. We request use of the small conference room right outside this court room at this time, if it please the court." Flint did not look like a man about to lose a case, but then he was going to get paid a handsome fee regardless of the outcome.

Judge Mitchell directed his gaze to Jeff. "Mr. Baxter, are you agreeable to a settlement conference with Plaintiff for purposes of final settlement today?" he asked.

Jeff, still standing, smiled. "Absolutely Judge. Our only stipulation is that counselor for Defendant be allowed to join us, since the future of his client Maxwell Cohen will be greatly affected by today's outcome."

"Granted," Judge said, without even so much as a glance in Flint's direction.

"Your Honor, I must protest. We resist the notion that …" Flint said, starting to show agitation.

The Judge cut him off mid-sentence. "You wanted a settlement conference, those are the terms. Do you wish to adjourn to the conference?"

Flint sighed. "Yes, Your Honor, we will adjourn to settlement conference, agreeing to the Defendant's stipulation."

Once again the gavel came firmly down on the wooden block. "So ordered," the Judge said. He gave instructions to the bailiff to notify him as soon as a final settlement had been reached, stating he would be available to sign the order until 2 p.m. that afternoon.

Both attorneys began gathering their documents and preparing to relocate. Pamela stole a glance at Eduardo, whose face revealed no emotion. She gave a confused look to Jeff, who motioned her to be silent. "We'll talk in just a minute," he whispered. She got up to follow him as he exited the courtroom and took up a new station on one side of the conference table.

Miguel joined them at the table. He and Jeff greeted each other cordially and Miguel asked, "Do you really think Cohen and his attorney are going to settle? I would have bet my life they'd go down fighting to the last."

Jeff laughed. "I've seen stranger things happen in court. I knew our case was strong but I never expected Cohen to cave. I don't plan to let my guard down, Flint is a snake and I don't believe for a minute he's going to come in here and give us everything we want. Thank God the judge made it clear, his way or the highway. I don't see how even a lawyer like Flint can get much wiggle room out of that."

Just then Eduardo and his attorney entered the room, taking their seats at the opposite side of the table. Eduardo didn't look nearly as arrogant as he had presented in the courtroom. Instead, he looked almost bored and totally disinterested. But there was something about his demeanor that betrayed uncertainty and dread. Miguel went around and stood directly beside Eduardo. "Cohen, I've waited a long time to see this. For what you have done to your children, especially to your young son who is as emotionally wrecked as any kid I've ever worked with, you deserve to go down." A flash of fear passed briefly over Eduardo's face. He stared wordlessly as Miguel made his way back to his chair, sitting down heavily with his arms folded. Pamela's eyes opened in wide-eyed astonishment. What in the world was going on? She was stunned, unable to process that they were in settlement mode instead of battling it out in court.

An hour and forty-five minutes later, Flint directed his client to sign the handwritten settlement agreement Jeff had hastily scratched out on his legal pad. Flint had done his usual dodging, delaying, and arguing over every 'and' and 'the' in the agreement. Jeff wasn't about to let them out of the conference room with a simple verbal agreement to be drafted later and then have Flint try to make last minute changes. He insisted on an executed legal document, signed by both parties, and instructed them all to wait while he sent the bailiff down to the clerk to get the agreement file-stamped and copies made for all parties. Within fifteen minutes the bailiff was back with four file-stamped copies.

Jeff looked at Flint. "Did you bring your checkbook? I'd like to collect my fee." Flint nodded and pulled a large leather business style checkbook from his briefcase. For several seconds all that could be heard was the soft scratching of his pen. When he was finished, he carefully lifted the check out of the book and handed it over to Jeff. Then he looked at Eduardo and stood. Eduardo stood also, straightened his tie and said, "I'll just step in the hallway to check my messages and then we can go." Flint joined him as they left the room without a further word. A smiling Jeff began packing his briefcase, giving Miguel a big hug as he left for an appearance in another courtroom.

Pamela studied the agreement. Eduardo had voluntarily given up custody of his children, agreed to pay all her attorney's fees and counseling costs, was legally bound not to have any contact with Lily and limited contact with Max only as specified in the agreement. Only a guilty man would do that. She had been given full custody of the children without a word. After all this time, this back and forth in the form of papers and email, it had all been a bluff to get her to back down. Neither she nor the children had to get on the stand to testify, a huge answer to prayer. It was hard to get her mind around the fact that it was over. The nightmare was over. Whatever else she had to go through she knew she could face it. There was still much trauma work to be done for the children to be healed, and single parenting was still the most difficult job in the world. But she could now face those things without the burden of Eduardo's legal harassment and the weight of debt to the most wonderful attorney in the world, Jeff Baxter.

Jeff gave her a hug. "It's over!" he said. "You won. You and the children have the legal protection you need, and the rest we will leave to the Almighty."

"Amen!" Pamela replied. "Hopefully the three of us can move forward and begin to put this all behind us. Is there anything else I have to do?"

He clasped her hand. "Just begin the business of living again," he said softly. "Your life won't ever by the same, but we serve a God who can heal our brokenness and restore the years the locusts have eaten. Never forget that."

Pamela's eyes misted as she gripped his hand, then watched as he left the room. For several minutes she sat alone in the conference room, wanting to pray her thanks to God but not finding words adequate to express what she felt.

"Freeze!" she heard a loud voice say outside the conference room door. Startled, she went to the door, opening it halfway. The scene before her was something from a cop show on TV. Three police officers, guns drawn, faced Eduardo, whose hands were slowly going up as his cell phone clattered to the floor. "You have the right to remain silent. Anything you say can and will be used against you in a court of law. You have a right to an attorney. If you cannot afford an attorney, one will be appointed for you." Eduardo called out to Gary Flint, who was down the hallway on his cell. "Gary, call Dick Leboff, I gave you his number last week. He's my attorney in California." Flint nodded, quickly ending his call and moving away as he punched in numbers. Pamela was stunned. Neither Eduardo nor his attorney seemed surprised. This was incredible, real live drama unfolding before her very eyes.

She returned her gaze to Eduardo, hands now cuffed behind his back, his eyes sending silent daggers to the officer searching him. "You're coming with us, scumbag. Smart of you not to resist, those two nice young ladies in California had a LOT to say about you, and it wasn't pretty. Hope you had a good breakfast, the food where you'll be living is crappy." The officer's voice was fading as they escorted Eduardo to the elevator. Clerks and Judges alike were standing in doorways, mouths open in astonishment.

Pamela closed the conference room door and fell back into the nearest chair. She could not believe what she had just witnessed. Apparently Lily was not Eduardo's only victim. There were others. Horrified, her hands came up to her face as she began sobbing. *Oh no, Father, oh no.*

When she finally lifted her hands, sobs fading into sniffles, she had no idea how long she'd sat there crying. It seemed like years but was really only a few minutes. Reaching for her purse she found a handkerchief and blew her nose. Opening her compact, she saw the rivers of mascara running down her cheeks. She found a tissue and began to wipe away the black streaks. Suddenly the door to the conference room burst open and Jeff ran in, breathing heavily.

"Pamela, you won't believe it! Eduardo has been taken into custody and is on his way to jail in California. I don't know all the details but he's been charged with two separate counts of rape and I've been asked to send a copy of the SORS report when I receive it. I had no idea!" Jeff said, his voice loud and excited.

She smiled weakly. "Oh, I believe it alright. I witnessed the arrest out there in the hallway from this very room." She shook her head. "I still can't believe it. But it feels … true. All the way down to my bones I know it's true." Pamela looked up at Jeff, new strength showing on her makeup-less face. "Jeff, do you see what this means? Lily has been vindicated. Never again can anyone call her a liar or doubt what happened to her. My precious girl is out of danger. I will never forget that scene as long as I live;

it is permanently inked on the pages of my heart. I can't wait to describe it to Lily – when she is ready to hear it – and bring closure to this awful chapter of her life."

For a moment Jeff couldn't answer, overcome with his own emotion. "Yes, her name has been cleared and justice has been dealt. Eduardo has no power over her anymore." He sat down, a new realization dawning. "Pamela, this also means Max won't have to worry about visitation with his father. It won't be logistically feasible, and even if it were no judge in his right mind would allow it. I've got to go find Miguel." He stood up, pushing his chair back. "You going to be alright? Do you want me to get someone to take you home?"

Pamela squared her shoulders, standing to walk him to the door. "No, thank you, I'm going to be fine. Just need a little more time to let this all sink in and think about how I will tell the children." She gave him one last hug and smiled. "The Lord is here, right beside me. I have all the help I need." Jeff took a deep breath. "Amen to that," he said, and quietly left.

Phrases from Proverbs 15 began telegraphing through her brain. "… the mouth of a fool belches out foolishness … a deceitful tongue crushes the spirit … the earnings of the wicked bring trouble … the Lord detests the way of the wicked … whoever abandons the right path will be severely disciplined … how much does the Lord know the human heart … the fool feeds on trash … mockers hate to be corrected … better to have little with the fear of the Lord than great treasure and inner turmoil … the Lord tears down the house of the proud, he detests evil plans … for the happy heart, life is a continual feast."

Unable to pray earlier, the words of Romans 8:26-27 now came clearly to her, printed across a marquee that appeared in her mind's eye: "The Holy Spirit prays for us with groanings that cannot be expressed in words. And the Father who knows all hearts knows what the Spirit is saying." God had not only given her the victory but also provided the thank you when she was too overcome to thank Him on her own. At that realization the dam burst, and all the tears that had been held back by fear and worry came flowing forth in a river of gratitude. These were happy tears, clean tears, tears that had no makeup to navigate, tears that existed solely to glorify her Father in heaven. She let them come, freely, joyfully, flowing out to the One who had asked her to trust and wait. The One who would never leave her.

Chapter 34

Pamela's family and church family were very loving and supportive during the trauma years. They did all they could to protect Lily and show her love, compassion and encouragement. Pamela truly missed Cindy, but with the arrest and conviction of Eduardo, now in a California prison, Cindy refused to return her calls or letters. Pamela couldn't imagine Cindy severing her relationship with her granddaughter, but that is what she had done. Perhaps what had happened to her son had changed her, or maybe she could only manage her own pain by cutting herself off from the children. It didn't make sense to Pamela, but then nothing about that family made sense any more. She grieved for Lily's loss of her CiCi, but there was nothing she could do about it.

There were positive times during Lily's teen years as she threw herself into the parts of her life she could control, like making good grades and working on the yearbook and prom committees. She went on church retreats where she learned firsthand about the love of her heavenly Father through Jesus, who saved her on just such a retreat. She joined youth mission trips where she learned that she could begin to rebuild her own life just as she was re-building houses for those in need while on the mission field.

But the pain runs deep and Lily didn't feel the strength of the legal position in her world. Trying to manage the unbearable grief and loss while coping with adolescence and the stress of legal proceedings – depositions, constant rearranged scheduling, hearings postponed at the last minute – was just too much. Frequently she was withdrawn; sleep was difficult and sometimes she would slip out at night for a walk or to go to a friend's house, trying to escape the demons of her nightmares. Pamela was worried sick most of the time. She cried until there were no more tears, so concerned about her lovely teenage daughter, vulnerable physically and emotionally. The only place Pamela found comfort and hope was at prayer time, letting God hold her up and speak to her through scripture, especially the Psalms.

Lily began experimenting with cutting. Pamela noticed that Lily would wear long sleeves all the time or had plastic colored bracelets from wrist to elbow. She learned later that this was how young girls hide the scars of self-inflicted cuts on their wrists and arms. It was a way to replace the emotional pain with physical pain. This too, Pamela read, was common for abused girls and those with PTSD.

But the worst thing was the possibility of suicide. One night Lily tried to overdose on over the counter pain relievers. A week later she told a friend she wanted to jump off a bridge and end it all. The friend made a non-emergency call to the police who had an officer call Pamela because they were concerned. Pamela sat in silent shock after the call, glad Lily's friend was concerned but gripped by fear. How does a parent prevent her child from taking her own life? She could try to stand watch 24/7 but at some point she had to sleep, and as a single mom she had to go to work and keep her job. Then one night while Pamela was at a St. Luke's volunteer meeting two blocks from their house she got a call on her cell phone. It was Lily. She said she could not keep herself safe any longer, would Pamela come get her and take her to the hospital. Pamela left immediately and called her mom to come stay with Max. Then she called Julia. When they had decided where to take her, Lily went willingly.

Pamela was relying on the advice of Lily's psychologist and the group therapy psychiatrist, both of whom she had come to trust and admire. She also trusted her motherly instinct. Lily was in a dangerous emotional place and needed professional help. It was so scary to leave her in that place. Pamela knew nothing of the staff or how they dealt with fragile, at-risk teen girls. But she knew she had to do something. Keeping Lily at home was no guarantee of her safety. God had provided good doctors, so Pamela took the step of faith and admitted her.

The admitting process took several hours – interviews with various doctors and the paperwork. Lily was a minor and this was a voluntary admission, so Pamela handled the paperwork. Once admitted to the facility, they were taken to the adolescent suicide-watch floor. The staff was kind, and although Pamela and Lily were scared they both sensed this was a place that could help Lily. The staff was extremely serious about keeping the kids safe. Many typical hospital-stay items were prohibited, from the obvious things like shaving razors and sharp objects to shoelaces and drawstrings from pajama pants to makeup compacts allowed only without mirrors. In addition, once Lily was assigned to that floor, only the people on an approved list, as determined by Lily, could contact her or come for a visit. If Lily didn't want someone to visit her they weren't getting in – she would have to feel completely safe to get the full benefit of the treatment and they were serious about that too.

Pamela felt so scared, so helpless, so out of her comfort zone. She wanted to be the one to help her daughter, not these strangers. She wanted to hold her, stroke her hair and comfort her, to tell her how much she loved her and that she would do anything for her. She wanted that to be enough to fix everything. But Lily was desperate for help that mother-love alone could not give.

It was incredibly hard to do. Sitting in the car in the hospital parking garage that night, Pamela couldn't imagine driving home alone or trying to go to sleep knowing she had just committed her teenage daughter to a place where professionals were concerned she would kill herself. And the only way she, as the parent, would get to visit is if her child gave permission. No younger siblings were allowed in. Try those logistics as a single parent, Pamela thought, especially when she had already relied so much on family, church family, friends and co-workers for help. But her child had bravely reached out for help, and Pamela would do whatever it took to get her the help she needed.

That week was a turning point for Lily. In that place she felt 100% safe and could open up about her feelings and fears in the healing context of a group of others her age with similar issues. She gained the strength to start using the survival skills she was taught. Pamela visited every day and was happy to see the changes. When she picked Lily up at the end of that week there was a marked difference. She wasn't out of the woods yet and there was still a long road to complete healing, but Pamela could see in her a new resolve and confidence to go forward. Pamela was grateful to those dedicated people who had helped her girl want to live again. Thank God Lily had listened to the advice of her psychiatrist to ask for help instead of trying to escape the pain permanently through death! Pamela firmly believed that individual and group counseling through the right professionals God put in their path helped Lily immensely and equipped her to survive.

After she came home from the hospital, Lily began to take life one day at a time and was able to let Pamela be there for her. Pamela's boss granted her much flexibility with her hours, another God-thing. Lily threw herself into schoolwork. By now she was in high school and achieving academic honors became her passion. She spent time with her best friend Vivian, listening to music or babysitting, and things started to feel more 'normal.' For Lily.

Max's Story
Part One

Chapter 35

During all the chaos surrounding Lily, Pamela never lost sight of the fact she had another child. She tried to make sure Max had plenty of sleepovers with his close friends Andrew and Turner, and that he got a chance to go to their homes as well. She knew he was troubled about it all, and sleep became a real issue. But Pamela never dreamed that her teenaged son would get arrested. Yes, Max was from a divorced home, his father had never been a disciplinarian, and Pamela knew she wasn't the strongest or most consistent single mother around. But Max had good friends, Pamela made it a point to know their parents, and he was in a good school. She made every effort to be there for him. Other boys came through similar circumstances without getting arrested. That possibility was the farthest thing from her mind.

When the phone rang at 5:00 a.m. one February morning from an unknown number, she wasn't prepared for the caller at the other end of the line. Max was spending the night at Andrew's and she'd hoped to sleep in until 8:00. The call was from the Dade County Juvenile Justice Center. A lady named Annie asked for Pamela by name, wanting to know if she had a son named Max. As Pamela said "yes", fear started to rise inside her.

Annie's voice began to register as Pamela's brain jumped to full alert. Her words were brief and to the point. Max had been arrested at 1:30 a.m. on charges of burglary of a residence. Two other boys had been arrested too. He would be released on conditions. Juvenile would recommend deferred action and no charges, possible community service. In juvenile there is no bond. Here are the directions, and you do not qualify for a public defender.

What does all this mean to me, Pamela thought? She grabbed her purse, googled directions to the Juvenile Justice Center downtown and got into her car. She arrived at daybreak and found the entrance for released offenders at the back of the parking lot. She entered the waiting area and was greeted by a Correctional Officer. Pamela gave her name, showed her driver's license and waited for Max to be brought out. She had already called Andrew's mom, who had been to pick up Andrew by the time they talked. Neither of them could believe what had happened – a junior high prank pulled on the very wrong, cranky neighbor. Pamela had no idea how to handle this.

She heard voices and turned to see Max, led out by a different CO. Max looked at her sheepishly. "Thanks, Mom, for coming to get me. I'm sorry," he said. Pamela gave him a quick hug and walked to the desk where she was given release papers.

"We'll call you with the hearing date," the attendant said. "And you'll want to get an attorney for your child. The neighbor is pressing charges." She handed Pamela a form to sign then said good night.

On the ride home Pamela had more questions than Max had answers. He was tired, but not remorseful enough in Pamela's opinion. Where was her precious son inside this awkward adolescent boy? The little one who wanted to make his mommy happy, the sunny disposition that had always brightened her world. She had the sinking feeling things were going to get much worse before they got better. Little did she know how right she was.

⌘

I cannot control the path my child chooses

⌘

Chapter 36

Pamela sat on the cold gray metal bench and waited. She scribbled her thoughts on a yellow legal pad, her pen pausing only briefly to consider how best to express how she felt. She'd begun doing this on her second visit to the Juvenile Detention Center. Writing about the experience helped her process it all, helped her find focus in the chaos surrounding her son that was now her life. Her words on paper described the visits, journaled her feelings, poured out her prayers.

God, how I hate being here. The staff is polite and helpful for the most part, but this sterile environment is awful, cold, gray neutral. Waiting alone, unable to relax after a long workday. I don't belong here! My son does not belong here. I know You have a plan, Lord, but I wish it did not include these trips to juvenile jail.

I can always spot the moms who are seasoned visitors, who know the drill. They arrive early, carrying only car keys and an ID because no other items are allowed inside. We wait for the guard who will come out and begin the sign in and verification process. On nice days we wait outside, leaning against the wall or just standing. When the weather is cold or bad, we are allowed to wait inside in the small foyer inside the detention facility.

This type of waiting is not like any other kind I've ever experienced. There is no small talk; there is simply nothing to say. Each of us knows why the others are there, to visit a child or sibling or grandchild who is in jail - what can you say about that? For the most part we stare at the wall or the floor, not wanting to make eye contact. There is no desire for the short-term bonding that occurs in other waiting lines for a movie or tickets to a concert or at the DMV.

Finally the guard comes out. We have to line up, much like prisoners ourselves. We wait quietly and patiently while he checks in each person. He checks ID's against the Approved Visitors List, and if your name isn't on the list he calls Control. If they don't come back with a "10-4", you don't go in. Period. It's that simple, no exceptions, doesn't matter the circumstances, everyone has a story. We each go up in turn, sign in, and return to our seats to wait some more. After another period of silent waiting, we are told it's time. We stand in line single file, and move on to the next room where we are required to leave personal belongings in a metal cabinet. We get the routine warning not to give prisoners anything - food, candy, books, notes - nothing is allowed in, not even a scrap of paper. Violators risk losing their thirty minute visit.

From there it's on to the search room. Once again all of us are in single file, legs slightly spread and arms stretched out to the side, waiting our turn to be patted down and have the wand moved over us. When all have been searched, we hear the dreadful sound, that heavy metal sound of the prison door.

So many different feelings are crashing around inside me. I don't want to be here, yet you couldn't keep me away from the chance to see my son. I am hurt by his behavior that landed him here and angry at the amount of time I have to give to these visits. I am hopeful that his attitude will be positive, that he'll take his consequences in stride and that this time he'll resolve to truly clean up his act. I see parents waiting to give their child the big "talking to"; others will blame "the system" for their child's misbehavior; others are like me, hopeful but anxious. I wish I could go back in time, before Miguel predicted the storm, before the storm broke.

They filed into a room with tables and chairs, the heavy metal door locking shut behind them. Each visitor staked out a table and sat, waiting to see if the loved one they had come to visit would be brought down. Prisoners don't have to see visitors, so you don't know until they walk in the door whether you'll get to see them. Through large glass windows on one side the guards kept a watchful eye on the visitation. More silent waiting - the silence was deafening. Occasionally family members at one of the tables would whisper something to the other but it was ever so slight. Then Pamela saw the movement out in the courtyard - the kids were coming. All she could see was shadows on the other side of the thick block glass windows, and she heard the guards call down some of the inmates who weren't behaving in line. With a loud metal clang the door on the other side of the room opened and the kids began to file in.

Pamela noted the now familiar orange jumpsuit, the line of feet in white socks and the one-size-fits-all cheap plastic tan shower sandals – God, how she hated the site of her son in that uniform. The kids knew what to do: move slowly; hands behind their back with thumbs and index fingers meeting to form a diamond shape; count off as you cross the threshold. Max was number three this time, and he greeted her with a hug. Moms in crisis never know if their child will come to visitation, and they never know if they'll be greeted with a hug or an angry face that silently registers hurt and resentment and defiance. She was pleased to hear that he has been on Level 3 this time. Levels of behavior are assessed constantly - level one is the worst and three is the best. Once he got a "59" for talking back – that meant 59 minutes in a cell with no furniture and you weren't allowed to sit on the floor. You simply stand and wait until the time is up. On Level three he has been able to watch a TV, access the book cart every other day, and the gym. Most of the time he reads or does pushups in his room.

Max asked his mom what food was waiting for him at home. Food is important to a fifteen year old boy, and prison food is nothing to write home about. He was annoyed that he missed out on a brownie because he was called down for one of the many random UA's (urinary analysis). He wanted to know if his friends had called, and did the school know he'd been doing school work while in juvenile. His attorney has visited him and that went well; his counselor's visit didn't go so well. Pamela wished for the one hundredth time she didn't have all these professionals involved in her son's life, but it was the only way she knew to try and handle what was happening to them. For it was happening to all of them, not just to Max. That is what she couldn't seem to get across to him, this adolescent in his self-absorbed world, that his actions had a direct and significant impact on those who love him. It concerned her so much that being arrested <u>once</u> wasn't enough of a learning experience to keep him on the straight and narrow forever. How could that be? It was almost as if he needed cement walls and steel bars to contain what was going on inside of him. He was taught right from wrong, he was being held accountable, why was it not making more of an impact? Her mind circled back to the same answer it always did: because this wasn't just about rebellion. This was also about stuffing feelings, trying to ignore them and do whatever it took to not feel them and deal with them. Or maybe he was trying to find some feelings. Pamela didn't blame Max. She wished she was able not to feel her feelings. But she had to be strong and stable for her kids. She was determined to help their little family of three survive.

Max's time was almost up; he was to be released any time after 6:00 a.m. the following day. He urged her to pick him up at 6:01. Ah, the humility and determination to obey that surfaces after he had been in jail. He was even eager to attend church and youth group again, and told Pamela he'd been reminded about being respectful to his elders. His eyes darted around; although he could look her in the face, it was obvious he was uncomfortable in this setting and would like to be home again. Pamela tried not to see the almost-tears in those big blue eyes; it was important for him not to cry right now. Time enough for tears late at night on the pillow, just like she did at home. They talked about what would be expected of him at home when he returned. He said the stay was good for him, that it reminded him of why he hated being there. She wished it didn't take this for him to be reminded – again she thought surely once in his life should be enough to stick with him forever.

The guard in the room gave the five minute warning. Pamela glanced around to see the visits of some of the other moms. Some were sitting silently at table with a child; some were smiling and talking earnestly together; some were crying and hugging, feelings visible almost to the point where no words were necessary. Max asked again what time she would pick him up, and she told him she would do what she could to get him early.

I'll be there when I get there, she thought. Pamela was past the point of completely inconveniencing herself to meet his demands. He had repeated this pattern too often – break the law, get arrested, promise to do better. She would get hopeful and accommodate him, wanting to avoid conflict and try to keep peace in her world that had so few peaceful moments. He would be "good" for a day or week or month, and then violate probation and there we go again. He had lost his right to expect anything of her other than the basics of food and shelter. But of course she missed him, and she didn't want him there. She told him that. He assured her he was ready to go back to school and do the work, without skipping. Pamela wondered whether his teachers would be willing to work with him after he'd blown them off, but that was Max's problem, not hers.

The guard called Control, visitation was ended. Visitors are instructed to remain seated while the prisoners stand and get in order. One last hug, Max bravely smiled and stepped in line. The two girls were having trouble not clinging to their moms; tears were flowing on both sides of the table. The room was quiet except for the sounds of sniffling and shuffling feet; moms and kids silently mouth an "I love you" across the room to each other. Max tried not to look in Pamela's direction; leaving was so hard. Right before they began to march and count off he looked in her direction and she winked. She had learned he needed to see her brave with a smile on her lips as he walked out. She didn't want him to see her crying as it would only make the return to his cell that much harder. And she wasn't sure she could stop the tears if she let them start. It broke her heart to see him there, to think that this might not be the last time. She was frightened for his future. What if he never broke this pattern? No, better to be strong - show him how to endure hard circumstances and draw strength from a Higher Power. Besides, he'd seen her cry plenty of other times. She had her good days and bad days too.

The last child had left, and that awful clang of the metal door locking shut echoed in the room. No one moved. They knew they must wait for a guard to come in before they could move. Some held back tears, some were openly weeping, some quietly distressed; but one thing they all had in common. They were leaving to go out into the sunshine and freely go back to their homes while their children stayed locked up, each in a cell, left with their own thoughts and feelings and no mom to hold them or tell them it would be alright.

Hold back the hugs, the time isn't right

Keep to self the kisses, they hinder the fight

Restrain the tears, they can only come out at night

Stand firm your ground, maybe he'll turn his life around.

Two months later Pamela was back at Juvenile to visit Max. The visit was not good. He hugged her when he came in and seemed glad to see her. But she didn't want small talk today, she wanted a "come to Jesus" meeting. He said he would quit skipping school. When she asked how, he said by remembering how much he hated it there. She shook her head. Things were different now that he'd stolen from her. He denied it, said the "proof is all circumstantial." It went from bad to worse – he didn't miss her because she "bitches all the time"; he wouldn't bring friends home because she would "freak 'em out". He hated her once he found out she took his driving permit. On this visit he cared nothing for her inconvenience and wait at Detention Hearings, and said he was fine there. At the end he got up to be the first in line - no hug, no goodbye. She hated seeing all the other visitors get hugs and tearful goodbyes while she got nothing. Max's back was turned to her and he waited to count off. He had said he would be back in jail eventually "'cause I'll make mistakes." He had no goal, no vision. How did her son, raised with much love, get so unfeeling and uncaring? What she wanted from him she couldn't have – reciprocal love and respect.

Last January she had wanted nothing more than for the three of them to move back in and enjoy their home after the remodeling. By February Max had been arrested, and by April Lily moved out for a short time. In April he was suspended from school, arrested in May, June brought home detention and probation, in July he was ordered to an Intensive Out Patient drug rehabilitation program after he ended up in the ER dehydrated from drinking cokes laced with bourbon, and in August a new school. Here we go again, she thought, still the same cycle.

There were no answers, only questions. Max didn't want her to tell his dad or his best friend's dad. He said he wanted people to give up on him. She used the word repent, and he had told her he'd rather stay than go home and hear about God. That really hurt.

Five days later she arrived to pick up Max who had been released. On the way home, for the first time he talked about that night when he and those other boys got arrested. He talked about it in detail, and seemed to be looking back at how he could have done it differently, seeing clearly how it played out and why. For the first time he seemed to get it when Pamela told him about the possible adjudication of the felony hanging out there if he violated probation again. He said he thought it had been dropped to a misdemeanor, and she reminded him that would happen only if he successfully completed drug court and probation.

Max said that after a week to think about it he had a plan for changing his ways, his life, his habits at home. He seemed eager to get to school. He talked about the church ladies who visited them in jail, and fed them cookies, and came to tell them about Jesus and what He had done for them.

Pamela was pleased that morning to see the guard who had been so kind to her on Monday at visitation. He remembered her and the situation with Max's dad. She was so grateful to be able to thank him in person. He wished her luck and said he hoped Max did not come back. *Thank you God for hope.*

Max was still very angry at his dad, but even after three days to think about what he could say to him he couldn't come up with anything new. Pamela reminded him that his dad was out of practice in doing the right thing, and Max seemed to think about that. She told him she believed his dad loved him.

Again and always the tears and disappointment. After being home only one week he missed school again, had quite the story – no bus, bike broke down, his ride overslept then locked the keys in the car, ran out of gas, no money for gas, everything except a grandparent that died. Pamela was sick with guilt, why didn't she come get him when he called and missed the bus? At least he would have been in school. She hated knowing maybe she could have turned his day around. But she knew he could just as easily left school the minute she dropped him off and found another way to make his day a mess.

What was inside him, a little boy who was floundering? That night they argued. He asked why she didn't kick him out? He said he didn't understand her view at all, he didn't feel sorrow or remorse; she grieved for the way his feelings were so shut down. Why did he have to miss his counseling appointment last week? But even if he had gone to school, he was still out tonight. The temperature could get close to freezing according to the weather, with a winter storm warning. Unbelievable weather for Florida, but then her life was becoming unbelievable.

Pamela thought of two great evangelists who told their rebellious sons "you're no longer my responsibility, but God's." And in the Old Testament look at Aaron's sons, Eli's sons, and King David's sons. The enemy challenges our children.

So many tears, how does the human body produce so many tears?

Father, I feel so much better that he listened to me, all my tears and thoughts, and even almost cried himself. I feel like the ultimate yo-yo, one minute furious and worried, the next full of empathy and sorrow for my "lost" child. I don't even care if he's playing me, I want so badly to give him another chance. Is this a glimpse of how much You love us?

As she sat at her prayer bench this morning, Pamela heard a flutter outside the window. It sounded like the wings of a very large bird. She looked out just in time to see the neighbor's cat carry off a white wing dove, its wings still trying to flap in hopes of escape. Her first thought was why couldn't it be one of those annoying grackles instead of a pretty, peaceful dove? There are way too many of them, they aren't pretty, they eat the cat food, and they don't make the lovely cooing sounds of the dove. She understood the laws of nature and was not mad at the cat – he was working on instinct. But she felt so sad for the dove, especially as she saw another one close by in a tree and wondered if they were mates. The dove was helpless once in the jaws of the cat. Immediately she thought of her precious daughter, molested by her father. Why does God allow the innocent to be harmed and to suffer, particularly when it comes to hurting children? At once God placed the answer in her mind and it rang true in her heart. It all goes back to each individual person's heart in relationship to Him. He loves us so much He created us with a free will, and when we choose to respond to God in love and our hearts are right with Him it is practically impossible to perpetrate harm to another of His creatures, especially the innocent. But if a person without God follows his basest instincts, dominated by sin and evil, it is only natural for the innocent to be harmed. A person whose heart is not right with God cares not for His creation, or His desire for us to love Him and obey His laws. Does God have the power to intervene and stop such harm? Absolutely. Then why doesn't He? Pamela couldn't answer that. She only knew He was <u>not</u> the author of evil and He hurt more than she did when children were harmed. She also knew that her love for and commitment to Him would not be possible if He simply commanded or programmed people to love Him, because the depth and magnitude of love given freely, unconditionally, having no end and <u>regardless of circumstance</u> is what real life is all about. That is how He loves us, and how our hearts desire to love Him. None of us has the ability to comprehend why God acts or does not act in our lives, she thought, but she had experienced His great and steadfast love for <u>her</u> and could not deny it. She could look through tears at the devastation of sexual abuse or drugs in the lives of her own dear children and honestly say the <u>only</u> thing she knew for certain was that God existed, He was in control, He loves us, and it is enough. It has to be enough or she couldn't rely solely on Him as He wanted her to. The answer to stopping all the hurt in the world was <u>every</u> single individual on this earth getting his heart right with Almighty God. Then innocent children wouldn't get hurt, and we wouldn't wish hurt on others. How could we get right with God? That answer she knew well: get in His Word.

For the word of God is alive and powerful. It is sharper than the sharpest two-edged sword, cutting between soul and spirit, between joint and marrow. It exposes our innermost thoughts and desires. Nothing in all creation is hidden from God. Everything is naked and exposed before his eyes, and He is the one to whom we are accountable. (Hebrews 4:12).

Lily's Story

Part Two

Chapter 37

Toward the end of Lily's senior year in high school she began talking about moving out. Pamela was so disappointed, so very sad. She wanted her to have some 'normal' years at home to finish high school and attend the local university. Lily had stopped attending church and youth group and Pamela was worried about the direction things were headed. Lily also had some new friends whom Pamela had never met. Lily's best friend Vivian told her the new friends were pressing her big time to move out. Pamela and Lily had had several heated conversations and Pamela spent many sleepless nights in prayer, asking for guidance for her and for Lily. Her heart felt like it was breaking again, but she knew she could not keep her from leaving. Pamela decided to do whatever it took to keep their lines of communication open. The night Lily decided to move out Pamela told her how much she loved her, how she wished Lily would stay but how she would rather her leave with them on good terms if she was determined to leave. She watched Lily's little white car back out of the driveway, a box containing a few clothes and treasures in the back seat, and crumpled to the couch in tears. Pamela didn't even know where Lily was going, all she had was her cell phone number and the hope she'd stay in touch.

Father, am I a horrible parent not to fight with everything in me to keep her at home? I could take her keys, lock the steering wheel, chain her to her bed! Anything to prevent her from going to stay with an older guy I have never even met. It can't be right, something is terribly wrong. I should fight and scream and declare how wrong it is, not calmly talk to her. I fear she is going down the hardest path, and I do not want to break off communication. This looks like the picture of a defiant selfish girl who is not honoring me or You. But I know her heart, I love her, and God, NO one loves her more than You do. I see her as my precious daughter who as a little girl baptized our dog, who as a teen suffered much at the hands of her earthly father, who feels the pain of loss of her grandma whom she can no longer visit, my girl who is straining at some invisible leash as though it would break. You know I want the best for her. Last night she said I couldn't stop her; I said I could, but I don't think it's true. Maybe these next few weeks will give her time to change her mind. Will I look back in regret and grief? I don't know. I have been unable for months now to "control" her choice of friends, where she spends her time. I couldn't force her to spend her free time here — it's almost as if she's being lured by demons anxious to get her away from my influence. Have I unwittingly played into the hands of Satan by not physically trying to stop her? Forgive me if this is so! Somehow I feel almost relieved that the anxiety of wondering if she will come home each night and when she'll move out is gone. If I have helped her future to become dark I pray Your mercy on my soul. But I am accepting what I will never have: an innocent young girl going off to a college dorm, happy and well and full of hope for the future. I grieve the loss of her involvement with her church family; it used to mean so much to her.

I've prayed and cried and agonized over the decisions she has made. I see the soul You created — smart, sensitive, caring, a Christian, a good friend, a loving sister and daughter. She is a battle-scarred soul, Father, and right now she's not walking close with You. Yet I believe You have a plan for her. I pray mightily You will protect her, use her life to bless others, bring her back close to You. I believe You can bring something wonderful out of this life. This situation is in Your hands; I commit her to Your care and protection, every day of her life. Forgive me if I've handled this wrong, if I've not done enough to protect her. I couldn't protect her from her own father, so please take care of her now. Teach her the lessons You have for her without too much pain please. Hold her close.

Pamela ached the next morning, waking to a house without Lily's sweet sleepy face to peek in on or her little car in the driveway. I miss my girl, oh how I miss her, Pamela thought.

Kneeling at her prayer bench, she felt like a total failure. She hadn't even tried to stop Lily from leaving, what had she been thinking? She was a weak, pitiful excuse for a mother. If anything happened to Lily it would be all her fault, she would never be able to live with herself. For the first time, she had a sense of what it was like to not want to live. She didn't want this pain, didn't want this horrible sense of failure, that nothing would ever be right again, and didn't want to think about anyone who might need her. Pamela just wanted it all to be over. She couldn't pray, didn't deserve to talk to God. How ashamed He must be of her, He wouldn't want to hear from her. He couldn't forgive such awful, irresponsible parenting. She knew she should get up and do something but her body felt like lead; she had no energy to move. With effort she raised her head; her eyes fell on the Bible on her prayer bench, open to Psalm 13. Her eyes read the words as her brain slowly registered them: O Lord, how long will you forget me? Forever? How long will you look the other way? How long must I struggle with anguish in my soul, with sorrow in my heart? Turn and answer me, O Lord my God! Restore the sparkle to my eyes or I will die. Don't let my enemies rejoice in my downfall." Realizing she was praying without meaning to, Pamela read the rest of the Psalm aloud: "I trust in your unfailing love, I will rejoice because you have rescued me. I will sing to the Lord because He is good to me." Rescue, yes that was what she needed, what Lily needed even if she didn't know it. Pamela had come to the end of herself, and only God could rescue her now. Wearily she rose to her feet, the burden not lifted but somehow more manageable. She walked into the kitchen and began to load the dishwasher.

Two awful days and three nights passed before she got her girl back. Little did Pamela know how much danger Lily was in or how God's grace would empower her to rescue her daughter.

The phone rang at 1:30 in the morning. It was Vivian, crying and telling Pamela she'd heard from Lily. The guy she was with was beating her and wouldn't let her leave to come home or go to school. Pamela told Vivian she didn't know where to go. Vivian said she had been to the house once when the man was gone and thought she could find it again. Vivian's mother brought her over to their house and Pamela got in her car to follow them. She was scared to death, worried they wouldn't find Lily, that this dangerous stranger would take her away and Pamela would never see her again. Vivian found her way to the house but was afraid to park in front of it so they parked down the street. She was also afraid for any of them to confront this man she had heard was so dangerous. All Pamela knew was Lily was in danger. She had to get her back, and her God was more powerful than any man.

Pamela got out of her car, walked up the dark street and into the driveway leading to the garage apartment Vivian had pointed out. She didn't know what to do – go knock on the door? What if he wouldn't let her in or Lily out? Pamela got the idea to call Lily's cell phone and she answered. Pamela announced she was there to get her and asked Lily to come outside. Amazingly, she did. In the few minutes before he followed her out Pamela told Lily how she had found her and Lily admitted she'd wanted to come home but he wouldn't let her. As the young man came down the stairs Pamela told Lily to go up to gather her things and get her car keys, that she was coming home. Pamela knew she would never forget the gratefulness and relief in those hazel eyes.

Even in the darkness with just a nearby street light to partially illuminate his face, Pamela knew immediately that she was staring in the face of evil. His smooth, oily voice oozed words of assurance that all was well, that he didn't want Lily to leave and she didn't want to. He said that he could understand Pamela's concern since they had not met, but assured her he was a good person and even had a grandmother who went to church "too". When he realized Pamela was not buying his prepared speech, he changed his tone. He objected to her taking Lily, reminding her that she was not welcome there and that Lily was eighteen, old enough to live where she wanted. He seemed eerily confident that Lily would not leave.

Pamela did not remember later all he said, or anything she said. But they had quite the discussion and she stood with her feet planted firmly on the gravel, determined to take Lily home. One thing she did remember: her words and inner strength that night did not come from her. Nothing she could have said or done would have been any match for this strong, young, slick-talking man. All she knew was that as she stood toe to toe with him, calm and unyielding, something caused him to simply step aside as Lily came back outside with her box of possessions in her arms. Pamela helped her load it in the back seat and told her to drive home, that she was parked on the street and Lily was to wait there to follow her. Pamela clearly remembered walking past him as she headed down the driveway toward the street, aware of his muscled arms, the glow of his cigarette, and the calculating way he watched her. He could so easily have overpowered them both, there was no one around strong enough to stop him. But the power that night wasn't his – it was the power of God's grace, giving her a boldness and resolute stance different from anything she had ever experienced. Grace that erased Lily's wrong turn and her weak parenting and rescued them both from themselves.

Vivian and her mom went home, Pamela's fervent thanks still hanging in the air. Their caravan home was uneventful. At home Pamela hugged her girl for a long time, told her she was safe now and that they would talk in the morning. Drained from the intensity of what had just happened, they both slept.

Pamela took a personal day off work the next day, unwilling to leave Lily unattended when he knew where they lived. She and Lily talked, and Pamela learned how he had beaten Lily, hitting in places that don't show external bruises. Pamela would learn later that he had a criminal record. Lily was shocked to learn of his background and all the more grateful for rescue. Pamela kept thinking of those evil eyes she'd looked into and how God prevailed through an exhausted, weak single mom against an agent of the devil himself. The good news was Lily was back home, safe, and had been spared what could have easily turned into a kidnapping, or worse.

For a long time after that Pamela would get furious when she thought of this man wooing and charming and flattering Lily right out of her home. It made her crazy to think of how close Lily came to disaster. But years later Pamela learned something about him that caused her to be grateful to him. She and Max were in Miguel's waiting room, and something about their conversation caused her to mention that man's name.

Max looked at Pamela with surprise. "Mom, during those weeks Lily was with him I had started dealing drugs at my high school. I got in with some very dangerous thugs, and after one particular deal where I didn't give them their money, they came for me. I was stupid, I thought I could cheat those guys. If it had not been for that man's intervention I probably would have been killed."

Pamela's mouth hung open in shock. The very man who had hurt Lily had saved her son.

She wished she had done many things differently at the time when she suspected something was amiss with Lily. She wished she would have taken her car keys, locked her steering wheel, anything to make it logistically more difficult for her to be with the guy. She wished she had offered to go with her and help when she decided to leave home at his urging; perhaps in the process she could have removed the blinders Lily was wearing. She wished she had followed her when she left that day; at least she would have known where she was. She wished she had talked more about the obvious problem of a 'boyfriend' who did not want to even meet Lily's mom, at least tried to draw Lily out on that and expose some of the lies he was feeding her. She wished she had asked more about why Lily wanted to leave rather than assume it was simply because she was eighteen and about to graduate high school. But God moves in spite of our inaction or wrong action. He sees the bigger picture and can use any situation for His purposes. God works in the details, and even in our worst choices we are chased by grace that can turn events and use people in ways we would never dream.

I must discipline yet love unconditionally

⌘

Max's Story
Part Two

Chapter 38

Pamela felt old way before her time. Single parenting wasn't getting any easier. During his high school years Max was in and out of Juvenile Detention and continually on probation. He had periods of seeming stability and good behavior, then he would start on a downward spiral again and get arrested or be detained for a probation violation. Max's Probation Officer, Cassie, and Pamela became friends and worked together to try to guide this troubled boy through his difficult times. Both of them hoped the combination of accountability, a good recovery program and consistent discipline at home would, over time, bring Max out of his emotional pit and into normalcy.

Pamela tried all the usual ways of communicating with her teenagers: talking, nagging, reminding, listening when they wanted to talk, yelling when they didn't, and writing notes to them. She found that Max responded best to notes, and they began to write to each other. She would leave reminder notes for him to see when he woke up. He left notes on her Bible for her, usually asking for help with school work or for her to bring projects to class or buy supplies. There were even occasional notes of apology after an argument. The beauty of this method was that each person could have their say without interruption, and the other had time to think about what was written before responding. For them, it worked.

Their correspondence continued during Max's periods of confinement. Visitation was not the best environment for them to communicate. Pamela expressed herself better with the written word anyway, preferring old school handwritten notes over texting or email. She wrote Max regularly when he was away, and sometimes he wrote back. But she knew he read her letters because there was a lot of free time in detention. She felt she had the best chance of getting through to him in letters while he was a 'captive audience.'

On this April afternoon when the free world was bursting with spring, she put down her pen and reviewed her latest letter.

Dear Max:

Things are getting more serious for you now and I hope you will use the time you have while locked up to think about where you want to go in life, what kind of person you truly want to be. It may seem like only another week in detention to you, no big deal, and if it does – well, that's part of the problem. You can only go on like this so long; eventually, you'll violate your probation enough that you will lose your freedom completely. I do not want to see you end up in State Youth Commission or adult jail on a permanent basis, and I would hate for you to be taken from our home and placed in a residential facility. But to me it looks like you are heading down that road.

I urge you to re-think the values you hold, some of the friends you hang with, and your lack of discipline in attending class. These things really will make a difference in how your life turns out, and what you do during your high school years can never be undone. You and I are already to the point where I no longer have reason to believe anything you say, and rebuilding my trust in you will take time and hard work. I am very willing to work on it, but you will have to be willing also. More importantly, you will have to begin being honest. May sound corny, but becoming a person of honesty and integrity will result in much more satisfaction in life and will allow you to have people in your life worth having.

Always remember that no matter what you do, or how far you stray from doing the right thing, God loves you – He loves *you*, Max, much more than you can ever imagine. Nothing you can do can separate you from that love – you can't earn it, you can't make Him stop loving you – it is always there for you; all you have to do is accept it and He will change your life, one day at a time.

I've heard you say you just want to hang out with friends and flip burgers in the future. I have bigger dreams for you, and hopefully one day you will have different goals for yourself. But to be able to do whatever it is you want you have to keep your freedom and stay out of trouble. I don't know why you are skipping school. All I know is that is <u>has</u> to stop, and it has to stop now. And if you don't start going to <u>every</u> class <u>every</u> day, you're going to lose the luxury of skipping and going to detention every other month or so while living at home. You may think it is not going to happen to you; understand, it *will* happen if you don't change your ways.

You're my son and you know I love you. Because I love you I can't allow you to continue enjoying the privileges of home life while lying, stealing, skipping, and breaking curfew. We'll have to make some changes when you get home, different changes than we've made before. I'm not talking just about removing things from your room, although that may be part of it. Cassie and I are discussing various options, and I will do what I think is best for you. You simply need to understand that the pressure on you to obey the law is going to increase until you either comply with the rules, or get locked up again. It's up to you. Love, Mom

As she folded the letter and addressed the envelope she sighed. Her thoughts went to the other kids she had seen in juvenile jail, and of the other parents at visitation or in the courtroom. Regardless of the guilt or innocence of the juveniles, they all seemed to have one thing in common:

the lack of an involved or healthy father. Not because the dad was dead, but because he was not being a responsible parent, or because he too was a criminal and either locked up or prevented from any contact for safety reasons. The jail population in their community was made up primarily of black males. Pamela believed it was because they were the most likely to be without fathers in their lives. She didn't believe it was about prejudice or race or unjust arrests, although she knew those could be factors. She thought it went deeper than that, that it was about young men growing up without a father, or with a father who is unsafe. Like Max. Who was not black.

It was the end of May. Max had been out of jail for a couple of months when the call in the middle of the night came. It was never easy, but she was getting better at handling the calls from the local police department in the middle of the night telling her that they had her son. Probably due to Al Anon, she laughed to herself. There was nothing like being awakened by the phone at 2:30 in the morning, especially by the police department. The conversation always went something like this:

Pamela: Hello? (trying to wake up)

PD: Is this Pamela Cohen?

Pamela: Yes. (who can be calling at this hour?)

PD: Do you have a son named Max?

Pamela: Yes. (the old familiar grip of dread brought her fully awake)

PD: Officers have your son at the 7100 block of Little Creek Road. You need to go there and they will explain everything to you.

Pamela: Can you give me a specific location please? (I can't believe this is happening again...)

PD: The parking lot of the Conoco on the corner of Little Creek Road and Pine.

It was almost impossible to look decent at that hour with no "get ready" time. She threw on a pair of jeans, slipped into a clean T shirt, ran a brush through her hair, grabbed her purse and left. She was now used to crisis so her brain immediately went into emergency mode. What did he do? Was he stealing? Is he cooperating or resisting arrest? Is he high? Is he violent? Oh God, will a felony go on his record? She drove the few minutes to the scene.

There were two cop cars. Max was cuffed in the back of one of them, his bike resting upside-down on its seat and handlebars in the parking lot, his backpack on the hood of a cop car. They had found cigarettes (is there no limit to the number of citations a teen can get for Minor In Possession of tobacco?), cans of spray paint, drawings and markers. She heard Max thrashing and cursing the cops – she refused to look at him. The officers were nice, asking the usual questions. They told her he gave his incorrect phone number and address. She was surprised he had given his real name this time. She hated having to say he was on probation. They asked if he had a dad and if he was involved in his life. Pamela shook her head No, his dad was a sex offender, also on probation. They nodded knowingly. As she apologized for his disrespect to them, one of them said it was common, especially with boys where there is no dad around. But it still upset her that Max was so dishonest, disrespectful and defiant. She had tried too hard to raise him just the opposite.

They took her name and called in to "check for involvement". Great, she would be a suspect too. They checked for a record and found a report of family violence. Of course – the time he had been so high on drugs he had threatened her with a chair and she had felt compelled to call the police on her own teenage son. He had taken off on his bike and nothing had ever happened like that since. But now they were concerned to release him to her. It would almost be a relief, Pamela thought, if they took him to the Juvenile Center. But that would mean she would have to go down to get him later, more time off work for another Detention Hearing. She felt sick – he was so close to being off probation. Now he had traffic tickets for bike violations, another MIP and a curfew violation. The last two were probation violations; the Juvenile District Attorney would love that. She convinced them to release Max to her. She was thankful that the local police officers had always been polite, kind, courteous, considerate, compassionate, mature, professional, patient, understanding, and truly wanting to help, a credit to their profession.

The officers calmed Max down; he was ticked off about "violation of my rights." Pamela could already hear what he would (and in fact, did) say to her on the drive home: "The police officers work for me. You pay their salary. They aren't protecting, they stopped me and I wasn't doing anything." How could he *not* get it that he'd broken the law in several ways and it was not anyone's fault but his? It seemed to escape him that he had violated the law, that rights and safety of other people were involved here too. Though he argued with them, miraculously they released him to her, making sure she was not afraid of him. I'm glad to see he's been crying, Pamela thought. Thank God he can feel, can cry. For so long he couldn't. Thank God they didn't haul him in, but called her instead. She didn't know if he really went to see his sister, or if he was lying. What is it they said in Al Anon parent's groups: "If an addict's lips are moving, he's lying." All she knew was the Serenity Prayer, and the reality of uninterrupted sleep, tears and sobbing; heartsick grief as she fought off the feeling of being a complete failure as a parent. *Thank God I am not alone, You are with me. God, You must have a pretty big bottle of my tears by now... I comfort myself with "I'm not afraid of a storm in the hands of my heavenly Father. God's love brings hope to my heart."* Pamela recalled part of Psalm 56 the way The Message paraphrased it:

You've kept track of my every toss and turn through the sleepless nights,
Each tear entered in your ledger, each ache written in your book.

Once again Max returned home, and the first few days went well. Later that week to help out another single mom, Pamela decided to take Max and a friend for burgers and then drop them off at the local electronics store where the friend's mom would pick them up and bring them home. She left her cell phone with Max in case plans changed. Within a half an hour he called her on the home landline – from the back of a cop car, in tears because he'd been arrested and they were taking him in. He had shoplifted some video games - a total value of $59. The life cost was going to be so much more. He was detained overnight, released for school Friday, and a new hearing set to review his probation, which now probably would not be released.

Pamela shook her head in disbelief. Max was just weeks from being completely off probation, yet he had done something so obviously designed to get him caught. She had been stupid to think he could handle a few minutes waiting for his ride without getting into trouble, but she couldn't help but think there must be a reason, something only a counselor could find. Shoplifting wasn't Max's "thing", and none of this made sense. What was clear was that she had been an idiot to leave him unsupervised in public, even for a few minutes, even if he had seemed to be on the straight path.

Chapter 39

It was always so much better when Pamela could have a good visit with Max. Three days later at their visit he was in such a good mood – smiling, relaxed, and almost happy. He said he'd gotten her first letter and did what she said, gone from mad to sad and made the best of it while he was in. He spoke of Mr. Arnold, who taught him to play dominoes two and a half years ago, and now gets beat by Max. He talked in detail and matter of fact about what it was like there. He spoke about things that don't have any bearing "out in the free" but are a big deal on the inside. Things like:

If two inmates are in one cell, the door must stay open.

It's hard to sleep because of the lights on 24/7 and loud talk of the staff.

If you do manage to fall asleep, noise wakes you frequently. All you can see on every wall is brick, brick, brick.

It's nicer if you're alone because you can close the door and get some sleep.

20 squares of toilet paper, to be used one at a time, that's standard issue

If even a pencil is missing in school, the whole unit is padded down until it's found.

There was lots of racial tension between inmates – just like on the outside.

You must count off –every time you enter or leave a doorway

Hands are always held open behind the back as you walk through the facility, forefingers and thumbs touching, open palms.

They joked about each knowing the drill, their drill. Max's drill - when he had a dirty UA and got detained, he would have to tell a PO in training where to write the information, which form to fill out, and how long the process would take. Pamela's drill - the drill for visitation: get someone to let you in, give the name of the child you're visiting, show your Driver's License, sign in, your name checked against the approved visitor list, put your stuff in the locker, how to lock it, how to line up, go in single file, pick a table quickly. They weren't really joking, just making the best of it. Max was able to laugh about the food. How small the portions were, how everyone wolfed down the food because they were so hungry. "You know how I hate cabbage, Mom, the purple stuff in salad, but I even eat all that and scrape my plate too!" And then as if on cue, everyone would eat their dessert exactly the same way – save it for last, cut one small sliver of a bite of cake at a time and eat very slowly to make it last. The same with the three and a half graham crackers for snack. Unlike at home gobbling Oreos or chips, here he nibbled tiny bites of cracker to make it last longer.

He talked of school there - easy for him - playing spades with some of the staff and the "jail rules" of the game. He talked calmly of his dad. Good strong hugs coming and going. Genuine connection. *Thank You for that, our visit with laughter, not tears.*

Change is about bringing new sense to your circumstances. Pamela was always reminded what kind of week she'd had by how many handkerchiefs were in the laundry – too many tears for mere tissues to handle. It was an emotional rollercoaster. She never knew if what she was feeling was due to PMS, menopause, emotional fallout of teenage rebellious behavior, emotional fallout of the addict/alcoholic behavior, her own emotional makeup, family circumstances, stress at work or just being human. Her thoughts roamed as she sorted clothes for the wash. When your child is an addict, do you ever get over the grief at not having a "normal" child? One who goes to school, participates in sports or music or clubs at school, or a church youth group? She missed 'normal', especially since he did those things for a while when he was younger, then one by one quit them all and had begun to drift aimlessly through life.

She remembered something she had heard from a young man, eighteen years old and living in a recovery community: "It's scary to think of going through my whole life sober." As a parent, it was scary to hear that.

Thank You for never giving up on Max. Don't ever let him feel hopeless. Let him know deep in his soul how much he is loved. He is my gift from God.

"Sooner or later we all sit down to a banquet of consequences"

R.L. Stevenson

Chapter 40

Sometimes God literally rings the doorbell to wake us up to what our child is doing, so we can take action, and they can receive consequences – it's a good thing. Eight days after Max's arrest and release Pamela was awakened at 2:30 in the morning by the doorbell. She went to the door, but no one was there. She checked Max's room, then the garage, and discovered her car keys, purse, car and her son were gone. She called the cell phone which she had left in her purse and he answered. She told him to bring the car back, and he did. He said a friend called him (although the phone hadn't rang) that another friend was in trouble and needed Max. As she had learned to do, she called his Probation Officer and informed her of his violations (curfew, taking the car without permission – not to mention without a driver's license) and a warrant was placed for his arrest for violating probation. Pamela told Max what the PO had said, that it would be better if he let her take him to turn himself in. But he refused, saying, "I'm screwed." He was found, picked up and taken in later that day. It was three days before Pamela's birthday.

When she visited him in juvenile jail this time, Max seemed constantly close to tears. At the Detention Hearing the day before and now at visitation he cried **real** tears. During the visit he cried off and on, and he said, "It's different this time." He confessed one of his friends had advised him not to take the car. He seemed hurting and broken. But had proven to be an excellent liar; she had to disbelieve everything he said until it was proven true. Pamela knew it was the only way to protect herself. It was awful, the despair at not being able to discern whether he was telling the truth, but she had to stay smart to keep her sanity.

"Lord, let him come to You in repentance, true repentance that transforms his life and shows in actions when he gets out. Thanks and praise he can feel, cry and say, 'I'm staying home so I don't have opportunity." He needs rigid structure – help me provide what he needs, Lord. Love my child. I believe You are breaking his rebellious spirit bit by bit – break him so he can find You. What is it You say in Your Word? 'The sacrifice you desire is a broken spirit. You will not reject a broken and repentant heart, O God."(Psalm 51:17) Teach him that he can't run far enough from You without running right into You."

A week later she retrieved Max from juvenile. It made her really sad to pick him up when there were no hugs, and she couldn't honestly say "I'm glad you're home". She was already worried sick about how soon he would be back there, or how she could keep things at home from being stolen. It was obvious Max was out of control. Pamela couldn't bear the thought of sending him away but having him at home like this was no way to live either. She was so concerned about the underlying unresolved emotional issues that she knew were driving his behavior. The initial counseling had helped him through the shock and pain of the early days in those crazy years, but she had seen that court ordered or forced counseling does not work with an adolescent who wasn't sure how he felt and didn't want to face the scary process of finding out. She had suspected he was doing hard drugs, whether to feel or not to feel she didn't know. That worried her too, not just the illegality of it but the danger. From the classes she had taken on the neurological science of addiction medicine she had learned that marijuana was indeed a gateway drug; that it was addictive and capable of re-carving the brain's pathways especially in a young person under 25. His decision-making would be greatly hindered. She knew it was only a matter of time until the next incident or crisis. But nothing could have prepared her for what happened next.

Chapter 41

Pamela was leaving the office for lunch on a hot summer day when her cell phone rang. The local police had answered a call about a disturbance of the peace in Lily's neighborhood. They found Max lying in the street, unconscious, evidence of being beaten. He had no identification on him so he was taken by EMS as a John Doe to the Emergency Room. For some reason their family dog was with him, and the dog tags had their home phone number. The police located their home and found Lily, who had stopped by to check the mail. She gave them Pamela's cell number. "This is Officer Hansford of CGPD. Your son was picked up on the street as a John Doe and we've taken him to the ER." Pamela called the hospital and the ER information desk told her EMS was bringing Max in and that she should come immediately.

She could not have prepared for the experience. By the time Pamela arrived Max was no longer unconscious, but he was disoriented, confused, did not know who she was. He had to be restrained because he was uncontrollable. At admittance the doctor ran a CAT scan, X rays, blood tests – all was normal. Max's vital organs were functioning and there was no evidence of illegal drugs in his system. The diagnosis was an overdose from some type of over the counter medicine. This seemed logical since Pamela had found several empty packages of Coricidin in his room. But because the doctors had no idea what he had ingested, and he couldn't tell them, they felt it wasn't safe to treat him. They did insert a catheter – it took three strong young male aides to hold him down – and gave him some kind of charcoal treatment. Max's screams and cries could be heard all throughout ER.

Pamela did not find out until years later that he had overdosed on a plant called Datura, a common yard plant also known as Jimson Weed or Stinkweed. Its leaves can be smoked, or the seeds eaten orally. The plant's effects when made into teas or ointments have medicinal properties, but when ingested in moderate to large doses the results can be dangerous, even fatal. Pamela couldn't miss the irony that her son who was now involved with illegal drugs – everything from alcohol to pot to cocaine – was in the hospital for an overdose of a drug that can be plucked from a front yard.

Max had all the signs of an overdose – eyes dilated and darting everywhere, the shakes, picking at his clothes and the bed sheets, paranoid, hearing and seeing things, looking for things, repeating himself, thinking he was in a car or another place, not knowing what day it was or where he was, and very afraid because he didn't know what was happening. Even in his disorientation and confusion he was strong, and the restraints bound his arms and legs, even his head was strapped down. Pamela sat by the bed, wishing there was something, anything, she could do to alleviate his pain. But all she could do was watch, and listen, wishing this was all a very bad dream.

During the worst of it he babbled excitedly and she learned a lot, much of which she wished she did not know. At times he spoke to her as if she was one of his cohorts in crime, and she unexpectedly received explanations for things she had found or seen at home. He was hallucinating, talking to people who weren't there, seeing bugs, answering imaginary phones, leaving messages, mumbling to himself. He talked of stealing, of tagging, and let out a stream of cursing, then tried to talk about events but mixed them up with each other. He thought he was locked up again, talked about getting no sleep, doing 'shrooms' because you can't test for that, again with the no sleep, sneaking out. He had absolutely no memory of waking up that morning, or anything that had happened. Pamela was engulfed by sorrow and worry – was there permanent brain damage? He was messed up - cut and bleeding, his shirt cut away from his body, his lips cracked, swollen and black from the charcoal treatment. But mainly she was in anguish for this young boy who ingested chemicals to the point of being found unconscious on the street, at risk by molesters and other types of criminals, jeopardizing his very life. She couldn't bear the sight of him so incoherent and vulnerable but couldn't make herself leave the room, so she stayed at his side and cried on the inside. She determined that the next day she would get with his Probation Officer to form a plan for residential treatment, and use this frightening episode to try and get his consent to treatment. If he was willing to go, he could be accepted into the places that would only take those who came for help voluntarily, places more pleasant than a lock-down facility. She had to try.

The sights and sounds of the ER were so strange, the passage of time unmarked. The way he was strapped down, the monitors beeping constantly, IV's dripping, urinal bottles ever ready, nurses and aides in and out, the repeated questions, each time from a different doctor or nurse, the way Max was not himself – Pamela hated all of it. Yet she was absorbing every detail because she didn't want to forget. It was important that she remember because he wouldn't, and he was the one that needed to know what this was like, for him and for her.

After six hours he came down from his "high". The ER doctors decided to keep him overnight for observation. Since he was only fifteen he had to be admitted to Children's Hospital. He was almost six feet tall, physically more suited for an adult room. Pamela couldn't miss the incongruity of this tall, teenage boy in a room designed and decorated for someone five years old. His frame maxed out the bed, and it was odd to see his head resting on a pillowcase decorated with dinosaurs in primary colors. Yet it was somehow appropriate; emotionally he was still a child. Unfortunately the Children's Hospital staff was very experienced in overdose cases. Perhaps there was a reason for this environment after all. He fell asleep and Pamela decided to go home and get some sleep too. Tonight he would be in the care of skilled nurses - who could say where he would end up tomorrow.

He slept through the night, and the morning found both of them somewhat rested. When Pamela arrived with coffee, he was awake and seemed 'normal'. They would have to talk, of course, and this would be a difficult discussion. He didn't do illegal drugs or technically do anything that would be a probation violation except skip a day of summer school, but Pamela knew that he was in a very bad way. If he was finding a legal way to meet the need for drugs to medicate his pain, he wouldn't last long and she couldn't keep on living like this.

They greeted each other and he was genuinely glad to see her. She had decided if he showed any remorse or concern about what had happened, it was time to make a major move and find a residential rehab facility for him.

They had a brief talk in his hospital room before he was released. He didn't think he did anything wrong, except skip school, and didn't admit he took OTC drugs to get high. But even he knew he had a problem, and he agreed to go to a residential place like boarding school or a boy's ranch if he got that option rather than incarceration. He felt the weight of his situation, and the pressure, but said "drug rehab isn't the answer." Well, what was the answer? She thought it was obvious they had to change his environment. After she described places like the Boy's Ranch he thought that sounded like a good alternative to jail. He admitted he was scared, didn't know what to do or why his life was out of control. He agreed to let her try and find a placement for him within thirty days, and she agreed to let him try and finish the summer school term in the meantime. He said he wanted to change and acknowledged he needed to leave home for that to happen.

Pamela had already been talking to Valerie, his Children's Advocacy Center case manager, about her concerns. It was Valerie's professional opinion that the drug use was not the problem but a symptom. She suggested that residential placement was what he needed. Because he was in the hospital from an overdose, he was willing to listen to his mom. Pamela helped him see how an objective person would view the recent chain of events in his life, and he became willing to leave home and go to a residential facility for a time. *Oh God, how can I ever thank you for this miracle? Help me to help my son, please guide me.*

I must try to be Christ-like and look into my child's heart,

past the blistering bravado of adolescence to his fear and hurt.

Chapter 42

The note Max left that night almost destroyed what was left of Pamela's heart.

-Mom-
Nothing to lose ...
Hopefully I get arrested
or hit by a car
- Your horrible son-

It was ten days after his release from the ER, and he had run away. For twelve hours she didn't know where he was. When he finally called at 4:30 a.m., crying, saying he needed to come home, Pamela was glad he had called and glad to know he was safe. She drove to pick him up and brought him home. There wasn't much to say, but he made it clear he felt he had nothing more to lose. When they got home he went straight to bed and to sleep. She tried to sleep, but it was fitful and she arose early to communicate her feelings to him the best way she knew how, in a letter.

My Dear Max-

You said last night you have nothing to lose any more, and you asked me to write down for you what you have to lose by running away, getting arrested again, etc. As I see it, here is what you have to lose:

Chance to have some control over where you will live.

Freedom to live at home between now and your new place.

The support of your PO, Case Manager and others in the juvenile system who want to help you.

Hope

Keeping safe

Longer probation if you fight the consequences

More chance of jail if you keep violating probation

My precious son, I can only imagine how hard this time is for you. If I could, I would take away your pain and bear it for you. I know you must be hurting greatly inside, feeling lonely and scared about what it's going to be like living at some "place" that isn't home, not knowing anyone. I'm sure this is not how you want your life to be, but the only way to change things is to change things, as they say in the program. Change can be painful and difficult, but sometimes it is absolutely necessary, like with you. You can't keep on living this way or you will surely end up dead or in jail, and that is not where you belong.

Please trust me and work with me on this plan. I love you and I don't want you to leave home; I've worked hard to find a good place to take care of you while I cannot. But your behavior has limited my choice in the matter. I believe you can get through this, Max, and become a better, happier person. If you will live at home without running away, getting arrested or getting hurt and ending up in the hospital, here is what you have to gain:

Daily building of trust with me and others in your life

Chance to live temporarily at a place that is not a lock-down or drug rehab but is a home set up for young people with similar problems who want to have a better life.

Live at home between now and the new place

Learn to be happy

Learn to enjoy things other than illegal activities or sneaking out

Chance to live at a place where I can come visit and you can visit home

Continued support of family and friends who want to see you do the right thing

Shorter probation than if you run or fight the consequences of your actions

Chance to get real help rather than just an orange suit

Whatever your pain and problems are, they won't go away until you deal with them and work through all the stuff. It's hard work, but it's worth it when you can be happy and successful rather than living life in a tailspin. I can't change your life for you, but with God's help you can. He loves you, values you and wants you to be happy.

<u>You can do this, Max</u>. You can make it through whatever changes you have to and it will be worth it. Your real friends will always be glad to hear from you and want to see you when they can. You will make new friends that may like and appreciate you more than anyone ever has. You can choose to try this new place and make it work, and not have to worry about going back to detention every time you violate probation. Or you fight it, run away, or just do something really bad and go straight to jail. For me, I want you to be somewhere where I know you are safe and where people are trying to help you get your life together, not just guarding you so you don't get out. You are young, smart, and have an incredible personality. Please help me help you to turn things around before it gets really bad. You can never screw up so much that I won't love you, and God loves you way more than I do. Read the Big Book, read the Bible, get that truth into your heart and mind so you have something solid to hang onto when times get tough.

I don't want to have to worry about where you are, or if you are safe and okay, and I'll do everything I can to find a place that will help you make your life better. The sooner we set that in motion, the sooner you'll be able to come home. It occurs to me we haven't talked about what the Boy's Ranch is like. I've printed out some stuff on it that may help. Remember, I have your best interest at heart more than juvenile court, and I pray you will work with me to make this happen. I love you more than I can say, want you to be happy, and want things to work out for you. And I believe in you, you <u>can</u> get on the right track and I'll be there along with many others to congratulate you.

Love,

Mom

The next morning they talked about the Boy's Ranch. Max had looked over some of her information and began to ask a few questions. He still didn't want to leave home, but it seemed her words had an impact. He realized she was serious about making a major change. They reached a tentative truce, and for the next three weeks lived on the edges of hope and fear. Max was careful to always let her know where he was and Pamela loosened the reigns of accountability just enough to give him some breathing room. Pamela worked with Cassie, Max's Probation Officer, to get on the judge's calendar for a probation hearing about where Max would live. Then she got on the phone to the Boy's Ranch. They said they weren't sure when they would have room for him. Pamela asked for the pre-admittance paperwork and prepared it as quickly as possible. Time was critical here – if the judge ordered Max to the Boy's Ranch but they couldn't accept him, the next hearing would take him away from home but Pamela would probably not have any say as to where. Pamela sent off the paperwork and began praying that there would be an opening in time. Two days before the hearing she received the acceptance letter – if she could get Max to the Ranch, he was in. At the hearing, the judge sentenced Max to eighteen months additional probation to be served on the Ranch. The court would consider letting him come back home at the end of that year and a half, depending on his behavior and progress. The Boy's Ranch had a school and a drug rehab component, and Max was to be an active participant.

Chapter 43

Max wasn't the only one nervous about his going to the Boy's Ranch. As Pamela gathered the things she was to pack for his stay, the reality that he was leaving home set in. What would his life there be like? Would they take good care of him? The location was so remote that she knew he wouldn't be running away, so that was a relief.

Although he did not want to leave home and go the Ranch, Max was relieved not to have been sent to jail. The days between his sentencing and the final paperwork for transferring to the Boy's Ranch were tense. Max was restless, and Pamela was concerned that he wouldn't make it until then. She walked a tightrope between discipline and accountability and trying to keep him hopeful and encouraged about his future. Andrew's mom, his "second mom", was a wonderful sanctuary for him in those days; he felt calmer at her house and would often spend the night there. He was better behaved, helped out willingly with chores, and seemed to have found a niche, so she was thankful that for two weeks he had an alternate place to stay that was safe and a good influence.

The day came for Pamela to drive him to the Ranch. He was packing in his room when Valerie, his case manager, stopped by to say goodbye. She was another godsend, a precious Christian young lady who had been with them through all the court stuff. She was a tremendous help to Pamela and they had become friends. She had been helpful many times when Max needed an advocate, both personally and in the juvenile system. She went in to Max's room to say goodbye but he was upset so she came back out. Together they prayed for him and asked God to help him make this difficult transition. They were both concerned that he might bolt at the last minute and knew that only divine intervention would get him into the car and on the road. As she stood to go Pamela sensed that indeed their prayers had been heard and she knew that God was in control of this situation. Valerie left and Pamela called to Max that it was time to go.

He came out and Pamela could tell he was struggling with whether to get into the car or jump on his bike and take off, as he had so many times before. He opened the back door of the car and tossed his bag in. Pamela watched his every move as she tried to stay calm and got into the driver's side, praying hard that God would get him into the car. Closing the back door, he turned and walked over to his bike, backpack over his shoulder, and grabbed the handlebars. Then, amazingly, he removed his hand, walked back to the car, put his hand on the passenger door handle and got in. Pamela didn't waste a second backing that car out of the driveway, her heart racing as fast as the wheels were turning, and finally they were on the road.

Pamela recorded in her prayer journal how she later found out that Valerie had pulled off the road just a few blocks from our house, convicted of the need to stop and pray for several minutes that Max would get in the car. Max told Pamela later that his plan was to take off on the bike at the last minute; if he wasn't allowed to live at home he'd find some place to live better than a Boy's Ranch in the middle of nowhere. He said he didn't know what made him get into the car; he couldn't explain it, but it was a power greater than himself. Indeed.

During the first days and weeks he was gone, it felt very strange at home. Pamela thought about Max constantly and how he was doing. His first calls home were tearful, pitiful, and tore at her heartstrings. He hated it, the other boys were mean to him, the Home Parents were unfair, his friends would all forget about him. But gradually she began to get used to being able to sleep at night again, having a measure of peace about her daily life, and not having to take off work for hearings or hospital visits or court dates. She even started doing some things just for herself. She joined the Sunday Singers, one of the choirs at church that she had always wanted to be in but could never commit to practice times because of the chaos at home.

One weekend Pamela went to a women's retreat with some friends at church, and it was wonderful. The pastor for the event shared a message that struck home and reminded her of their current situation. In her youth Pamela had been the prodigal daughter. Now she was the parent waiting for her own son. The prodigal betrayed his family by wishing his dad were dead and requesting his death benefit. He discovered that in the world identity is found in looks or achievement – conditional love. In the world he had to prove his worth – like Max on the Ranch – but at home he had worth because he was the son. At home, there is identity in relationship – unconditional love. As a Christian believer, Pamela knew she had worth and identity and the ultimate home because she belonged to Jesus Christ. Living in guilt would not heal; when we hit bottom we start looking up, and that is where true healing comes from. She hoped it was only upwards from there for her and Max.

Depending on behavior while at the Ranch and progress in rank, or lack thereof, residents were allowed occasional phone calls home, letters from pre-approved family members or friends after the initial settling in, and eventually Home Visits if they were merited. Max's first Home Visit came after six weeks of living on the Ranch. It was a disaster. Pamela recorded the episode in her prayer journal so she would not forget how long true transformation takes.

"On the way home yesterday I tried so hard not to get my hopes up, to realize it was too good to be true that the Ranch would have changed him for the better already. It was his first night back. I awoke during the night. He was gone. I drove around searching, worrying he would get arrested or do drugs and not be able to go back to the Ranch even if I did find him; he had vanished. I cried myself to sleep, just like the bad old days when he was living at home. Only worse, this time I had had some hope and the disappointment was so huge and heavy I did not see how I could bear up under it - it was crushing me." *Father, thank you for the flood of cleansing tears I cried over Max last night. It seemed different than the sobbing and weeping I did earlier in the weekend. My eyes aren't swollen, and I feel as though some of the pain of loss was dealt with. I miss my son, grieve over his behavior and yet I can't miss the obvious fact that he must not, cannot, come home for a long time. Help me stay strong and learn what You have for me in this.* Max came home the next day and Pamela drove him to the Ranch in silence.

Max didn't have another Home Visit for three months. Another hard "first". Pamela had to tell him herself that she wouldn't allow him to come home for the Thanksgiving holiday, even though his behavior on the Ranch had improved and they would have allowed a short visit. Too much broken trust, too many times wishing she had held the line and had been tougher. She had to try to make him see she could do tough love, for as long as it took. Thanksgiving was hard that year, for both of them, but it was the right thing to do. The hard thing usually is.

Pamela took refuge in her letter writing, pouring out her thoughts and feelings in an effort to help Max do the same.

<u>Letters from Home</u>

Dear Max,

I am remembering happy times with you and thought I'd share them in case you'd like to enjoy the memories with me.

Waffles for breakfast with faces and hair made out of banana pieces

Early morning walks to Mr. Doyle's after your big sister went to school – you played with the leaf blower, got a real slingshot, picked up pecans and cracked and ate them, asked him questions about all the things he had in his garage

T-ball, soccer, WAYA flag football – I went to every game ☺

Learning to ride your first bike – you just did it! Immediately!!

Boy Scouts – making yard candy canes, camping out, pinewood derby cars

Countless sleepovers with Andrew and Turner, your best friends since first grade. When they moved away, we bought their bunk beds and sheets for you and you were so happy ☺

Your birthday parties – always family, Andrew and Turner

Your love for video games, from when you were five – your first SNES, game boy, Sega Dream Cast, Play Station, Xbox, Play Station 2 – you've always been excellent at them. Is there a career in testing video games before they are marketed??

Going to the park – you loved to climb on the playscapes

Playing with cousin Brayden at all the family gatherings – walking from Aunt Riley's to the truck stop for snacks

Sierra the cat slept with you every night for years. He was your comfort and companion during those bad years of sleepless nights

You and Lily making tent houses with every blanket and sleeping bag we had, under the piano in the pink room at Greenleaf house

Re-creating the YMCA Park camp in the mountains out of Lincoln logs

Building cities and cars and families with Legos

Singing and dancing to Joe Scruggs, or The Jungle Book, or Sharon Lois & Bramm, Sam & Dave – oh, how we loved music and dancing!

All the bazillion photographs taken of you – we couldn't get enough pictures of "our boy", the one who would carry on the family name, especially your Grandma CiCi.

You answering "yes" to Mrs. Penny, the Asst. Principal's, question: "If everyone else jumped off a cliff, would you?" You said, "Yes, because if I didn't I wouldn't have anyone to talk to."

You and Andrew -

Riding bikes all over the neighborhood

Building a tree house - that was hard but you were so dedicated

Drawing plans, buying lumber, and designing your bike ramps; working hard to build the ramps, then biking on them into the late hours of the evening.

Inventing the Tapler – a combination of a stapler and tape dispenser

You building your bike – you were passionate, patient, and you persevered – good job

You made an excellent spinach quiche from scratch for your eighth grade French class – without any help!

Decorating Christmas cookies, taking special ones to your teachers in elementary school

Watching the only TV show I watched, 7th Heaven, with me

Baking cookies, lots of cookies, on every occasion and no occasion

Birthday cakes – remember the Sailboat, Clown, the Guitar, Pizza, Dart Board?

All the visits to Aunt Riley's

Max, I don't know what you are feeling these days but you've been through a lot in your young life. Divorced parents are hard enough on kids, but on top of that you've had to deal with the junk thrown in by your dad – how many thirteen year olds have to give a deposition to their dad's criminal attorney? Dealing with Grandma CiCi as she pulled away from your sister, tough times at school, more counseling than some adults will ever have, in and out of the orange jumpsuit, and two trips to the Emergency Room for alcohol or drugs. I'm kind of rambling in this letter, but I guess what I'm trying to say is you probably have a great mixture of feelings down inside that keep your innards churned up even when you don't know it. What I'm learning in my counseling is to <u>feel</u> my feelings. Sounds stupid at first, but I didn't realize how much I try to *not* feel sad or mad or frustrated. I find that when I let myself feel that stuff, it brings it up but then <u>out</u> of me, and if the feeling is brought out into the light it can't hurt or control me anymore. So now, if I'm feeling sad because of time lost with you because you have to live at the Ranch, I <u>feel</u> sad, maybe sit with it a while or write it out, then I can get on with my day and appreciate the happy memories. Because I know of God's great love for us and plan for our lives I can anticipate more happy times in the future. Just gotta go through this valley first.

Always know how very much you are loved, Mom

Dear Max:

After your phone call last night I realized I needed to write this letter. You mentioned that you would probably be allowed to come home for Thanksgiving. What you need to understand is that even if the Ranch says you can, I will not allow you to come home for Thanksgiving. After your last visit, I don't know when I will be ready to try that again.

You may not want to talk about what you did on your home visit, but let me assure you that your own wrongdoing has been brought down on your head. Home visits are a privilege, and you have shown that you cannot yet be trusted back at home. You lied, were gone most of the weekend without permission and without letting me know where you were, not to mention deceiving me, doing drugs, and taking the cell phone. And all that was after six weeks of good behavior at the Ranch. So I am not foolish enough to think that after eight more weeks of good behavior you would be ready to come home and be honest, obey the rules, and do what is required of you. I do not know how long it will take or what all it will take for you to truly change your ways, but I do know that you are not coming home again until I am convinced you have made some <u>real</u> change. No more games, no more manipulation, no more lying or "working" me to get what you want. You've shown me no remorse, no evidence that you would do anything differently, made no effort to begin to apologize for how you have grieved me.

I say this not to hurt you, but to make it clear how I feel. No matter what happens between now and then, you will spend Thanksgiving at the Ranch. I have not yet decided what I will do about Christmas; much will depend on your progress between now and the end of the year.

The only thing more difficult than not having you live at home is having you home and out of control. You have chosen to do this the hard way, and it will be hard on both of us. It is time, past time, for you to get right with God, with yourself, and with me. It won't be easy, it's not something you can fake, and I am not changing my mind. I am absolutely committed to doing what is best for you, and your staying on the Ranch is it.

I will be at Grandma's either the Friday or Saturday after Thanksgiving. I would like to come for a visit; I'll let you know when as it gets closer to time. Love, Mom

Years after it was written when she read that letter, Pamela was struck by the strength of tone and conviction. She remembered how she had been during his really out of control days, knew how incredible it was for her to be able to write that letter. Only after repeatedly being deceived and lied to and deciding to surrender to whatever *God's* plan was for her son could she hold firm to the things she said in that letter. The miracle was that she had. She had needed to do it for herself, regardless of the outcome for him.

Leaving the house one night about three months after Max left for the Ranch she glanced at the bike ramps in the driveway, unused for months now. Would Max ever jump his bike off the ramps again, or grind down the side of the longest one, or re-build the worn kick-ramp? She felt sad, but those things didn't matter now. When he started them it was about building them, that process and the time and effort he put into it, and trying to channel his time and energy on things fun and challenging but healthy and beneficial. So it was with his life now – even if he never came back home, it was about the building of his character and his learning to surrender to God, face life's challenges, get through them, and become a decent accountable member of society. Even if he never came back home.

Dear Max,

It's been over a month since I had a letter from you, and I've really wanted to hear from you. You know, it's funny. I got your letter today, and in the past I always rushed to open letters from you – couldn't wait to hear from you. But this time, I decided first to read your other letters and balance what you said against what you did after you wrote. It was very interesting. I started with a letter you wrote last July while you were still in Juvenile Justice Center for stealing and probation violations. In that letter you were very honest – about your feelings, how depressed you feel most of the time, the things you did and involvement with people who stole, etc. I don't think you were 100% honest because you left some things out, but you were trying hard to have a fresh start, new beginnings, and begin to earn trust. Your letters from the Ranch have had some honesty too, and I am very glad to see that. I know you don't like living there, and I want you to tell me how you feel – about the place, about the other boys, about school, sports and teachers. But I also want you to <u>really</u> think and <u>accept</u> why you are there. In your first Ranch letter you said you had no one to blame but yourself for being at the Ranch and still being on probation. That is absolutely true.

In the same way, you have no one to blame but yourself for your behavior right now on the Ranch. Your letter today said you are doing "bad" because you have nothing to look forward to. That's not correct – you are doing "bad" because that is what you've chosen to do. Until you, Max, decide you are going to do well and get your life back on track it's not

Kim Robinson

going to happen. You must decide to turn your life around for the sole reason that it's the <u>right</u> thing to do and the <u>only</u> way to be truly happy and fulfilled. Actually, you have it backwards: you aren't going to have anything to look forward to because you're not doing good. It doesn't matter who your home parents are, which home unit you live in, where you go to school, or even which city you live in – those things don't dictate your behavior, you do. God created us as beings with free will, and He lets us go along and screw up as long as we want to. But there comes a time when most of us realize the fallout from messing up and just living for pleasure without accountability is not worth it. It doesn't make us happy, we end up miserable. Your dad is a perfect example of a miserably unhappy person, but he's not willing to do what it takes to change his life and find true happiness. That would require honesty, apologies, accepting his mistakes and need for help, and deciding never to repeat those mistakes – in Christianity we call it repentance.

You, however, are in an excellent position to change things. For one thing you are too young to have screwed up very much, and there is time to redeem yourself (although none of us knows how long we have to live, so you don't want to wait until it's too late to get things right with God.) And you have an <u>overwhelming</u> amount of love and support – me, your sister, all my family, your church family, your counselor, the staff at the Ranch (who truly care about you) and your friends. By the way, I hope you've been able to really think about who your friends are. Anyone who continually encourages or assists you in doing things that are unhealthy or illegal is not a true friend. And, my son, you are bright, charming, witty, intelligent, funny, athletic, and friendly – characteristics that can take you anywhere in this world you want to go. To quote your Grandma Rogers, "You've got <u>so</u> much potential!" I continue to pray and believe that you will decide to make a real fresh start, a life characterized by honesty, decency, accountability and faith. You can do it, and God is waiting every moment of every day for you to come to Him for help, comfort, strength, and endurance. I believe you want to do better, and that you don't plan to mess up on your next home visit. But you must show true remorse by being good long term even when you don't get what you want or there is no immediate incentive.

Your letter was all about wanting to come home for Thanksgiving, how you have learned your lesson, how you want to show me, Jared and Cassie you can do well, how you want another chance, how you want to come so much you even want me to lie and say you can. I'm glad you wrote me, but I do not believe you have learned your lesson. What I really think is that you are hoping to be able to see your friends and you'll say anything to try and make it happen. I know you <u>can</u> do well – heck, you

166

were <u>exemplary</u> the first five weeks at the Ranch, then came home and proceeded to do exactly what you wanted when you wanted with whomever you wanted with no regard for my feelings, your probation rules, or the consequences. It's that short-term thinking, Max, and it will get you in trouble every time. And I see it in your letter – you <u>say</u> you'll do good, not sneak out, you'll listen to my every word and be honest. I hear your words, but I'm watching what you're doing and it doesn't match. It's been six weeks since the home visit, and what I hear from the Ranch is you are either just doing what it takes to get by or getting into trouble over little things. I am <u>very</u> glad you are not in major trouble, but if you were really contrite and remorseful you would have started the day I brought you back being on your best behavior and doing the very best you could to earn back the trust and respect you had at first. You need to realize that while rewards are good, the true incentive must come from inside you for good behaviors to last. I do a good job at work and try to please my boss because it's the right thing to do and it makes me happy and satisfied inside, not just because I need a paycheck. I try to treat others with respect and dignity because it's what I'm supposed to do and I feel good doing the right thing, not because there is any immediate reward. I attend worship, teach Sunday School, pray, and do mission work because when I do those things God asks of me I am happy, and blessed, and I feel good knowing I'm doing my best to obey. My heart is gladdened, and the more I do the right thing the easier it is to do it. But you have to start somewhere; there is a recovery saying: "Do the next right thing." Do the best you can, even a little improvement each day will make a difference. Start with attitude. Remember to be grateful to be alive, that you aren't in detention, that you have the opportunity to excel at school, sports, and FFA, that you can be an encouragement to another boy who is suffering worse than you are. Show respect to your Home Parents, Teachers, Coaches and Caseworkers. Be honest in all things, with yourself and others. Find something to laugh about, every day. And rather than concentrate on yourself and your own problems, pay attention to others and their struggles and see what you can do to help. Be patient, and kind. Listen. Max, I <u>know</u> these things work because I have tried them over time and have seen the results. I have made many mistakes in my life, and I reaped the consequences of them all. It seems to me that for some reason the consequences you have experienced just haven't been severe enough to result in a true change of heart and behavior. I love you too much to let up on my own brand of tough love – more than anything I want my precious beloved son to grow into a good responsible man. That means doing my part in teaching you life's lessons, even the ones that are so hard I think I can't bear it at the time. You are going to have to face and accept the truth that you are not coming home for Thanksgiving. I will not lie, and I will not change my mind. I meant what I said: until I see some real evidence of change in you I cannot allow you to come home.

I'll see you at 10:00 am the Saturday after Thanksgiving. I want to come see your basketball game next Friday, if I can get off work early. I love you more than I can express, and miss you always. Never, never give up!!

Love,

Mom

Chapter 44

It was the first Sunday of Advent and Pamela sat in worship trying to settle her mind and surrender her feelings of the moment so she could engage in the service. As the pastor talked about it being the first Sunday of the Christian Year, she thought of how this coming year would be a whole new year for Max. The message was on John 18:3-7, about the power syndrome versus the rule of God's grace. As she listened it was as if every word was meant for her, for Max, for their future. "If you let Jesus in," pastor said, "as the King of your heart and life and knock down those 'mini-lords' who have been ruling in your life – dishonesty, fear, stuffing the pain of your feelings – you will find yourself happier, at peace, hopeful, and able to face <u>and</u> <u>defeat</u> the fear and pain. Let His love and grace shape your attitudes. Take charge of your own life by letting Jesus take His place on the throne of your heart." It's ironic, she thought, that taking charge equals surrender to God; it sounds backwards, but <u>it works</u>. We are being chased by grace and we have to let ourselves be caught. We can make the ultimate "power play" by relinquishing our power of will and following Jesus Christ, who is all-powerful. If she had a difficult time surrendering her will, how much more difficult must it be for Max with his background of family trauma and the devil of addiction?

Later that evening, reading some Al Anon literature, she found this:

"You don't know what is going to happen. Be thankful for every moment, look for things to be thankful for."

She realized her gratitude was obedience and that pleases God. Let my testing turn me to faith, she thought, not to temptation. God is still and always on the throne. Our life before the Ranch was the pits; now it's better. Be thankful!

Chapter 45

Letter from a Friend

Pamela,

My son probably started drinking around the age of twelve. Started when he would go over to a friend's house up the street to spend the night and such. The wife and I had no reason to believe that anything was happening. Up until the time that he started getting into trouble, in the spring of his freshman year in high school, he was a normal kid that had not been exposed to drinking in the family. I used to drink, but stopped when he was around three because I didn't want to be a bad example... Ha, for all the good that did. There have been numerous incidences. Juvenile court, municipal court, criminal court, jail, drug rehab, therapists, psychologists, and some kind of mental hospital in another city. Then there are the numerous episodes of running away from home and the utter despair and pain of knowing that your kid is out there doing no telling what with no telling who at no telling where. This small town doesn't seem all that big until you're out there at 3 o'clock in the morning driving around trying to find someone and you don't even know where to start.

I haven't even scratched the surface actually. This email would be a million words long if I continued with everything that has happened in the last five or six years. To make it short...... kids with opportunity + alcohol + Pot + any other drug of their choice + questionable friends = problems.

It happens to the best families in the world. Addiction, curiosity, rebellion, peer pressure ...it's there every day. It's not YOUR fault, Pamela. It happens. You already know about the one day at a time stuff. You have to be strong because it won't get better overnight by some miracle. You have to have boundaries that he knows he can't cross. Don't be afraid to enforce them. By now, he knows what your values are and what you will and won't allow. You have to know that you have raised him the right way and one day he will decide that your way IS the best way. Imagine that. Be honest with him. Tell him your feelings and let him tell you his (if he will). Remember that, in his opinion, you are probably really, really stupid. Don't let that keep you from continuing to watch over him and make him aware that you love him more than anything in the world and that you are there for him unconditionally.

I wish that I could tell you that A.A. for teenagers is a good thing but, I honestly don't know if it is or not. From my experience, most of the young people that I've seen attending are being made to go either by the law or their parents or by the drug rehab folks, or whatever. It looks to me in many cases that until the person is READY himself to change then all the A.A. meetings in the world won't do much good. At least for kids of his age. Please don't get me wrong, every person is different. It won't hurt him to go. Don't rule it out.

Try to get him to UNDERSTAND that continuing on the wrong path can RUIN his life. Good luck. My son is now twenty-one. He is not married and has a two year old son of his own. He is on felony probation for burglary of a habitation. He has missed going to prison by the skin of his teeth. He still drinks. He still smokes pot. It's still day to day. I'm still not sure when it will stop. But, like I said, it's up to HIM to decide. No one else.

On the bright side, he's working part time while going to a technical college. He hasn't been arrested in years, although he's still playing with fire, and his son is a beautiful, intelligent kid that, I know, has helped to curb his wild side. I don't recommend Max have a kid. Do you agree? Ha.

Write back if you want, I'll be here.

David

Dear David:

I know the holidays can be an especially hard time for those of us with kids like … well, kids like ours. I did not let Max come back home for the holidays, and though he wasn't happy about it I think he benefited. He knows now that coming home for a visit and going AWOL with sex/drugs/rock and roll results in staying at the Ranch for many months, even on Thanksgiving and Christmas when most of the other boys are gone and there is "nothing to do". I still remember your email to me about your experience, and I continue to try to go to new lengths of tough love. Max's behavior is much better, but his counselor at the Ranch is still looking for that inward attitude change that tells them the behavior changes are here to stay. They don't want to be just a holding tank where he does his time then gets out next year and goes right back to his old ways, and the jury is still out whether they'll let him stay the full amount of court-ordered time. They've said they may release him early if he doesn't start taking responsibility for his own actions however small and quit blaming others. All of which sounds familiar to you I'm sure.

I thought of you also in a recent AlAnon meeting – regular AlAnon meetings are designed as support groups for those with a friend or family member struggling with constant dependence or addiction, but I'm fortunate to have AlAnon for Parents meetings in our town where the support is specifically for parents. Someone brought their AlAnon version of a Christmas letter they wish they could send. You know, where it's a good year because their kids are alive, not in jail, and not living at home!! I think of that when my family gets frustrated with Max because he's not doing perfect on the Ranch, or they dismiss his report card of all A's for three six-weeks in a row because the Ranch curriculum is easy enough that "he should make all A's". I have to remember they haven't lived with him through all the 4 a. m. phone calls from police department, the driving around at night, searching hoping to pick him up before police do, going to truancy court because he's skipped so much school I have to go to court for it, constant calls to his Probation Officer to check the status of the latest Minor In Possession tobacco or theft charges, times off work for juvenile court dates, visits to him in detention, counseling appointments and of course the day in ER watching him suffer the effects of an overdose after being picked up by the police who found him lying in the street with only the tag on our loyal family dog to tell them where he lived. After all that you bet I think it's FABULOUS he's alive, attending class at all, making A's, showing a steer in the AG program, and playing basketball on both the JV and Varsity teams. I would have killed to have that kind of involvement while he was in high school here, and even if they kick him off the Ranch tomorrow at least I've had four and a half months of knowing where he is, peace at home (easy to do when NO kids are living with you), and seeing him try to do the right thing and keep trying even when he fails. I will always be grateful for the divine intervention that put Max in the car to make that trip to the Ranch last August – Max would still say he doesn't know why he got in, he had his backpack loaded and hands on the handlebar of his bike to bolt. Parenting is a relative thing – that is one reason I keep going to my AlAnon group, it's just for parents and they truly understand what it's like. As a Christian I am grateful to the God of second chances and the chance.

Take care, hope this year brings answers, and peace.

Chapter 46

Even after all the history, on Max's first Home Visit in over four months, it was still hard for Pamela to stand firm on the rules and be consistent. That told her how much she had been a part of the problem. She had to boil it down to keeping her word no matter what – no matter what she felt, no matter how good he was doing, no matter what anyone else said. This first time back she knew she had to show consistency and no bending. After all, it had been on her watch that he had foundered and failed at life. On the Ranch he was succeeding beautifully so far, but only after time, much time, of male authority and firm consistency.

She couldn't describe her feelings as she went to his room and wondered if he really and truly did not sneak out. Did he actually spend the night at home in his own bed? Waking up, hearing him get up at 2 a.m. and go to the bathroom, then hearing his bedroom door shut again – was he going out the window? She quietly opened his door – not anxious to see an empty bed, but not knowing how to react if he was in it. At first glance the bed appeared empty, covers bunched up on one side. But before her heart could do that old familiar plummeting to the bottom of the pit of despair she saw a small section of a leg. He was home! He had burrowed in where the covers were bunched and now she knew where to look. She saw the gentle rise and fall of the comforter, evidence of peaceful breathing. Oh the joy! Tears were instant, and gratitude to God, who was indeed changing the heart of her son. *Thank You for opening his heart to change.*

There is no feeling like that of hope for the future of your child when he has come back from the edge of total disaster. And there is no faith like the hope we cling to when the only reason we have it is because God tells us to wait, be patient, and hope in Him. As Pamela began her own journey in counseling to help her cope with everything, she found that what counselors say is true. Healing from trauma is a gradual process, like peeling layers of an onion, and long periods of 'ordinary' time can pass between the peeling of one layer and the healing of what counseling exposed. As some areas are healed it strengthens you; then you are able to handle the challenges that surface with the next layer.

Pamela came to appreciate fairly quickly how counseling could help her. She had been seeing her counselor for a few months, and was struggling with how to deal with her feelings regarding Eduardo. At one point her counselor suggested that she needed to find a healthy way to deal with her anger. The curious thing was Pamela didn't feel angry. Given the circumstances it was very strange for her not to be mad about what had happened. But all she could feel was fear, worry about the kids and her finances, and shock over the type of person Eduardo had turned out to be. Her counselor knew she was angry but unable to acknowledge or express it, and she gave Pamela some homework. She instructed her to go home, get a baseball bat and take a swing at the side of the house or a rock or some other object that she couldn't hurt. Pamela thought the whole thing was pretty silly but was determined to do what she had been asked. At home that evening, she located Max's assortment of bats and chose a thick, heavy, wooden one. She looked around for something to take a swing at and her eye fell on a broken VCR on a shelf in the garage. She asked Max to take it outside to the back patio for her. He asked what she was going to do with it and she told him. "Why?" he asked, looking at her as if she had lost her mind. "Because my counselor told me it would help me feel my 'mad'," she said, hoping she sounded more confident than she felt.

She selected a nice open spot on the patio. Pamela gripped the bat, lifted it over her shoulder and brought it down as hard as she could on top of the VCR. All it took was that one swing, and instantly she felt furious. She started beating that VCR and kept swinging until there were no more pieces left to fly. She hit it so hard even Max was impressed with strength he had never seen; he moved out into the grass to give her some elbow room. She didn't stop until one particularly well-placed swing actually broke the bat; its top half landed full force just below her left knee, painting a big purple bruise. Max ran over, picked up the remains of his bat and looked at her leg. "Mom, are you okay?" "Yeah, I'm fine, but I think I'll use your aluminum bat next time." They cleaned up the VCR parts that were strewn all over the patio, and when Max took them out to the trash Pamela went inside searching for more broken appliances.

That was the start of her journey to healing. She learned that stuffed or ignored anger was going to manifest itself one way or another; best to acknowledge it, get it out safely, and not let it hurt her inside, slowly poisoning her. Without the insightful help of a good counselor she trusted and knew wanted to help, she would have continued being broken. Instead, Pamela gained the tools she needed to mend her life and move forward. All that was left broken was an old wooden bat.

Chapter 47

Two weeks later Max got kicked off Ranch for fighting. Now he was back home, and Pamela had to figure out where to get him into school and how they were going to live this time around.

The first priority was to get Max enrolled in a local high school, and fast. It was mid-semester in the spring, not the best time to plug into the rhythm of high school. Max's school records – academic, attendance, behavior – would have to be gathered from two local high schools (one who had revoked his transfer after one semester), a rehab charter day school, and the boy's ranch school. He was supposed to be finishing his sophomore year. Pamela wondered how far he was behind academically and whether his credits would transfer. It seemed unthinkable to re-enroll him back in his original high school, right back in among all the old 'friends' and temptations. She considered whether he could get into Independent Academy. It had been a godsend for Lily, enabling her not only to graduate but to get a scholarship into a top university. She hoped it would be the same type of haven and hope-giver for Max.

Pamela remembered when she first heard about the Academy. Lily was going through a horrific time; once a star pupil she was having difficulty at high school. Attendance was slipping and the circumstances at school had turned quite bad for her personally. She told Pamela about Independent Academy, knew some kids who had transferred there and begged her mother to enroll her. At first Pamela said no, without even checking out the school. The thought of putting her in some kind of 'alternative' school went against every traditional bone in Pamela's body, and the fact that it was far from their house worried her greatly given the situation. But Lily was persistent, asking her to at least find out about it. Pamela mentioned it to a friend in her Sunday School class, who told her that it was a fairly new school that had opened up only a few years before. It was for at-risk students – kids who for a wide variety of reasons were considered likely to drop out, not just academic risk. Her own daughter was currently attending and doing very well. She could not sing enough praises about Independent. Pamela valued her friend's opinion greatly and she knew she wouldn't do anything for her children that wasn't first bathed in prayer.

The founder and principal had a background as Director of the US Department of Education and was determined to create a 'school of choice' environment that emphasized excellence in academics as well as personal accountability and civic duty. It was accredited, had individualized curriculum with teachers who truly cared about learning and about motivating the students to attend and learn. In the four years of its existence, a significant percentage of graduates went on to be accepted into and attend four year universities, including MIT and The University of Texas at Austin. It was a year-round school, contained students from diverse socio-economic backgrounds and all types of life experiences. If a student applying for admission was not willing to commit to regular attendance and the code of honor, primarily respect and responsibility, he wasn't accepted. The teachers gain the respect and trust of the students by their encouragement, understanding and expectations with accountability. Community service was a part of the required curriculum. The classes were small, the atmosphere both motivating and laid back against the backdrop of administrative structure. Fights were extremely rare, and the problems that plagued other public high schools were almost unheard of there in this small high school housed in an old former elementary school building on the poor and less-safe side of town. There was on-site day care for teenage mothers trying to finish school, work programs, and a smoking area outside – things not found at 'normal' high schools but that reflected the reality of the lives of the students. A limited choice of extra-curricular involvement was available - student yearbook, prom planning committee, Peer Assistance Leader (PAL) mentoring elementary kids, art. Academics were emphasized - sports programs, band, choir, orchestra were non-existent; the students there are focused on finishing high school and it takes everything they've got. At Independent the staff was dedicated to the success of each student – every step of progress, no matter how small, was celebrated and used to encourage and edify. There, teenage mothers, boys in recovery and victims of abuse or other trauma came willingly every day and were eager to do class work and homework. They learned to thrive on earning the admiration of the staff, support of their peers, and helping others through community service work. Hope abounded there. Independent Academy was not without fault, and as it grew to meet demand there were serious challenges ahead if they were to keep their admission standards high. But Pamela was proud to call her kids Independent students, blessed that this school existed in her city, and eternally grateful to the people who had encouraged her to give it a try.

Max seemed to have learned some good lessons at the Ranch. Although he was glad to be at home he was now sad that he had disappointed those at the Ranch who had worked so hard to help him. He really wanted to graduate high school, and knowing Lily's positive experience at Independent he thought it might be a good place for him as well. In order to be enrolled, Max had to convince the Asst. Principal that he could live with Independent's Code of Ethics: personal honor & integrity, choose peace over conflict, respect self and others. He had decided he could do those things, and spoke convincingly to staff. This was his fourth high school, and it was time to make it work.

He did ok for a month or so, then the old signs start showing up. Questionable friends, things missing from the house, stories that didn't add up – he was still in school but it was not looking good. At the end of June, Pamela took a weekend trip to visit Tessa. She made the decision to let Max stay at the house. It was the wrong decision. Their neighbor revealed the facts. Max had had a big party at the house, a loud late-night blowout that disturbed the neighbors and left some major debris – quite the collection of cans and bottles.

A few days after her return, Max came home late one night and asked to talk to Pamela. He had been using cocaine, and was on a very anxious "high". She didn't know why he told her except that he was so upset with himself, and knew he was out of control. He had been to an A.A. meeting, and stopped by a "friend's" house on the way home. While there, another "friend" offered him the drug and he did it. He felt so bad, despairing and wanting to come clean and tell her about it. "I keep messing up and I don't know why. I'm on a downward spiral again, I can feel it, and I'm scared."

Pamela had to call Cassie since she knew Max was using. She would have to take him in and when his drug test came back positive he would be detained. Here we go again, she thought, except this time with much more sorrow because he had had so many months of sobriety and things had been going better for a while. What was it going to take to bring the "real Max" back?

Chapter 48

Just half an hour ago she had brought her sixteen year old son in on an outstanding warrant for his arrest for a probation violation. Pamela knew where to go, where to park, what entrance to use if it was after hours, what information to bring, what not to bring – she knew the drill. She was no stranger to the juvenile jail. What she was a stranger to was this calm feeling, this matter-of-fact approach to the whole process, this reasonable demeanor with her son and the intake staff at the detention center. It had been months since they had been there, and she had hoped and prayed that stay would be his last. But he was back, and what was amazing was how she was handling it. Pamela loved her son, and on this day she could express that love by helping hold him accountable, doing her part to allow him to experience the consequences of his own actions and decisions, and for the most part detach herself from <u>his</u> feelings and emotions. Before, she would have been a trembling, teary-eyed, thoroughly anxious mess, worried about how he was feeling, when he would eat, would it be too cold, would he be able to sleep, would he cry, could he pray, would the other inmates cause him problems, what about school, what about his meds, would he call home, would he choose to see her when she visited. Now she knew he would be OK whether she was calm, cool and collected or a total basket case. How did this happen? She was still the mom, he was still the wayward son.

The difference was AlAnon. Going to meetings. Working the Steps. Getting a sponsor. It Works if You Work it. God's Plan A is other people, connecting in a healthy way with people who really can say "I know how you feel."

Pamela had attended her first Al Anon meeting under protest, unwillingly and only because Max's counselor at Intensive Out Patient told her she had to. Lola made her commit to trying it as a part of Max's treatment, saying it would help them both. Pamela did not want to go, did not have the time, had nothing to say and frankly didn't want to be around other parents whose kids were 'truly addicts' – not just good kids with a traumatic family situation like her boy. But to help Max she went. Over time she realized it was helping – helping him by helping her. She began to focus on fixing herself rather than trying to fix her son, and to see them both in the light of a more honest perspective. It was painful sometimes, but not as bad as she had feared, and the freedom of learning she could be OK even if he wasn't was the most valuable thing she experienced. What a concept – even if he was drinking and drugging, skipping school, hanging with the "bad" friends, stealing and lying, or arrested and jailed, she didn't have to feel his feelings or bear the consequences that came with those situations. Those were <u>his</u> circumstances, not hers. And detachment meant she could continue to love him despite his actions, keep praying for him, and do the best she could for him as his mom – turn him over to the One who created him and was, still and always, in control.

Pamela was on time as usual for Max's Detention Hearing the next day. She figured Judge Barker was almost as tired of seeing Max in front of his bench as they were of being there. He asked Max to view the stack of files on his desk, and compared Max's one file to a stack of five other files – both stacks were the same height. Max knew the Judge wouldn't tolerate lying or being played, and he confessed to using. He said he was doing so well he thought he could handle using. "I didn't realize how good I had it. I started hanging around with the wrong kids and messed up and ended up using," Max had confessed. The Judge told him that was the addict way – one mistake and you feel all is lost.

Cassie questioned this "annual" mess-up cycle – two years prior had been the incident where Pamela had to call the police on Max for violence. Last year it was the arrest for shoplifting when he was just five weeks away from getting off probation. Cassie thought something was going on deeper that needed to be ferreted out and dealt with in counseling. She told the Judge that Max was invested in school and his part-time job, and requested furloughs for him to go to school and work while in detention. Judge asked if Pamela was willing to do the transportation back and forth. She said yes, if Max was willing to truly invest in recovery she could do that. The Judge detained Max until he had a clean UA, hopefully for just a few days.

On the way home she thought of things to be thankful for. Thank God he could cry. Thank God he could feel and express his feelings. Thank God he was scared about being sent away. Thank God he looked vulnerable and seemed approachable. She was grateful she could observe his tears, the orange suit and ankle cuffs with compassion and sorrow but also with the conviction that he had chosen his consequences, she did not. To try to interfere with those consequences was not love – it was controlling and trying to change him, hoping he would see things her way. She had to learn to get out of God's way – Let Go and Let God – and let Him work on her son, His son, without her. It was so hard to do, but it was the thing she absolutely must do it if she wanted to aide in his recovery. This was a spiritual program, and to try to work it without God did <u>not</u> work.

I cannot save my child from his consequences

Chapter 49

She had thought it would get easier, taking Max in to be detained. But this time it was awful. She felt so horrible, almost deceitful, though she did nothing wrong. In fact, she did the right thing, the thing his Probation Officer told her to do. But this was different from calling Cassie when he was high or violent; different even from taking him to the Ranch which he hated and rebelled against but at least he knew what was coming. This time he thought he was coming in for a PO visit, and she knew they would probably detain him but he didn't suspect it. To him it would feel like they blindsided him, but in reality it was his deserved consequences finally catching up with him. He had started skipping school again, Pamela could tell he was using, he'd started breaking rules at home, and Cassie was very concerned that if they didn't come down hard on every probation violation and try to find a way to intervene in this latest downward spiral, he was not going to live much longer. Pamela was afraid she was right.

When they arrived at her office Max refused to talk, even to Cassie. When he saw his other Probation Office, Justin, he admitted, "Yes, I violated probation but not bad enough to be brought in." How could he say that, how could he feel that, when he had been told by many people many times that one more slight violation would bring him in. He still thought he could get away with it. And because today had been a good day for <u>him</u> – good at school, good with friends, good on the way to see Cassie, Pamela felt like the unjust sheriff hauling him in. Why was that? He skipped school, used hard drugs within thirty days and took the car without permission or a driver's license – all obvious violations – and yet she felt like the bad guy because she hadn't told him he may be detained when they arrived – something he knew could happen. He knew he could get detained, he just always thought it wouldn't happen to him. Then it did happen and he had immediately played the blame game. God how she hated drugs and what they do.

Cassie and she agreed that all the signs were there that he was using and about to bolt. With his seventeenth birthday coming up they had a short three week window to get him into a local lockdown rehab program that accepted kids up to sixteen years old - if they could get him in. Amazingly the program had one or two beds coming open in one week and Pamela got an interview that day with the director, who would interview Max on Monday. Cassie said it was never that quick to get into that program. Right now she knew Max thought he would get out the next day, but he was going to be surprised, hurt and very angry to hear Probation recommend residential treatment. He would look at Pamela during the

Detention Hearing and see in her eyes that she agreed. Even knowing he needed help and deserved confinement it would still hurt beyond measure to have him gone. She already missed him – his wit, his smile, his conversations, the evidence of his just being there. She wept. But he was not happy, he was skipping school and not honestly communicating with her. Her dream, that he would have a happy, normal home life, was still just a dream. And he would lose Independent Academy and his job. He would feel it was totally unfair at first. When would he realize there comes a point when even juvenile judges play hardball and your actions catch up with you? She would pray and grieve; drugs had stolen most of his youth and she couldn't get it back. She hoped he would choose recovery. *God, I want my drug-free boy back.*

Chapter 50

Pamela was singing this afternoon - Praise God from whom all blessings flow! She was amazed at the extreme range of emotions within forty-eight hours. Max was in detention and she was able to visit him today, just the two of them in the visitation room. He could feel, and was thinking of his future. Genuine tears flowed freely about being locked up, missing school at Independent, missing the school break with his friends, not wanting to be locked up over his seventeenth birthday, wishing he could be back on the Ranch: " I didn't know how good I had it." She loved him so much, but she could only work her program. She was able to be glad he could feel and cry, for that was progress. She could observe his sincere sorrow without shedding tears of her own. She had shed billions of tears, and now it was his turn. She had serenity because she knew God had a plan for her precious son. As they said in the program God has no grandchildren. She knew that her prayers were heard and would be answered according to God's will and timing, not hers or Max's. She could empathize; tell Max of her sadness and missing him at home, express her hope that he'd be released to resume his job and high school when the time was right. She could hug this thin, sad, 6'2" young man with all her strength, tell him she loved and missed him and truly mean it, and then walk out to go home to have her own life. She could encourage her son, make sure he knew she would do whatever was in her power to help, and then leave. She still thought about whether he was in a cell alone, or could sleep at night, was he hot or cold, would the nurses be kind if he was sick, but she no longer cried herself to sleep over those questions. He was in juvenile detention because of his actions, not because she was the one who had physically driven him there. The real guilt over her past mistakes as a mom when he was young had been completely turned over to the One who forgave and by the power of that same One she would no longer let false guilt take up residence in her heart. In the midst of sorrow and pain and regret and what-ifs and discouragement, she was able to honestly say, "Nevertheless, not my will but Thine be done." The pain was still there, and more tears would fall, but the intensity of those paralyzing sobs of grief over a child going down the wrong path was now born by the only One with the strength to bear that kind of pain. In her experience, trying to navigate life without Him simply didn't work.

The next night when Max made his evening call home, most of it was spent in tears. He was probably the oldest boy there, how awful it must be to cry in front of the others. He was feeling like he couldn't take it, Pamela could tell. He didn't know what was going to happen, was hurt because Cassie couldn't talk with him before the weekend, and the inmates were telling him how awful the Options program was so he already had a bad taste in his mouth about going there. It was hard to hear the silent sobbing over the phone, imagine the tear-stained face and know how much he hated being locked up. But it was harder to know that he's still not quite ready to do the hard work – A.A., counseling – to help him get out of this pattern. 'Tough love' didn't begin to describe it.

"Don't look back, your future's ahead of you."

Juvenile Justice Staff Member

Lily's Story
Part Three

Chapter 51

Lily was still living on her own, working and attending the local community college. She and Pamela stayed in touch. She had had a lot of counseling, most of it during the immediate aftermath of the trauma. She had stuck with her group therapy group for a while and was doing well but school and work made scheduling appointments challenging. She had made progress followed by pockets of ordinary time, but peeling back some of the layers didn't change the fact there was still an onion. Even after all her progress, Lily began to exhibit some signs that concerned Pamela. Lily went back into counseling for a few months, then stopped. She started working a lot of overtime, and signed up for more college classes than usual. By this time Pamela recognized the signs that feelings inside were bubbling up out of Lily's control. Lily immersed herself in school and work to keep busy, trying to prevent unwelcome thoughts and feelings. She had started drinking and hanging out with friends who were known to drink a lot; sometimes at night she would call Pamela, sad about something and wanting to talk.

Pamela got the call one night around 2:30 a.m. that Lily was at a friend's house, had a knife and was threatening to kill herself. She drove across town, praying for God to stay Lily's hand and spare her life. Surely Lily hadn't made this progress for it to end like this. When Pamela arrived, she found Lily curled up in a ball on the sidewalk outside, softly moaning for help. Pamela's heart went out to her – soul damage was so deadly. Her daughter had come to another festering wound that must be brought to light, cleansed, and allowed time to heal. Lily let Pamela help her up and get her into the car. That night Lily spoke more of her pain than she ever had before. She talked of how much it hurt, how she wanted to be happy but couldn't, how she wanted to want to live, of her love for God and Jesus who had saved her, questioning why must the pain hurt so but knowing that God loved her. She spoke of her love for Pamela, how she wanted to make her proud and not cause her pain. But mainly she asked for help – over and over again she would cry, "I need help, I need help". What strength of spirit to ask for help! When she was so down she could hardly believe help could be found, and the world told her to just pull herself up by her bootstraps and not to show any weakness. Praise God Lily was able to ask for help!

When they got home Lily was exhausted. Pamela put her to bed, anxiously wondering if she should have taken her straight to the hospital. But Lily was over twenty-one now and would have to admit herself. A new school semester had just started, decisions would have to be made, and the fact she let Pamela take her home suggested she was willing to receive help. Pamela would need to keep watch, pray and be ready to talk with her in the morning. She slept in the next room so she could easily hear if she stirred. The night passed without further incident and Pamela was up early the next morning, seeking the Lord's guidance and checking local listings for a psychiatric hospital. There was only one facility of this type left in their city, and she didn't know if they had any beds available.

Chapter 52

When Lily woke the feelings of despair were less intense but still there. She and Pamela talked and agreed she needed to admit herself for care. They arranged for her to withdraw from school and called her boss to get a leave of absence from work. They spent time just being together, distracted by a light-hearted movie on TV and enjoyed simply feeling close like they had in the early days when the craziness began. Back then, often Lily could find comfort in just being at home with Pamela, reading and playing games or watching a movie. Those days that Pamela took off work to be there for Lily had been very precious. She was so happy to be able to do something and to show that she valued her daughter over and above the commitment to her job.

Later that day when it was time to go Lily seemed reluctant, and Pamela wondered if she would go through with it. But she did. It was a very different admitting experience this time. As an adult, Lily was responsible for all the admission paperwork and her interview was strictly confidential, Pamela was not included. After she was admitted, they let Pamela accompany her to the adult suicide watch floor. Again, they removed all laces from shoes, all compacts with mirrors, all drawstrings from pants, camera cell phones (for confidentiality), and would allow no visitors that weren't on the list. It was a very scary time; somehow they both knew this really was serious, truly life or death. The demons were back and battling for possession of their lost ground.

Lily stayed in the hospital for a week and on her second night there attempted to strangle herself with a bed sheet. She was taken back to the lock down part of that floor for two nights, to stay there on doctor's orders until she was deemed safe enough to move back to the main section. There simply was no way to make lockdown a pleasant place. In that area were the deeply disturbed residents; being around them was frightening and disturbing. Pamela spent much of that week with Lily – visiting hours were generous. Lily wanted to do jigsaws puzzles and they spent hours at the sitting room tables putting together the colorful ones Pamela had purchased. They talked about what life was like, what her options would be when she got out, and her future. One day she asked to speak with Pamela in front of her counselor, and it was powerful. Through her tears she spoke of how her acting-out behaviors had been to try and manage the pain or find her worth. For the first time ever, in words spoken to Pamela, she connected the abuse by her father to her feelings and behaviors. It was a major breakthrough. For her to recognize and acknowledge that what happened to her was not her fault, she did nothing wrong to deserve it, that it was the aftermath of trauma that had driven her to unhealthy behaviors was a huge step. Pamela was so proud of her; such difficult things to speak but such great strides in healing because she spoke them.

In the remaining days of her stay, Lily worked with her doctor and Pamela to form an exit plan. She would move back home, return to a light work schedule, and wait a semester to resume classes. She wanted the structure and accountability of home, and agreed to participate in a workshop on healing. In a way, this was a more fragile time than her days as an adolescent. She knew she had to make the hard choices in life now to get on the path to wholeness, and no one else could do it for her. It was up to her to be responsible with medications while they were needed, maintain healthy relationships and ditch the harmful ones, and be able to confidently discern between the two.

What if Pamela hadn't chosen to believe? Would Lily be alive? If so, what kind of life would it be? Their path had been hard, Pamela mused, but she wouldn't have traded any of it if it meant not having her beautiful, loving, sweet-spirited daughter.

Max's Story
Part Three

Chapter 53

Options was a unique program. Housed in one of the juvenile justice complex buildings, it was a lock-up facility for juveniles sixteen years of age and under that involved accredited high school curriculum, a twelve step substance abuse program and behavior modification techniques. The director was an imposing man, highly educated and deeply committed to the principles of recovery. He was strictly a by-the-rules leader, and consistently held the boys accountable for their words and actions. His influence on Max was profound and he earned his respect in his seven months there. He firmly planted recovery seeds in Max and gave him the tools to graduate high school and go out into the work world.

At first it was hard for Max to be grateful that he had made it into Options instead of youth prison. Life at Options involved a shaved head, a small cement room with metal cot for a bed, and very close quarters with other teenage boys of all races, most of whom had some serious attitudes. Personal freedom was non-existent, and structure was rigid. The realization that he would be there for a minimum of six months depending on his progress was a bitter pill to swallow, and there were times in the beginning when Pamela got the call not to come for the weekend visit because his behavior had lost him that privilege. But in time he began to be a more willing participant, and Pamela learned to look forward to the weekly family group sessions on Wednesday nights. They received not just information on addiction and recovery, but took part in exercises on how to communicate within the family unit and how to better relate to one another, appreciate each other. Slowly Max's resentment, rebellion and resistance to authority was being chipped away – a process that would take years but got a good start in that place.

This would be another year without Max at the family table for Thanksgiving, or Christmas Eve candlelight service, or waking up with sibling and cousins to stockings and presents on Christmas morning. But the visits during the holidays held promise. Max used pretty paper to fashion a Christmas card, writing of his love for the family and hope for the future. That was a gift in itself. However the truly amazing thing was the Christmas play he wrote and directed, persuading eight of the other residents not only to participate but to work together to pull off the final production. The play, entitled "I'll Be Home for Christmas," centered around an army company in wartime and how the soldiers' individual decisions impacted their fellow soldiers and family members back home. It had all the elements of an engaging drama – action, intrigue, deceit, tragic death, consequences, rehabilitation and recovery, and reconciliation. The acting and dramatic reading was what you would expect from teenage boys not trained in theatre but it was quite entertaining. The fact that they worked as a group to present a play when there was nothing in it for them except the hope of applause from a small group of parents was amazing. Max told Pamela later that at the rehearsal, right before the parents came, he had almost given up and thought there was no way the guys would cooperate. But they did, and she was proud of their effort and courage.

By early spring he had successfully completed seven months at Options; it was time for Max to come home. Four more months passed and found him a high school graduate of Independent Academy and released from juvenile probation for good. He was working, paying his own rent and bills, and on his way to adulthood. His road was still rocky at times, but she had learned that it was *his* road, not hers. She would love him enough to allow him to experience the consequences of his actions and learn from them, even if they are painful, and know that in doing so she was helping. She was free to feel her feelings, and grow in the process - one day at a time.

As she said goodbye to members of the juvenile justice staff she had become close to during the last three and one-half years, she thanked them for all they had done to help keep her son alive and get him on the right path. A note she received from one of the Probation Officers a few weeks later was a special treasure.

Dear Pamela,

Thank you for the kind words. It is these words that we can only hope for when we get into this business. Without them I think we would always feel like we are spinning our wheels. Thank you again and keep smiling. "A mother is her child's only true friend, who will never leave when others who claim to be the 'best of friends' will". My mother told me this when I had my most terrible moments as a teen. As for my plight to work with the youth in the capacity that I do now ... it will continue. I am taking a field unit position with the County Juvenile Probation Department in another state. So, I continue….. please be safe and never falter in your love for your children. *They will surprise you someday……*

Justin

Chapter 54

Pamela put down her pen and sat back thoughtfully. Was it what she needed to say? Did the letter convey all the hope and help she intended? Her Al Anon sponsor had asked her to reach out to her sister who lived out of state. She knew Pamela's story and wanted her sister to have the type of support that only someone who's "been there" can give. Pamela had chosen to write a letter to this mother with teens in crisis who was just starting down a road she had already traveled and knew only too well. Email wasn't the perfect form of communication, and a phone call would put her on the spot to talk to a stranger about her personal problems. But a handwritten letter was different. That could much better convey tone, personal interest and empathy without requiring an immediate response. The letter was extremely long, though not as long as the famous "Joan Anderson letter" written by Neal Cassady, but Pamela couldn't bring herself to scrap one word of it. She had been through so much and those experiences she had a *lot* of words to share.

She picked up the white legal pad and re-read what she had written.

Dear Jesse,

Your sister is my beloved Al Anon sponsor and I am delighted to reach out to you at her request. I've been down the road you are starting, and if the lessons I've learned can help you in any way then I offer them freely to you.

You may be where I was seven years ago. As adults involved in the daily lives of our kids, sometimes it's hard for us to see the signs of trouble. My journey involved numerous crises and tests of faith. A child who gets involved with drugs, is arrested, runs away from home, makes outcry of sexual abuse, or is hospitalized for an overdose or suicide attempt presents a crisis of unbelievable proportions. I wish I had had something or someone to tell me what to <u>do</u>, what to expect, when the signs started showing up in my home. Having some tools and a close relationship with Christ can mean the difference between survival and defeat. In parenting there are no guarantees - every child and situation is different. I share some of my experiences here as practical suggestions, options you might consider. Keep in mind that the words "he" or "him" in my examples could just as easily read "she" or "her" depending on your situation.

Lying

Good kids lie at times. Even with the best parenting. But habitual lying means a deeper problem exists, one that needs to be addressed with urgency. I raised my kids in a healthy Christian church, taught them right from wrong, good manners, to always be respectful and honest. We had a loving extended family that supported those values and helped instill them in my son and daughter. Lily was never very good at lying, even as a small child. Max, on the other hand, took lying to a new level, almost an art form. For him, lying became second nature; he lied when the truth would have served him better. He lied the first time I found a bag of pot and a pipe made of modeling clay in his room when he was in seventh grade, and he lied about practically everything for the next four years.

When you realize your teen has lied in a big way and there is no way to deny it, you feel hurt, angry, betrayed, shock and confused, like a failure as a parent. The broken trust is devastating because it takes only seconds to destroy and years to re-build.

If your teen is a habitual liar, recognize it and deal with it. Don't try to rationalize his excuses - he's under a lot of stress, he felt really bad that he lied to you, his friend pressured him into it, he was being loyal to a friend – it's a never ending list. If you do, you are making things worse and sending the message that lying works. Acknowledge it, address it, and hold him accountable with consequences. Once you know he has lied repeatedly, adopt the stance that if his lips are moving he's lying and let him know up front that you will always verify anything he says or does until over time he has proven himself trustworthy again.

You can love him while holding him accountable – letting him face the pain of his own actions IS love. The inconvenience of enforcing consequences is harder on you than it is on him. But hold firm on this one. If there is a problem and you tolerate dishonesty in any area, it's going to be almost impossible to help him when the crisis breaks.

Don't beat yourself up about believing his lies either. Some kids, and addicts in particular, are excellent at fooling and manipulating even the savviest parents. You have to accept it and do your part not to enable or excuse it. Let him know that regaining his credibility is critically important, and totally up to him. Honesty – model it, insist on it, maintain your standards.

Skipping School

Even the best of kids can get caught breaking rules, skipping or get caught up in circumstances that result in being suspended from school – once. You know your teen, you have to evaluate what you know and handle it accordingly.

But if you've gotten a call about absenteeism or he's been suspended more than once for skipping, or found with drugs / paraphernalia or with kids who have drugs, take action. Meet with the principal, the campus cop, your kid's teachers and counselors. Make sure they KNOW you care and you want to hear from them about anything. Take your teen with you if he'll go; let him know you are going to stay in touch with the school. Set a day a week to pick him up and have lunch during his lunch period.   Know the names of his teachers and their contact information; call or email them often. Give them your home, work, cell and email. Ask about grades, homework assignments, upcoming projects, attitude, and attendance. Don't depend on the administration records, especially regarding attendance. Often they are weeks behind in entering data and it's not until report cards arrive that you realize he's had excessive absenteeism. If he is skipping with the same person or group try to talk to them; enlist their help if possible. Let your teen know all you're doing to hold him accountable. Get involved in school – volunteer in the office or library, offer to prepare docs or study aids at home for a teacher. Your chances of helping your teen stay in and succeed at school are much greater if you are a known parent at school. I'm talking about in addition to Back to School night or conferences called by the teacher. You can't prevent your teen from skipping or failing or even being transferred - my son lasted one semester at a school I worked hard to have him transferred into, only to have the principal refuse to answer my call and letter and revoke his transfer for excessive truancy and failing grades without ever talking to me about it. BUT you can do your part. Ultimately it will matter and does help for your teen to know you are involved in school matters.

Runaway

Typically a child is not officially classified a runaway if she has not been missing for twenty-four hours or more. As a parent, we worry if they've been missing for one or two hours. Each of my children ran away from home during our crazy years –

fortunately not at the same time! How you handle this one depends somewhat on the child, age, gender and the circumstances. I was frantically worried about my fifteen year old daughter when she ran away because she was suffering from Post-Traumatic Stress Disorder and having suicidal thoughts. Being a female automatically put her in greater danger, and I had no idea where she had gone or who she was with. I was less worried about my fourteen year old son when he ran away because he left a note, I knew his probation officer would help me try to find him, and I figured I'd hear from him sooner than later because he'd need something from me. I'll describe my two experiences - you can take what you need and leave the rest.

<u>Lily</u>

I came home after getting off early from work the day before Thanksgiving. Lily was gone. Her little brother didn't know where she went. I called the parents of some of her friends and they had not heard from her. I asked them to call with any news. Shortly I heard back from one of her best friends. All the girl knew was Lily left in a car with some guy she didn't know. My child was gone and I had no idea where. Her clothes and medicine were all in her room, so obviously it was not planned. I searched her room, found no clues. I called other friends, casually asking if they had seen her and they hadn't. After about an hour and a half, I got a brief call from Lily saying she was ok but she couldn't tell me who she was with, where she was, or when she would be home. I spent a sleepless night, crying, praying, clutching my Bible for comfort (it helps), and in the morning called the police and reported her as a runaway. It was Thanksgiving Day.

I had to decide whether to keep to my plan of driving to my mother's to be with family. It was agonizing – what if I left and she showed up at home, needing my help or medical attention? On the other hand, what if I stayed home the entire four day holiday and she didn't come back? And what about my other child, who was upset too and ready to go visit his cousins? Ultimately I decided to go ahead and make the drive. It was only forty miles away; she had my cell phone and my mother's number if she needed me, and she knew I'd come to get her if she called. If the police picked her up they knew how to contact me. It wasn't fair to my son to miss the trip, and I absolutely could not stay at home and pace in front of the phone waiting to hear from her. She returned home four days later, on the day after we got back into town. We dealt with the situation and fortunately she did not run away again.

Looking back, I wouldn't change how I handled it. It was absolutely the right thing to do in that situation. Even though I was worried sick I had to recognize that the situation, especially over a holiday, involved a lot more people than just Lily. She had made the decision to leave, I had no way to find her, and I knew she knew how to find me or find help if she wanted it. If I had been planning to drive further or be gone for a longer time I might have stayed home, but it was best for my son and me to try and keep some routine during all the turmoil.

I had slept very little or not at all while Lily was gone. When she returned I felt relief that she was safe, then anger at what she had put us through. But my job at this point was to assess the situation and determine my next move. It was late at night and we were both exhausted, so I decided to simply say that I would address the issue the following morning when we were both rested, after making it clear that I expected her to stay at home through the night. If this happens to you, you have to decide when to talk about what happened. Be sure you have thought out ahead of time what you plan to say and how you plan to say it. Consider her attitude, her actions upon returning home, her degree of sincerity or rebellion, what emotions are displayed, and your own limits before deciding what the consequences will be. If you are in a custody or legal battle, or involved with a county agency, you need to know how your actions will affect those areas as well. And whatever punishment you decide on, determine to stick with it and follow through or don't even discuss it.

A friend of mine once asked for advice on what to do when her son returned home after running away the night before. Here is what I wrote to her.

"My dear friend,

I am so sorry for how hard things are for you. I can sense the incredible weight of the situation on you. How disheartening to have to face that treatment from a child you brought into the world and whom you love with all your heart.

First, try to eat well and sleep as best you can while he's away. You're fatigued already, so just give it your best effort to take care of YOU. Second, I think you were 100% right in your conversation with your son. You have given in as much as you can, and it is obvious that a later bedtime, more phone and computer privileges aren't working to change his behavior. He is being disrespectful and as much as it hurts you must continue to stand up for your position. You have raised him better than that, and he knows it, but he's chosen to be rebellious. He says he wants to be treated like an adult, but he's acting like a child having a tantrum who needs supervision. He has shown he isn't ready for more privileges by not respecting the ones he already has. I doubt he truly wants to be treated like an adult - adults have to provide their own transportation, their own food and shelter, and be accountable in life. But he does know how to push your buttons, as my son did and as most of them do. Stick to your statement; if he bucks his punishment then he can do without computer access or transportation that isn't absolutely necessary, etc. You are responsible to provide food, clothing, shelter and love; those other things are luxuries.

All of us as moms have 'failures' because no one is perfect, but these things that are happening are NOT because of any failure on your part. You've gone above and beyond to provide for your children, going without things yourself. You have tried to help them emotionally, academically, and financially and from what I can see you are doing a great job. You just don't have anyone standing there to remind you of that at the moment! But you are drained, and of course you have no fight left - there's hardly any 'you' left.

I can still remember how scared I was when faced with the possibility of losing my children to Eduardo in a custody battle and how much that worried me for their sake. I cannot imagine how much you must be hurting. All I know is that you have to keep on keeping on. I've learned that when I have no fight left, when I am just done with it all, I can turn all the hurt, fear, fatigue and worry over to the Lord. That is how I made it through. God has all the strength in the world, and He is just waiting to bear these burdens for you. Crazy as it sounds, I've sensed His presence and help more when my times were dark than at any other time. And it's really true that He speaks through His Word. I read the Psalms when I was the most scared or worried - especially Psalms 46, or 27, or 18. I would read the words as a prayer, taking it very personally, and found that only the kind of peace that comes from outside of myself was able to soothe my soul and help me wait on the outcome.

You must not lose heart. Just do the best you can each moment and trust God to work things out. I don't know why He allows some of the hard things we have to go through, but I do know I don't have the big picture, I can only see from my viewpoint. Let go of the things you can't control, continue to be a good, firm mom to your kids and stand firm on your convictions, and never, ever, ever give up hope. Ever.

Take care of you, Pam"

<u>Max</u>

I woke up in the middle of the night and by now it was habit to check my son's room to see if he was there. Sure enough he was gone, but this time he'd left a note on his pillow. It was winter, and cold outside – fresh snow was on the ground. The car was still in the garage but his bike was gone. Even a jacket wouldn't keep him warm for long. I didn't want to call a friends' house at one in the morning and alarm a parent, and I wasn't sure where to start anyway. I knew he had lots of friends, and even though he was only fourteen he was big for his age and wouldn't be in immediate danger like a young girl would be. I knew I would have to wait until a decent daylight hour to call anyone, so I grabbed my worn Bible and began to pray - tears too, of course, and no sleep. Around five a.m. he called, crying, saying he wanted to come home and would I come and get him. I said yes and drove the short ten-minute drive to an apartment complex nearby to pick him up. He was very remorseful, said he kept on doing "stupid stuff" and didn't know why. I was just glad he was safe and back at home.

I handled my son's runaway experience much differently. By that time he had been on probation for several months. Probation rules included curfew and being accountable at all times to your parent. I knew his Probation Officer had to be called, but I didn't want him to be locked up in juvenile detention again. I also knew he probably hadn't been truthful about his reason for leaving, and if I let him get away with this episode without repercussions it would just be worse next time. I called his PO and she had me bring him in to spend the weekend in detention. Some kids have to learn the REALLY hard way, not just the hard way, and each time I did the right thing it helped him a little bit. He eventually learned that I was not going to tolerate outright defiance and illegal activity from a child living in my home.

<u>Arrested</u>

This is never easy to talk about, and the first time it happens the shock can be enough to nearly disable you. No one wants to get prepared for a child's arrest. But there is a process, and I wish had known a little about that process so I could have gotten through it better.

My son's first arrest happened away from our house. Here's what you can expect if this happens to you. You'll get the call from the police department that your child has been detained or arrested. Get the person's name, their direct call back number and the exact location of the facility. Ask if your child is being charged with a crime or just detained for questioning. Ask what you need to bring with you and if he is being released to you. He will have been handcuffed, driven to the jail facility, fingerprinted, searched, and any personal belongings confiscated. He will be treated like a criminal, but the staff at juvenile detention centers can be very kind; many of them have known kids in the system and want to help. You'll need to take these things with you:

Your driver's license

Any medication the child is on, in the original prescription container

Your child's Social Security Number or Driver's License Number, if applicable

If he is being charged with a crime and detained one or more nights, ask with what crime(s) he is being charged. Ask what information his school will need and how his schoolwork will be handled while he is detained. Ask about the visitation procedure and obtain a copy of the guidelines. If he is going to be in for weeks, ask if he can receive mail and if so how it should be addressed. Get the phone number for the intake desk. Ask if a detention hearing has been set, and if one has not ask who will contact you with details and when you can expect to hear from them.

I've only had to call the cops on my child one time, and it was one of the hardest things I've ever done. It was also a good thing for both of us.

My son was using and dealing pot at the time, and his behavior toward me had gotten out of control. One afternoon he came home high, began cursing and threatening me, and I was afraid he would get violent. I could no longer tolerate that behavior and I had warned him if it happened again I would call the police. So I did.

When I made the call, he quickly packed a backpack and took off on his bike – the police car passed him on his bike as they came to the house. When they arrived I told them he had left on his bike, and they chased him, caught him, and brought him home.

The officers who responded to my call discussed the situation and Max's history with me while he was restrained in the squad car. They asked me questions about my concern for my safety, family history, custody issues, and any legal history with the child. They asked detailed questions as to violence, drugs, family circumstances, things along that line. Max had personal items on him at the time of arrest – cell phone, backpack, bicycle – so they asked if they could leave those with me. That saved me the hassle of trying to retrieve those items later.

They had to determine whether the situation warranted taking Max into custody. They asked if I wanted him arrested or just talked to and left at home. My son was caught with several ounces of marijuana and a nice chunk of cash, but in our county that is so common the police officer said it might not be enough for him to even be detained overnight. He let me decide whether to have Max detained. I did not want my son back in jail, but I had also taken the stand that I would NOT tolerate drugs in my home so I asked them to take him in and book him. They drove away with my son in the back of the cruiser, cussing me and making hand gestures as the squad car drove off. One of the officers made sure I saw the gestures he was making - I think he knew I was having a hard time staying strong and wanted me to see that my son needed confinement.

The drama of having the police at my house was a new experience for me. The speeding police car with its flashing lights, the authority of the uniforms, the sight of my child handcuffed was way more 'excitement' than I ever wanted. To make it worse I was close to my neighbors and I knew there was no way they could avoid seeing what was going on at our house. Even in the midst of my fear and worry about my son I was embarrassed and wondered how I would respond to their questions. One sweet neighbor called and simply said she saw my son being driven away in the police car, was their anything she could do. The young man who lived next door to me came over the next day and was very kind, telling me that he had been through something similar as a teenager and expressed his sympathy. At least I didn't have to endure critical neighbors on top of my embarrassment.

I learned that it's ok to cry while talking to the police. It's a tough deal and emotions are right at the surface. They are used to it; I was not the first one they'd seen in this situation. I was as matter of fact as I could be when stating what happened – they needed to be clear on the offense, not my feelings about what happened.

Jesse, stand your ground – DO NOT tolerate drug use or possession of drugs in your home. It will only get worse if you don't maintain a zero tolerance position. Call someone you can trust to talk about it - your mom, your best friend, a prayer partner. You need support. Not talking about it or trying to cover it up will only add to your stress. At work, tell only those that need to know for the purposes of your time off work. Do not spill your guts to everyone at work. Not everyone is sympathetic, not everyone is interested in your personal life, and not everyone can keep from gossip or ridicule.

My daughter was brought home by the police one night, quite to my surprise. When it happened to me, I was awakened by the doorbell at 1:30 a.m. by a policewoman who asked if I had a child named Lily and was she out. I replied, "No, she's in her room." The policewoman asked to see, so I took her to Lily's room. I opened the door, and the bed was occupied. The policewoman asked me to go over and check – and sure enough, there was her favorite childhood life-size doll. Then I noticed one of the windows was open. It was only then that the policewoman told me she had picked up Lily for a curfew violation in our neighborhood park. She had known all along my teenage daughter had snuck out and was wandering in the dark alone, but she let me discover it for myself. The impact was much more dramatic than just ringing the doorbell and presenting Lily, and I learned quickly about my naïve assumptions.

I listened carefully to the officer. Many times you can get a quick education and benefit from their experience. I knew to ask if Lily was being ticketed or charged with anything and for a copy of any citation. I asked if she was found alone or with others.

When the officer left, I had to assess whether Lily could be safely left alone. If not I would have to stay up until she had fallen asleep. I had to make sure she was safe and that she did not leave again. It was a school night so I tried to prepare myself mentally to drag us both out of bed in the morning. If this happens to you, TRY to get some sleep – warm milk, soothing music, prayer, reading – whatever it takes. You'll need to think clearly the next day.

If your child is high on drugs, lecturing is useless. Save your words until they have a chance of being heard. Decide on your consequences before you talk to your child the next day. When you talk, stay calm and be very clear about your expectations. For example, begin with, "I expect you to stay in the house all night every night after bedtime." If she has a 'story', to tell, listen; you may learn something that will help you in the future. But be aware, you're likely being manipulated.

There are a number of non-traffic or alcohol related offenses a minor can be cited for. These include but are not limited to:

- Violation of park curfew

- Minor in possession of tobacco

- Minor in possession of alcohol

- Truancy

- Defacing public property

- Possession of small amount of marijuana in a drug-free (school) zone

- Possession of drug paraphernalia

- Possession of illegal narcotics

If your child is caught violating any of these laws, he will receive a citation at the time of the crime. Unless your child is on probation or forthcoming you won't know about it until you get a notice in the mail. Note to self: get to the mail before my child.

The main thing to know about these citations is that since your child is a minor, taking care of the tickets involves you. A lot. Your child committed the offense, but you are responsible for his actions since he is a minor. It can mean money to pay fines, time off work to attend hearings, time off work to take your child to classes and/or community service to fulfill court ordered requirements, money to pay for the classes, and scheduled meetings with school administrators. It can also mean time off work to stay home with a child who is ordered to stay away from school but who must be supervised at home. There are truant officers who check up on these things, and they can arrive at your home any time of the day or night. When court dates are set for the tickets, you must be there with your child. Make sure the court administrator communicates with the juvenile probation department if your child is on probation – you will have to keep in touch with both offices to make sure this happens and records are properly documented.

Just like adults, juveniles need legal representation to assure their rights if their arrest leads to charges. If the court advises that you do not qualify for a free court-appointed attorney, you have several options: hire an attorney, consult your county's legal aid office for free services available to you, or take no action on your child's behalf. When Max was arrested I wanted the benefit of legal advice to help my child. Before you obtain a lawyer for your child, consult with your child's PO. Ask questions.

- Was your child read his rights at the time of arrest?

- Is the arrest report readily available to your PO and you?

- Are the charges valid? Maybe he was guilty of some charges, but not others – get clarification.

- What about fees, now and later.

- What are your child's options? Why?

Try to obtain a lawyer familiar with juvenile court and its judges. A family friend may desire to help but may not be the best one for this task. As with counselors, word of mouth referrals are best. It should be someone who has you and your child's trust.

Juvenile Probation

If your child is placed on juvenile probation, the rules of juvenile probation will rule your life. Your child's Probation Officer will become your co-parent. Try to get a good one, one with experience and a heart to help kids, one who's not overloaded beyond his or her capability and whose hours are not defined by "eight to five" but by need. If your county has a Child Advocacy Center your child may get a court representative advocate assigned to him. A good Child Advocacy court representative can make or break your child's progress.

When your child is in the juvenile system, your life becomes directed by Detention Hearings, court appearances, visitation, school liaisons, drug testing, judges, PO visits and recommendations, and paperwork. Prepare as best you can for time off work. For example, a DH can start at 9:00 a.m. and depending on when your child is on the docket it could mean a half day or more off work. If your child violates probation and is arrested or detained repeatedly you'll need a very understanding and caring boss.

Work with the PO and within the system. Your goal is to get your child back on track in life.

Commit to cooperating with probation rules. Enforce curfew and restriction. Call the PO when your child violates any probation rule. Be reasonable –5 minutes late for curfew is not the same as sneaking out after curfew – but don't ignore violations.

Always be there in court for your child. You may be saying, "I work two jobs, I can't make it" or "I have transportation or health issues, it's too difficult." If you have a child then you must be there for him. Make every effort, impose on family and friends, work out a deal with your work – you can get back to normal later. You only get one shot at raising them when they are teenagers. Judges do notice which ones have involved parents and which ones don't.

Visit your child when he's detained. Even if it's inconvenient, even if you miss the first group and have to wait outside for thirty minutes, even if you're embarrassed to see someone you know on staff (that happened to me), even if he says he doesn't want to see you. He DOES. Be a parent, know his heart as best you can, and know how much he hates you seeing him like this. When you get a chance at a visitation table alone with your child, uplift him – even if only to say "I miss you, I'm glad to see you", then listen. Not to the surface things, but to what those surface things mean. It's awful to go to bed when your child is in juvenile detention; the only thing worse is being that child.

The social side of probation is hard. You are on probation too. If your child is on "house arrest" it means he's released to your home if you are there 24/7. Unless you are able to work remote you will have to be off work. It's difficult to schedule meetings, lunch or doctor appointments in advance because juvenile court takes precedence and you never know when he'll be detained and you have a hearing to attend. Just be as honest and professional as you can while being discreet. Always be open to positive things that can happen at the last minute, even when it looks like there is no hope. Be flexible, gracious, and patient, and know that God is in control. A judge once said to my son, "You have been touched by the hand of God" because of the reprieve he received. Judges have children too.

Drugs

The line between "normal" teenage rebellion and a teen in trouble is a fine one. "Experimenting" with drugs can shift to addiction in a heartbeat. My son started smoking pot when he was twelve, and by the time he was fourteen he was a full blown addict. His drugs of choice at first were primarily marijuana and alcohol; during the worst years he was into cocaine, a variety of pills, and speed.

Our journey involved arrests for a variety of crimes that placed him in the juvenile justice system for about four years. Eventually he made it off probation and out of that system, but during that time he spent many weeks in detention, was on a Boy's Ranch for six months, did seven months in a County lockup program for juveniles that was also a rehab facility, and attended four different high schools, including one that revoked his transfer because of his behavior. He was dealing drugs, and at the time I didn't know how dangerous the people were that he was in business with. I found out only recently that he almost didn't live through one deal where he tried to steal from his sources. All of this happened between the time he was twelve and eighteen. I am blessed to be able to tell you that today he is alive and well and active in his recovery program. But he is still an addict, and the pull of disease is strong.

If I had had this checklist when my son's drinking and drugging began, I could have checked off every single one. But I didn't consider all these things together; it truly never occurred to me that my son would even experiment with drugs, much less become an addict. When it is your child, the precious little one you gave birth to, watched grow up and love – it just seems incomprehensible. Now that my son is grown and by God's grace has so far survived this disease, I can look back and see how naïve I was not to put it all together.

Maybe you aren't sure if your teen is in trouble. You may want to look over this checklist I made to help you decide whether you need to take action. If your gut tells you there is a problem, don't ignore it. That's reason enough for concern.

Is There a Crisis?

• Is your teen accountable to you for who he's with and where?

• Does your teen lie? Is he good at it?

• Are his grades slipping, or failing?

• Has he been skipping school?

• Does he smoke cigarettes? Ever find a lighter in his pockets or backpack?

• Are his friends his age? Older? Do you know them? Do you know their parents?

• Do you have an uneasy feeling or outright distrust of his friends, even if their behavior toward you seems friendly and respectful?

• Have his friends / sleep hours / behavior patterns changed?

• Have things disappeared from your house / purse / car and you can't account for them?

• Does he sneak out? Are you sure?

• Is there unsupervised time at home with friends of the opposite sex?

• Does he participate in any sports or extracurricular activities? Are you sure?

• Does he have a hobby or obvious interest that he pursues? (For example, bike riding, collecting, working with tools, sports, music, reading, working with animals)

• Does he regularly take over the counter cold or allergy medication?

• Have you ever discovered drugs / paraphernalia or alcohol in his room?

• If so, did he say "it's not mine, I'm holding it for a friend" or "I don't know what that is or where it came from"?

- Have you looked at the computer lately? Does he have un-monitored Internet access? What sites does he visit?

- Does he have access to your credit cards? Are you sure?

- Does he have an over-abundance of markers? Do you see doodles of the same design over and over? Have you ever seen bags of nozzles, or caps from spray paint cans?

- Has he started frequently coming home late?

- Has he begun to take walks for no particular reason?

- Do you ever see him crack a book or study?

- Does he tell you "I never have any homework"?

- Does your teen get to the mail and / or answering machine before you do?

- If you keep alcohol at home, is it accessible to your teen? Have you checked the liquor cabinet lately?

- Have you ever gotten in your car and thought the settings didn't seem exactly right? Ever checked the mileage between bedtime and when you leave in the morning? Even if the only other person at home is fourteen and doesn't have a driving permit?

- Does he prefer his older siblings' friends?

- You've probably provided him a cell phone. Do you know all the numbers stored in it? Do you let him pass code you out of it? Does he make or receive phone calls after you go to bed?

- Does he clean his room sometimes without you asking? Have you ever checked the trash afterwards?

- Have your credit cards or cell phone ever been missing?

- Do you and your teen ever just have a conversation?

- What do other parents, church family, your family and neighbors comment about your teen?

- Does he deny all when confronted with any of your suspicions?

- Does he curse you?

• Have you noticed he has cash that you didn't provide, or video games you didn't buy?

• Does he listen ONLY to dark and angry music?

• Has he withdrawn from friends and family?

• Have his long-time friends that you know quit calling? Or he them?

• Do friends no longer call or come over anymore?

• Does your teen ask to have sleepovers or sleep over at a friend's EVERY weekend?

• Does your teen wear lots of bracelets, or hoodies and long sleeves in all weather?

• Is your teen having any problem sleeping?

• Do you think your teen is "just experimenting", and "it's ONLY pot" or "it's ONLY beer"?

• Do you find can tabs or bottle caps and he says "I just like to collect them"?

• Has another parent ever caught their teen and yours with drugs, sneaking out, or stealing?

You may have thought of others as you read the list. I realize that any one of these questions on its own may not indicate a problem, but trust me – there is always more to these kinds of behaviors than you think you know. Almost 100% of parents in the parent support groups, Al Anon for Parents groups, and treatment center rehab groups I've attended discovered that their teen was involved in drugs for at least one to two years before they found out about it. Some teens may "just" abuse drugs, but chemical addiction is progressive – if your teen is an addict you will eventually discover it, like it or not. He'll either get arrested, get caught with drugs at home or school, get busted at a party where the parents are out of town, or get caught stealing (drugs cost money). Perhaps she'll get picked up on a curfew violation, as a Jane Doe in the streets passed out from an overdose, or maybe even confess out of fear to you when another kid OD's, gets a DWI, or gets arrested. If you don't have a clue how to respond to one of these situations you are going to be thrown into crisis too, and at the very moment your teen needs you the most.

If you know or suspect your child is using drugs, DO SOMETHING. In our culture it is tempting to deny there is a problem, or say it's just "a phase", or think it's "only" beer or "only" pot. DON'T make that mistake – and remember, if he's under twenty-one alcohol is illegal, and pot is illegal in most states regardless of age. Do the hard thing, the uncomfortable thing; treat the behavior as the crime it is. Recognize it as a problem and lovingly confront your child with what you know, then seek professional help. See if he is willing to admit it and address the problem, and based on the outcome take action.

Experimenting with drugs can turn into addiction in a heartbeat, and as parents we must recognize that addiction can be a disease. Our actions need to err on the side of fighting the disease. It's never too early to take action, early intervention can make a difference.

Try to talk to your child first. If you have a good relationship with him and can talk to him, let him know you care. Tell him you are genuinely concerned, and ask what's going on. Listen. Listen with your head and with your heart. See how he reacts, what he says; if he admits to using drugs or alcohol, will he tell you how it makes him feel, or not feel? If he is overly-defensive, back off and know that that is part of your answer. If there is no response or he is completely shut down, monitor with care but from a distance (not too close).

Be willing to contact the school counselor or teacher and maintain a connection regarding your child's grades, attitude, friends and any concerns the counselors have. My children's counselors were immensely helpful to me in dealing with both academic and social issues that surfaced at home.

Know your resources - check out parent support groups like AL Anon for Parents, Tough Love, Disease of Addiction, local crisis hotline, and other parents. Search out treatment center websites and publications that have solid accurate info on the brain chemistry of addiction. Educate yourself. The 25 tips for parents on Palmer Drug Abuse Program's website are excellent. Take action when warranted. If your teen is blatantly caught in the act of dealing or using, don't hesitate to call the police. Ignoring the obvious and deciding not to get involved may very well be escalating a serious problem. Remember, addiction is a disease. It affects you – your work environment, your community, and your kids' friends. Decide to be part of the solution; do what you can to make a difference. Get him into A.A., or a good counselor, rehab, or deal with it firmly at home, but DO SOMETHING. Take an absolute zero tolerance stance on this issue. Drug abuse and addiction will take over his life and yours too. If you get the chance to help your child change the direction before it's too late it will be worth all the pain and effort.

My son went through an Intensive Out Patient program. The judge had ordered rehab and Max wasn't exactly happy about participating. But we were there, and I learned a lot about the inter-relationship of trauma, anger, adolescence and substance abuse. I soaked up the information at the sessions, took in more at AL Anon meetings, and read whatever I could get my hands on about teens and drugs.

Addicts are manipulative of others' feelings. The addict numbs his pain, and for a time feels none of it, or tries to feel it and can't. Either way, the loved ones feel the pain. I had to learn how to separate myself from her feelings. Twelve step programs call it detachment. I would need to become a master at it to navigate the waters of recovery and the court programs I became involved with.

Drug Court

Max had also been court ordered by the Judge to enroll in Drug Court, a program designed specifically to help young offenders and first time offenders and to prevent them from becoming just another teenage drug statistic.

At Drug Court those in the system can be detained for any probation violation or for any reason the judge thinks necessary. It is always painful to see your child arrested or detained, it never got easier. In fact, I thought it was harder in some ways because I knew what was coming for me emotionally, socially and logistically. I was also aware of the unknowns I would be faced with: when would he get out, when would the judge set a hearing, what would his behavior be on the inside this time?

Sometimes when a youth gets detained it is a very emotionally charged situation. The judge pronounces him detained, the young son or daughter is crying, hugging and clinging to his mother, saying how much he loves her. All the while the PO's and guards are moving in with handcuffs, trying to avoid an outright fight, and all the other parents and juveniles in the courtroom watch the drama being played out. The moms I admired the most were the ones who hug back, said I love you and meant it, and with compassion and sorrow in their eyes detached from their child so he could be led away to a cell. Those moms knew what needed to be done, and they had learned not to receive the false guilt their child tried to place on them. Whether you call the police on your child for unlawful behavior or the child is arrested and you find out later, the blame rests on the child not the parent. I learned from my own counseling to not ever let Max get to my heartstrings with "You put me in jail" or "You let them take me away". He wouldn't even be there if his actions didn't warrant it.

Oh, but how to describe how it feels when it is your child. When Max was detained at drug court the first time, I wasn't expecting it. But as soon as the judge said the words, Max stood up, put his hands behind his back in formation and went with the PO to the holding tank to be booked. My heart hurt for him, knowing there was no other option, wishing with all my might he could see how he was going down the very wrong path. As they led him away I got up from the table, not even worried about a graceful exit. There was nothing anyone in the courtroom could say to cheer me up and no reason to linger.

Occasionally juvenile offenders get a few hours of furlough for good behavior during an extended period of incarceration. As hard as it was for me to take him in to Detention, it was doubly hard to return him after five hours of really good time together. I had to remind myself that he was always "good" when he'd been locked up. I wished I didn't know that about my son! I love him – his sparkle, sense of humor – he was awesome when not on drugs or drinking. I wanted so much for him to get right and have a good meaningful life, to be fulfilled and be happy and know God and His love. I thank God for teaching me to separate the boy from his actions, the person from his mistakes. I started to understand why detachment was so critical.

<u>Overdose</u>

If your child is taken to the Emergency Room, they will call and let you know at which hospital to meet them. If your child is taken by the police, it may take a while for them to find ID and notify you. Remember to bring insurance information, and names of any medicines you know he is taking. There will be the usual

hospital paperwork, releases to sign, statements to acknowledge.
Be prepared to wait for or with your child for hours.

Nothing can prepare you for the experience. I was taken
back to a curtained room at the hospital. My son was strapped
onto a bed, with IV fluids and machines monitoring his vital signs.
He was conscious by the time I arrived but delirious. The doctor
could not give him any medicines because he had no idea what
Max had taken, and Max couldn't tell him.

It took six hours for him to come down off the effect of
the drug. When it was determined he was going to live he was
admitted for overnight observation. He was struck by the fact that
he was in for self-induced illness; the others were there for injury
or illness over which they had no control. It was a frightening
experience. When he was approved for release we both agreed he
needed serious help and I made arrangements to get it.

Residential Placement

My son was taken from home and placed elsewhere two
times, both times with my input and approval. The first one was a
Boy's Ranch facility for behavior modification. I was able suggest a
place and had everything in place for him to be enrolled if the
judge would order it. His PO had warned me that placement was
imminent if he had repeated arrests, and I wanted to try placing
him at a Boy's Ranch rather than in an institution if at all possible.
There are many good residential ranch type facilities for teens in
trouble, and it is worth your time and effort to get informed about
them. The web is an excellent source. Today as an adult, Max
states that the Ranch was the most effective in helping him change
his life.

The second was a residential drug rehabilitation treatment
program run by the county juvenile probation department. It was a
secure lock-down facility which offered the combination of jail and
a drug treatment program for kids in the juvenile probation system.
If you have such a program available in your county you are
extremely fortunate. There are private lock-down facilities, at-will
facilities for those willing to receive treatment, and jail for those
juvenile criminals who refuse treatment but whose drug addiction
ensures their continued crime and eventual capture. The program
Max entered, called Options, is different. Availability is limited, the
teen must be considered a good candidate for recovery and
rehabilitation, and the juvenile criminal record must be minimal
enough that the State Department of Corrections is still a step away

– but just a step. The philosophy is that it is worth extreme effort – incarceration combined with serious drug treatment and behavior modification – to produce teenagers that have a chance to make it once they are back out in the real world. In detention they do their time and are released, often to re-offend; but this program is incarceration with the emphasis on treatment and re-entry into community.

If your child is selected for this program it will have the same impact on your lives as if he were jailed. Once the decision is made for him to be admitted, he is held in the juvenile detention facility until a bed is available and all paperwork is done. He will be required to have dental and physical exams, get all school records, and you will undergo an intake interview. You will be interrogated about your family life, your habits, your use of alcohol, your background, and the circumstances leading up to your child's incarceration. You will be asked to commit to weekly family group rehab sessions, regardless of your work or personal schedule. You will not be given a choice about your child's teachers, nurse, or director of the program. You must agree to cooperate, or your child does not get a chance to receive this help.

Once in, there are no phone calls, no letters in the beginning and only limited correspondence later on. His head will be shaved, he will be issued a uniform to wear at all times, and any time he is out of his unit he will be in shackles, on his wrists and ankles. If he has a doctor appointment outside the facility during his residence there (as my son did), he will be transported in shackles by armed officers and treated as a prisoner. While living on the inside, he will have to get permission to do everything but breathe – move about the room, go to the bathroom, move to a different chair, everything. And when he finally gets visitation, you will have to schedule your hour well in advance. You will have to show up at the facility with your ID, be wanded by security and surrender your car keys and anything else you may have in your possession before you can be taken to see him. When you do visit, it will likely be in a big open room with no privacy, and all the parents will be seated in a row, waiting for the inmates to be brought in. They are brought in single file, open hands behind their backs counting as they walk through, and they are seated in a row in front of the parents. You are allowed to hug, but there are officers seated in the room during the visitation. It is awkward, difficult. In the beginning, your child may not even speak to you – punishment for 'your part' in his being in there. You have taken the time out of your day and gone through security, only to be treated as if you were the problem. Eventually he will speak to you, and he can only speak of what is happening on the inside. You don't even want to talk about "normal" life because it is so depressing to him – he has no windows, is not allowed outside often, and he desperately wants the freedom he once had. You get to know the other parents who visit regularly, and the kids whose parents don't come. You don't really feel like talking because none of you wants to be there, but you are in waiting rooms and elevators together and your kids are working towards improvement; some small talk is inevitable. You compare notes about how your kid is doing, has he moved up to the next level, and you wish with all your might you didn't have to be there. But you attend the weekly group sessions, visitations, endure sending letters with no response, and you get through it. Because you have to, and because it's worth it.

Sexual Abuse

If you have any reason to believe your child is being sexually abused – particularly if you discover information that points to abuse or outcry (notes, a phone number scribbled on a scrap of paper, casual mention from friends or other parents about odd behaviors, aversion to people or places previously enjoyed) – believe your child. The moment you suspect, believe. If you are wrong, there will be other, likely less significant, issues to face and you can take some time to determine the problem and address it. But if you are right, your child is in crisis and may be in danger; time is critical and action is required immediately. You may very possibly - literally – save your child's life, and you will be forever grateful you believed and acted on your belief.

If you're in doubt, I urge you to choose to believe unless and until it can be proven otherwise – your child's life may be at stake. Believe your child. She has much to lose and almost nothing to gain by false accusation. I suspect there are far more cases today of adults dealing with the trauma of childhood abuse than adults dealing with false accusations by children. Believe your child.

If you are unsure about any suspicion or outcry of abuse or molestation, consider these points:

• Get in touch with your local city or county agency and get a list of symptomatic behaviors of sexually abused kids. Does anything match what you are seeing? For me, reading the list was like turning on a light bulb.

• Does your child have anything to gain by making accusations against the person?

• What does your child have to lose by speaking out?

• What do your child's eyes tell you?

• What does your gut tell you?

• Is the accused person on the offense against your child? How much? Does his stance make logical sense?

• Does your child feel safe?

• How are the child's siblings reacting?

It's my understanding that there are no witnesses in most cases of molestation by a family member or close family friend. It is the word of the child against the accused. I chose to believe my daughter and that made all the difference.

Suicidal

No parent even wants to think this is a possibility for their child. I can only speak from my experience, but do not fool around with this. If you have <u>any</u> indication your child is even considering the possibility of suicide, take action. Call a counselor, a crisis hotline listed in your phone book or online, or a 24/7 counseling call center like 1-800-newlife. Do not wait, do not second-guess yourself, do not believe your teen's words that everything is okay if their actions and your gut tell you otherwise. Overcome your feelings of embarrassment or pride or busyness or denial or disbelief, or the idea that it can't happen in your family or to your child. Make the call – your child's life is at stake.

My first indicator that Lily was having suicidal thoughts was a note she had written to a friend which her eighth grade teacher intercepted. The school counselor contacted me, very concerned, and after our conversation I was too. She suggested we take her to a professional counselor and I agreed. That afternoon when she got home from school I confronted her and she told me it was just a joke, "dark teen humor", and she meant nothing by the note. I couldn't see any reason she would be considering suicide but my gut feeling that something was very wrong prompted me to find a counseling center (recommended by my pastor) and make an appointment for a "well check".

Shortly after I scheduled the appointment, I found completely by accident a suicide note to a friend of hers that I knew well. A scribbled 800 number on the desk in Lily's handwriting turned out to be for a crisis hotline, and I got really scared. Terrified. I wanted to do something, but what do you do to prevent a suicide? I called the counselor and changed the appointment to an emergency and we were in her office that day.

That appointment saved her life. I have since learned other possible indicators of suicidal thoughts or intentions:

• Cutting (girls wear lots of bracelets or long sleeves, no matter the season, to cover the scars)

• Bottle of aspirin, sleep aids, or other OTC pain meds disappearing from your medicine cabinet

• Casual comments about death or suicide, even "jokes", by your child or by peers

• Extra-ordinary aversion to social events or events they eagerly anticipated at one time

• Severe stomach-aches at predictable times (i.e., right before a scheduled visit to a friend or family member)

• Withdrawal, or shutting down communication

My daughter exhibited all of these, but I wasn't aware enough to put it all together until we worked with the county victim's services unit. Thank God I found the note. Thank God I believed my child.

Recovery Mom

In the midst of all the craziness I bonded with a few other moms who also had kids in crisis, and I dubbed us the Recovery Moms. Jesse, I didn't set out to become a Recovery Mom, but then my son didn't set out to be an addict either. He didn't intend for his actions to affect my life, but that's how the disease of addiction works. So whether he is in recovery or not, I need to be doing all that I can to make sure I am okay - even when he is not. Especially when he is not.

Recovery simply means that a person affected by the disease, either the addict or anyone who interacts with them on a regular basis, is or has been in the process of trying to recover. Webster's defines recovery as "restoration from sickness or any undesirable or abnormal condition; the duration of recovery."

When we recover something we reclaim or regain. In the world of addiction it is a process.

It is heart-breaking to learn your child has used drugs; devastating to discover they are an addict; unbearable to deal with overdose and near-death because of it. If you have a child involved in drugs or alcohol abuse, then you need to be interested in recovery. Your child will have to desire and manage his own recovery, but you have some things to recover from as well. When I was first introduced to the process by my son's chemical dependency counselor, I didn't think I needed to "recover" from anything, except maybe the shock of the situation I found myself in. I learned that there were lots of things I needed to recover from: my co-dependent behavior, my constant attempts to 'fix' people and things, my extreme people-pleasing tendencies, my blaming and lack of forgiveness, my anger at the disease, my unmanageable fear, my grief at the loss of a dream for my child, my unrealistic expectations of myself and others, my view of life from behind rose-colored glasses. You will have your own inventory.

Recovery programs that are based on Alcoholics Anonymous and the various affiliated programs have at their heart a twelve step plan. Addiction IS a disease. It is unique in that it is a physical disease for which the only cure is a spiritual one, one that must be lived out daily. No amount of money, education, professional experience, or self-will is enough to triumph over addiction; no plan that omits the need for help from a Higher Power is going to succeed. The twelve steps are a spiritual plan for recovery; their success depends on the degree and intensity with which they are applied, but recovery IS possible.

As I got to know other mothers in similar circumstances, a few of us were drawn to form a smaller support group. Becoming a Recovery Mom for me included occasional breakfast meetings with the moms in this group, where we could share a meal at our favorite Mexican food place, celebrate the latest step of parenting progress in an impossible situation, weep for the child who had relapsed or was living on the street, talk hopefully about the child who was currently working a recovery program, or maybe just talk about our own interests like writing or painting or making jewelry so we could have brief respite from reality. I am eternally grateful in particular to two courageous, wonderful women who made life bearable during the most difficult of days.

Recovery for each person looks different, but there are some key things you need to know for the process to be successful. Don't give up on yourself or your children, even when circumstances seem impossible. God can do impossible things.

I want to talk more about detachment. It was such a mystery to me and in some ways it still is, but it is so important. One of the best books I found on the subject was <u>Co-Dependent No More by</u> Melody Beattie. She says that detachment is necessary for survival, and that it means you separate yourself and your life from the addict while loving him "just as fiercely". That really nutshellized it for me. Going into crisis mode in reaction to my circumstances had become a habit, and I was ready to try something different.

Learning to detach is not easy. For one thing, it is both an attitude and an action, but there is no single plan of application. The how-to of detachment can be different in each case, so in the beginning it is a process of trial and error. That is frustrating enough, but beginning to detach and continuing to practice it goes against the grain. It's the thing you least want to do because it doesn't come naturally. Initially it seems to cause more open conflict, it takes great courage, and your addict will not enjoy the fact that you have a new plan that will result in his accountability for his own actions. No longer will he be able to cause the problem and have someone else – you – feel the consequences. Detachment done properly results in you being able to be okay even when your addict isn't. It results in the addict's problems being returned to him and placed squarely on his shoulders, to either live with or address as he so chooses while you live your own life.

When you first practice detachment, you may feel as if you are acting unloving to your child. But in reality it is the most loving way you can treat your child. It tells him that you are willing to do the hard thing now to help him learn the joy and satisfaction later of having put his life back on track.

When I was going through the early months of dealing with my son's addiction, I wanted some examples of how to detach. What specific things should I do? How often? Which behaviors do I tolerate and which do I take a firm stand against? How do I know if I've done the right thing? I know now why nobody in my Al Anon for Parents group was forthcoming with answers. It's not an exact formula that works exactly the same way in every circumstance. But I can give you some examples from my own experience that may get you started in the right direction.

Examples of Detachment

- Calling the police on your child when he is violent or drugged and out of control; watching him curse you from the back of a police car as he is driven away. (willingness to do what is necessary)

- Working with his PO to do an intervention that will get him locked up short-term for a probation violation and very likely long term into a rehab facility because he is spiraling down deep into drug use and it may save his life (surrender, willingness)

- Telling his PO when you learn of a violation such as skipping school or drug use, even though he begs you not to and promises he'll never do it again (openness, honesty)

- Not making false promises when he calls you in the middle of the night after running away, only telling him of your love and that you will do what is best for him (honesty)

- Letting him see your tears and broken heart in the midst of your love, even if he is high and ridicules you for it (humility)

- Granting forgiveness when in his brokenness he acknowledges his faults/crimes/pain/ failures and asks for your help (humility, willingness)

- Repeatedly refusing to let him come home from the Boy's Ranch for visits, even on major holidays, because he ran away on the first home visit for a whole weekend and because the Ranch staff lets you make the decision whether he gets a visit or not. Refusing to feel guilty when he is not there at the Thanksgiving table or on Christmas morning (practice, trust in God and in the process)

- Keep encouraging him to attend school, go to meetings, hang with sober friends, connect with family, and engage in healthy extracurricular activities. Invest in the process by being his taxi, getting to know his friends' parents, showing interest as he builds bike ramps or starts a tree house or modifies his BMX freestyle bike or edits a video of a family gathering (effort, in spite of fatigue)

Detachment does not mean watering down my standards just to try and keep peace or letting my parenting values be undermined. My stand has always been that it is my job as a parent to expose my children to the truth of the Christian faith by belonging to and attending a good church during their growing up years, requiring their attendance when necessary if they are under eighteen and living at home. They must have a chance to hear and ingest God's teaching and experience Christian fellowship. If they choose a life without God in their adulthood, at least it won't be because they weren't exposed to it. As a believer I am accountable to influence my kids for Christ for their eternal future, so how could I stand by and say I permitted them not to go to church with me? I couldn't.

I had good friends that advised me not to force them to go. But I knew it was important for their spiritual upbringing. When I do what God wants, I see rewards – like Max truly praying the Lord's Prayer, and singing in church, and being ready on time. If I give in to worldly standards he doesn't even have the chance to come and worship, hear God's Word spoken and experience God's love through other Christians. How glad I am my children didn't miss out on the love and fun of some of the members of our church! Some of those people are part of their support system still today.

Something that is absolutely essential to a Recovery Mom is Faith. Faith in a God who is real, relatable, trustworthy and available at all times. It involves spending time with the One in whom you have placed your faith, and much prayer. It brings hope and the ability to go on when you can't see where you are headed. Surviving the crisis depends on strength and stamina; my close relationship with Jesus and a daily prayer habit provided both.

At my lowest points, I have two choices: 1) Trust in God, or 2) Yield to Despair. I choose to trust in God. A change in attitude can lead to a change in action; oftentimes prayer has helped me change my attitude and I was able to do what was necessary. During times of adversity, you have to believe God will give you the victory. Times of trial are finite. Don't throw God away with the questions. One of my favorite devotional books is When I'm On My Knees by Anita Corrine Donihue. I read that one often during the really tough times.

Some of my own prayers have brought me comfort as well, like this prayer that I will share from my journal one December.

Father, in the quietness of my time with You, the wind chimes sing to remind me only You are in charge. You make the wind blow and cease blowing, solely at Your command. Who can comprehend Your power? And the constant steady ticking of the clock above my prayer bench reminds me of Your steadfast love and faithfulness. Through all our trauma and turmoil, You have been and continue to be the one unchanging constant in our lives. Thank You.

Other times it is the prayer of someone else spoken or read at just the right moment that touches my heart, and I know that God is speaking to me through the words of others. One evening I was driving and was compelled to pull over and jot down notes from a prayer for single mothers I heard Chuck Swindoll pray. My notes captured the gist of the prayer:

In that stormy place in their hearts enable them to persevere; show them they need only Christ, that He loves them and is working through them in ways they can't imagine. Those that don't have the affirmation of a husband, that are in such difficulty or in financial straits, be with them in their grief. Father, give them strength and fresh energy to go on.

I love what one of my former pastors said about being driven by faith, not fear. He reminded me not to let my past dictate who I am, to learn from the past but not live there. There is no future in living in or dwelling on past bad experiences, it breeds resentment and self-pity. I can use my God-given capacity to be special, to set a course for my future.

There are times when just a simple thought or sentence brings my faith home to me. I try to write them down or remember them so I can recall them when I need. These thoughts have been very helpful to me.

- No child is more fortunate than one with a Christian parent who prays.

- Focus on Christ, not circumstances

- Failure is the back door to success sometimes

- God has a purpose in our trial and tribulation

- Progress, not perfection (from the 12 step programs)

- When God is involved, there is always hope

- God's will is not about my plans

God's timing and His decisions don't always meet our expectations, but that should not keep us from trusting Him one hundred percent, every day in every circumstance. When you feel like you want to apologize for what God hasn't done, remember all the things He <u>has</u> done.

Jesse, you need to try and find some "time out" for you. If at all possible, get away – for ten minutes, half an hour, an afternoon, or even a whole day. Find a porch, a friend's country home, a beach house, the library, your favorite chair, a walk in the park – anywhere you won't be reminded of the daily obstacles. Even a few minutes helps. Your brain needs a break from thinking about it all. When you return, you will often have a fresh perspective, and renewed energy and purpose to tackle problems that now seem more manageable. I found getting outside was particularly helpful – the beauty of creation calls out to be recognized, and even on some of the worst days it proved to be a welcome distraction. I made a list of things I could do when I felt like running away but couldn't (can you tell I'm a list-maker??)

-Clean the kitchen drawer

-Count your blessings, starting with "I'm breathing on my own"

-Exercise with a video

-Flip through favorite photo albums

-Journal

-Listen to a CD of Ocean Waves

-Lock your door and cry your heart out for a time

-Paint, even though you don't know how

-Play the piano or guitar

-Pray

-Read

-Rock in a rocking chair

-Sing

-Sit on the porch or patio or front step

-Sweep the sidewalk

-Take a bath instead of a shower

-Trim the yard by hand with garden scissors and a rolling stool

-Watch old home videos of the kids when they were little

-Write a real letter

This may sound silly, but when your life is upside down it's the little things that can help. Things like going to bed with makeup on. You may have to drive to jail in the middle of the night, and you don't know how many hours you'll have to stay there. You can clean and curl in the morning. Here are some others that helped me:

- If you've cried all night, carefully dab Preparation H to the swollen bags under your eyes to reduce the swelling.

- Apply some Baby Powder to oily parts of hair close to the scalp and comb through – this can get you through the day when you don't have time to wash your hair.

- Sleep with your keys and purse by the bed. Better yet, keep a locking cabinet in your room for these items.

- Always make a mental note of the mileage on your car when you get out of it for the last time that day. Check it against what's on there in the morning.

- If you give your child money, ask for change and a receipt. Follow through. Every time. No exceptions.

- Remove the doorknob off the child's bedroom door. You can easily check on them and they can't sneak out as easily.

- Dispense any necessary medication at each dosage time – don't leave the bottle where he or friends can easily access it. It's inconvenient, do it anyway.

- Write notes to communicate to your child – sometimes it works better than trying to talk.

- Don't let your child make you think you are crazy. My son stole my cell phone for a time and had me absolutely convinced I had lost it. Items I KNEW I had were missing and he resolutely maintained he never saw them.

- Think before you Speak. If you can't think, don't speak.

- You've said it all before. Shut up.

Try to see past the behavior to the child in pain. Hate the behaviors, love the child. When the crisis is over and you've having "normal" time at home, and your teen snaps at you, or plays music too loud, or leaves clothes in the living room floor, remember Proverbs 12:16 – be slow to annoyance. It's a good day – he's not in jail, not using, and you know where he is. He's just a kid trying to get through life.

I mentioned briefly about counseling for your child. But you will need a good counselor also. An excellent counselor is worth her weight in gold. Before the events that led to my getting into counseling, I would have said, "Who needs a counselor, all you need is God and a few close trusted friends to tell your problem too." But now I know that emotional wounds and scars are real, they have a direct impact on me mentally and physically. Without the professional help I received to work through the problems and find healing I wouldn't be the happy, healthy, whole person I am today.

We are more than our problems. Life is about bigger things than just my circumstances and I have to release my grip on my circumstances. It's scary, but do it anyway. We must learn not to live at the mercy of our feelings, they can't be trusted. They are a natural expression and have to be channeled, but they should not be our primary guide to action. Be aware that the monster inside you can rise up and engage at any time. I would find myself behaving nicely with my son, where it felt like a truce was flowing between us. Then something small happen would happen and I'd snap. I remember once when the printer wouldn't print. I showed my impatience and frustration by griping out loud with lots of loud sighs. My son immediately reacted – shouting, telling me to "shut up", all his old behaviors surfaced. My old reactions spewed forth before I could even realize it. I was lashing back with hurtful words of my own, thinking only of myself and my feelings, and contributing greatly to ruining the moment. All my hours of self-control each day seemed as if they were for nothing. The old hurt and tears and pain all come flooding back – especially since I hadn't slept through the previous night, which is not unusual when you are living in crisis.

But it's not for nothing. Let the air clear and you can apologize for your part. You can't make him apologize for his behavior that hurt you; don't try, it will just make you feel worse. Just clean up your side of the street, as they say in Al Anon, and move on down the road. You are sowing seeds of change in your home when you do, and with perseverance you will reap the harvest.

Counseling

Do your homework to find a good one. Credentials are important, and references are crucial – word of mouth referral is best. Don't focus on insurance coverage, your child needs help. I've found the really good counselors will work with you on a payment plan if you need it. Make sure it's a good mesh for your child – my son had two that didn't resonate with him at all, but one that helped change his life. It may take a few visits to know if it's a good fit. Don't be afraid to change, and when you find a good one keep at it – good counseling takes time and unpacks layers of emotional baggage. Counseling shouldn't be a lifestyle, but it is sometimes a necessary tool for healing. Lily's doctor was an absolute jewel, and ultimately inspired her career choice.

You can't put a price on survival, emotional and mental health, and spiritual grounded ness – good counseling is worth the money.

Finding a good counselor or therapist takes some time and effort but it's worth it. It's critical if you are in crisis. Ask for recommendations from friends, your pastor, the local mental health agency. Call and interview them by phone first, then if you like what you hear and feel comfortable schedule an initial consultation visit. You are looking for someone you can trust who keeps confidentiality and who will invest in your health. It needs to feel like a fit; the counselor should demonstrate skill, compassion, patience, and discernment about when to listen and when to ask questions or give suggestions. Don't be afraid to change and try others if it's not working after several sessions. Seek the right one and stick with her when you find her. The true professionals won't expect to keep treating you forever as a lifestyle. They know this process is a tool for a season, maybe months or years, and when it's time to end it you'll both know it.

Expect to spend between $100 to $150 per hour and to have sessions once a week. In my case that was a huge budget item; during the worst of it all three of us were going weekly. I used insurance where I could, paid as I went when I could, made payment arrangements with the counselors that allowed it, and borrowed if I had to pay the rest. But it was worth every penny. It was money well spent and I would do it again in a heartbeat.

Forgiveness

I don't know about you but I had a lot to learn about forgiveness. I have learned that forgiveness is a process. It is about changes that need to happen in my heart, not what someone else needs to do. It does not mean forgetting what happened, or immediate regained trust, or staying around unsafe people. It does not mean removing all boundaries. If a person in denial has access to you, it is sick access and needs to be stopped until the denial is stopped. Do everything you possibly can to get them on the right path. But don't let them continue to have access to you and your emotions - that is not healthy. Forgiveness includes not forgetting and keeping a safe distance when that is warranted.

Anger is part of the process. It does its job, then afterward you have to let it go and grieve. Grief does its job, then you can begin to forgive. Own your part in things. Sometimes we are so disconnected we can't see clearly. We have to forgive ourselves for some things too. Hurts do matter. But move out of the law of revenge and demanding justice. Give up your right to demand punishment. As I heard often on New Life Ministries daily broadcast, don't excuse, forgive. That does not automatically mean that we trust right away, trust has to be re-earned.

We need to be willing to forgive, but we can't force others to be willing to ask for or receive forgiveness. It has been said that unforgiveness is like drinking poison and hoping the other person dies. I believe that. Even if the other person doesn't want forgiveness, you need to forgive for your own sake. It's one of God's mysteries, that when we forgive others we are the ones who benefit. Forgiving while not forgetting is a huge part of the healing process. It will take time, but forgiveness is key; seek it earnestly.

New Life Ministries' Ten Tips on Forgiveness outline this issue better than anything else I've seen. They offer all their resources on their website at newlife.com but I received this in an email when I first started supporting them.

"Forgiveness, when empowered by God's Spirit, is a process of detaching painful events from our emotional response to them thus facilitating the process of healing. In contrast, the refusal to forgive has far-reaching results spiritually, emotionally and even physically. Lack of forgiveness (bitterness, grudges, vengeful motives, repressed anger) is the primary cause of most depressions.

I have found that ability to forgive, both myself and others, comes in varying degrees. It is much easier to forgive my child when he comes to me broken and penitent and desiring my forgiveness than it is to forgive myself for faulty parenting (real or perceived) or forgetting something that was very important to one of my children. Forgiving someone who insulted you or purposefully tried to make you look bad is one thing; forgiving a family member who writes off your child as a hopeless case is something else altogether. Forgiveness IS a process. The freedom I feel from those I've been able to forgive is exhilarating, empowering and has taught me the importance of working on those areas where I still hold on to bitterness, vengeful motives and repressed anger. I am still trying to learn how to completely forgive my former husband. His actions caused our daughter unspeakable suffering, loss of relationship with his family, and almost cost her her life. He continues to live in denial, not acknowledging what he did or the need for help or correction in his own life, much less the need to be forgiven. I have to be willing to forgive should that ever change.

It is tempting for me to feel that if ever anyone had a justifiable reason not to forgive another human being it would be Lily, and me. But I know that I must try to forgive; I need that to be healthy and whole. So I acknowledge that such a person must be sick, may have had something horrible happen in his life to make him capable of such behavior, and must be as lost a soul can be. I pray for God to work in his life, for his own benefit and that of his children and his family. And I wait. When and if the opportunity comes for forgiveness, I want to be ready. It's never too late to start again. You start mending bridges by first assessing the damage. In Christ all things are new, all relationships reconcilable. In the meantime, I do everything in my power to protect Lily from someone who is not yet and may never be a safe person for her to be around.

Connection

You need healthy connections to help you through tough times. Stay connected to others going through similar circumstances. Al Anon, Tough Love, Family Groups at out-patient drug rehabilitation centers – these groups provide the kind of healing that can only be found in connecting with others who have been through it.

Stay connected with the things that make you "you". It can be almost impossible to find the time or energy to devote to interests like reading, writing, painting, playing a musical instrument, volunteering, exercise, etc., but it is important to do things that remind you of who you are other than the mother of an addict or a suffering child.

Stay connected to the wonderful times in your past. Keep pictures around the house where you'll see them often of the children were little and precious. It helps harness your anger at them if they turn into defiant teenagers.

Stay connected to hope. Write letters to your wayward or defiant teens, expressing your hope and your faith in them, confidence in the future and your love. Oftentimes teens are more open to communication by note or letter – they can read it when you aren't around, and don't have the pressure of responding immediately.

Stay connected to God. Have individual, daily prayer (hourly on some days!). Attend small groups – Sunday School, Bible Study, book groups – whatever keeps you around other Christians and those who care about you. Go as often as you can, even when you are tired or depressed or discouraged.

Hope

Any letter (or should I call this a booklet?!) about how to live in crisis needs to end on a note of hope. It is difficult to be hopeful in times of crisis, but you must find hope in all circumstances. Without hope we give up, become discouraged, think that our efforts don't matter, and in doing so we miss the chance to help ourselves and others through the situation. During all the crazy times there's frustration and a sense that as a parent I'm not making a difference in the lives of my children. But I must stand on faith, not my feelings. Feelings will pass; I need to remember that my parenting does make a difference. As long as there is breath in my body there is hope.

When I used to get caught up in the "why?" question of all that was happening to us, I tried to keep in mind what I heard Chuck Swindoll say in one of his radio messages about suffering. He said that why people suffer is the big question, especially following trauma or tragedy that hurts innocent children, and in his experience he found no easy answers. That has been my experience as well. All I know is that God is sovereign and He created mankind with free will, and sometimes that freedom is used for evil. I too have learned to turn to God in the suffering because He understands my pain, grieves with me and He is always available, 24/7.

Sometimes in the middle of the night the situation seems hopeless. Maybe you don't know if your child is ok or where your child is; or worse, maybe you do. You cry until you're exhausted from it, and you know there is not enough makeup to make yourself presentable for work in the morning. But get through the night, sleep or no, and it is better in the morning, even if just a bit.

Educate yourself – read books that address your circumstances; learn about addiction or the effects of sexual abuse or the rules for those living in residential treatment; ask other parents for resources, go to Al Anon!

Comfort yourself – the best source of comfort I've found is the Psalms in the Old Testament section of the Bible. A few of my favorites are listed in my Scripture Guide. Try them, find one or two that speak to you and memorize them, or write them down for when you need to call them to mind. It truly helps and is a great source of hope.

Talk with your friends, share some things with those who really care and are safe for you to do so. If you have family that is supportive and non-judging, and will love you through this, let them support you. Here is where a church family can be invaluable. The prayers and support of the faithful will sustain you in ways nothing else can. If you aren't in a church home that has small groups where you can be real, find another church.

The feeling of general ease at home when not in times of crisis is good, but hard to accept as lasting. It's like a guest who visits, stays a while and you enjoy it and wish she'd never leave, but you know she will, she must. Learn to enjoy and really live those days, those moments – cultivate a heart grateful to God for those evenings when your teen talks to you, shares laughter, you enjoy a "normal" supper, conversation flows. These are the times when relationships are strengthened and fortified so that you can both withstand the next storm. Because one day there won't be a "next storm", and you want to be left with a good, fun relationship that you'll both want to maintain. Ditch the anger, resentment, and self-pity – it's taking up space that could be filled with love.

I've received a great deal of hope and encouragement from the Turning Point Magazine & Devotionals from Turning Point Ministries. That's another ministry I support and I've taken their magazine for years. I found some great advice which I've kept over the years on hopeful parenting in one edition many years ago. Basically it said that we have to remember we can only do what we can do, we are responsible only for our choices and we can't take responsibility for the decisions of others. We can only do our part in working on relationships that aren't what we want them to be. Just do your best and let God do the rest. It ended with a quote from Ruth Bell Graham about trusting God for miracles because miracles are not in our department. After we have prayed and done our best, we must trust and wait. God's timing is different than ours, and as I have often said it seems like He is never in a hurry.

I have never forgotten the parting words of Justin, one of Max's former Probation Officers. He told me to never falter in my love for my children, that they would surprise me someday. He was right. We did live through it, life is better for all of us, and I continue to be surprised and amazed by my children. Have hope, love and listen, and never, ever give up.

I hope these lessons from my life experiences give you hope and help you to keep on keeping on, taking every day just one day at a time. I'm enclosing a list of resources and a scripture guide I devised so I could quickly get where I wanted to go in my Bible. Remember to love your children. Pray. Trust. Wait. Eventually this too will pass.

Waiting to hear your God-story,

Pamela

Resources

New Life Ministries
http://www.newlife.com/

Focus on the Family
http://www.focusonthefamily.com/

AL Anon
http://www.al-anonfamilygroups.org/

Tough Love
http://www.toughlove.com

Drug Information
http://www.erowid.org/psychoactives/psychoactives.shtml

PDAP
http://www.pdap.com/

All Things Possible Ministries
http://atpministries.org/

Intervention MD
http://www.interventionmd.com/

http://www.byparents-forparents.com/4troubledteens/

Suggested Reading

The Holy Bible	ESV, NLT, NIV 1984
When God Doesn't Make Sense	Dr. James Dobson
Parenting Isn't For Cowards	Dr. James Dobson
The Purpose Driven Life	Rick Warren
Life is Tough but God is Faithful	Sheila Walsh
How People Grow	John Townsend & Henry Cloud
Lessons I Learned in the Dark	Jennifer Rothschild
God Will Make a Way	Steven Arterburn
Tough Love Manual	Tough Love
One Day At a Time	Al Anon
When Your Child Has Been Molested	Kathryn Hagans
Power of a Praying Parent	Stormie Omartian
When I'm On My Knees	Anita Corrine Donihue

Pamela's Scripture Guide

Topic	Scriptures			
Acceptance	Job 2:10	Psalm 15:5	Proverbs 19:20	
Bearing Burdens	Psalm 68:19	Matthew 11:28		
Comfort	Psalm 23	Hebrews 13:5-6	2 Thess. 2:16-17	
Discouragement	Psalm 91:1-16	John 14:1		
Fear	Psalm 34:4	Psalm 56:3	John 14:27	Isaiah 43:1-5
God's Sovereignty	Psalm 145:89	Psalm 71:5		
Help	Psalm 121	1 Peter 5:7	Psalm 28:7	
Hope	Psalm 18:28, Psalm 31:24	Psalm 40:2	Psalm 71:14	Jeremiah 29:11
Patience	Psalm 27:14	2 Thess. 3:5		
Persistence	Galatians 6:9	James 1:2-5		
Refuge	Psalm 9:9	Psalm 46:1		
Rest	Matthew 11:28-30	Psalm 62: 1,5-8	Matthew 11:29	Hebrews 4:9
Revenge	Romans 12:19	Leviticus 19:18		
Sorrow	Psalm 119:28	Psalm 34:18		
Trials	James 1:12	Isaiah 41:10		
Trust	Psalm 37	Psalm 25:1	Psalm 31: 14-15	
Worry	Philippians 4:6-7	Psalm 55:22	Matthew 6:34	

Epilogue – Pamela's Prayer

Three Pennies

Father, I am still convinced that those three pennies I found yesterday on my walk are a sign from You. The first two, found fairly close together, symbolize me and my daughter. Mine, the first one found (dated the year I met her father) was dirty, blackened on one side, soiled and dulled with embedded grime. Yet it somehow survived the abuse of past decades and remained recognizable, serviceable, intact - in fact stronger. Just as I have weathered the marriage, divorce, custody battle, protective order, civil trials and years of counseling that helped turn my life around. All that dirty and messy past remains a part of my history, but You used it to shape me into a godlier, better woman and mother, the more effective Christian I am today.

Two blocks later I found a shiny penny. This one was dated the year Lily finished her counseling, graduated high school in the top ten percent of her class with honors, was accepted into the university; the year we moved back into our home after seven years of renovation. I had the joy of seeing my precious daughter – this one who endured such soul damage and then eventual healing by Your grace – cross the high school stage in cap and gown and smile during the celebration afterward in our newly decorated home. At the time I didn't know I would get to see her walk across again, seven years later, once again with honors but this time on a major University stage. Your love and the professionals You sent were like the finest steel wool, slowly and gently scrubbing her tender heart until the light of her spirit began to shine again, where it shines brightly still today.

I almost didn't find the third penny. I had returned home after the late afternoon walk, the heat turning my face red as I reached the front steps and checked my watch. Determined to walk for at least thirty-five minutes, I saw that it had only been thirty. The thought came to me to walk back out to the street and head east for a few minutes. I crossed our street and hadn't even walked fully past the next driveway when I saw the third penny. As I resumed my walk for the remaining minutes, I had been praying for my son. He was thirty-six days sober, owning his attitude and actions, admitting his weakness, and seriously working his recovery program of God and the 12 steps. The moment I saw the third penny, I knew it was a sign from God that my boy was going to make it. Finally, the youngest one of our little family of three was going to get his counseling, work through his emotional pain without the disease of addiction killing him, and be made whole. At first I could hardly tell it was a penny. It had been hammered, beaten, flattened, the copper metal cracked, flaked and scraped; so much so that it seemed with one more step upon it that it would disintegrate and cease to exist. Max was in that kind of shape when he came to me asking for help, knowing deep down if he didn't get into a treatment center he wouldn't survive his upcoming twenty-first birthday. But just like this penny here he was at our home, the grip of death unable to reach him. He, too, still has value, still the person he was created to be. Mis-directed and mal-treated for a season, now he was willingly in the loving hands of his Higher Power. He is headed down a new path, intact and ready to be shaped and guided by the Master. Rescued and redeemed, You brought him hope when it was nowhere else to be found. Max is solidly on his own faith journey and I trust You to guide and protect him as you have Lily.

Thank you, Father, for the gifts of love, lessons and life. Amen.

ABOUT THE AUTHOR

Kim Robinson is an author and speaker who grew up in central Texas. She and her husband have six children, fourteen grandchildren and enjoy spending time with family. Passionate about parenting, she writes and speaks about a variety of issues facing parents and professionals dealing with teenagers in crisis. She enjoys speaking at retreats and to various organizations.

Her interview with Steve Arterburn of New Life Ministries for a Club New Life CD was distributed to CNL members nationwide. Kim was featured during a local news series on teen Drug Court in her county. Along with various professionals in the field of addiction treatment, she was an author panelist at an event hosted by Disease of Addiction, founded to educate communities about addiction. The panel was presented to local ISD educators where attendees received continuing education credit. Panel members spoke about addiction in teenagers.

Kim is active in various ministries at her church, was formerly active in the Kairos prison ministry, and a past parent representative on the National Council of Juvenile Justice and Family Court Judges. She enjoys blogging, reading, gospel and blues music, singing, and keeping her grandchildren.

Chased by Grace – A Story of Victory is her first novel. Publication of her second book, Grace for Moms in Crisis, is expected in late 2015.

www.kimrobinson.co

Made in the USA
San Bernardino, CA
13 June 2015